GIRL
4

Will Carver is thirty years old and lives in Reading with his wife and daughter. *Girl 4* is his first thriller.

Visit www.willcarver.net for more information.

WILL CARVER

GIRL

4

arrow books

Published in the United Kingdom by Arrow Books 2011

7 9 10 8 6

First published in the United Kingdom in 2011 by Arrow

Arrow Books
The Random House Group Limited
20 Vauxhall Bridge Road, London, SW1V 2SA

Addresses for companies within The Random House Group Limited can be
found at: www.randomhouse.co.uk/offices.htm

The Random House Group Limited Reg. No. 954009

www.randomhouse.co.uk

A CIP catalogue record for this book
is available from the British Library

ISBN 9780099551034

Typeset by SX Composing DTP, Rayleigh, Essex

The Random House Group Limited supports The Forest Stewardship
Council® (FSC®), the leading international forest-certification organisation.
Our books carrying the FSC label are printed on FSC®-certified paper.
FSC is the only forest-certification scheme supported by the leading
environmental organisations, including Greenpeace. Our
paper procurement policy can be found at
www.randomhouse.co.uk/environment

Printed and bound in Great Britain by Clays Ltd, St Ives plc

For Sam and Paul, who believed.

GIRL
4

Prologue

———◆———

Cathy was taken in the spring of '85, from outside the front of our Islington terrace, in broad daylight. I was twelve; she was ten. Battered unconscious, she was driven only a quarter of a mile away, her broken body sullied and exploited, then dumped without a murmur of remorse for her tiny, shattered life. She didn't have time to scream or cry.

I was supposed to be looking after her.

'Jan, let's play blind man's buff, please, please, please!'

'Hang on, Cathy, hang *on*.'

As she drew her last breath, she was still pure; still an innocent girl. It wasn't until after she died that this was indulgently wrenched from her.

But she was never found.

So, you see, I don't actually know any of this.

There were no witnesses; there was no trace. No pile of bloodied clothes, no mangled twist of bones. Another body vanished; another soul obliterated. A family devastated.

Three months of intensive searching and questioning turned up nothing.

I was first under the spotlight. I can still see my father's expression, seething as the police questioned me over and over again, slightly altering the nuance of their queries each time, attempting to elicit a different response.

'I was in the kitchen getting us some juice. Cathy was outside counting to thirty. When I went back out, she wasn't there.'

I repeated the words endlessly. For my benefit more than the officers'. I had no idea what they were driving at; no clue what they expected of me. I was just a child. I could only state the bare facts; they were all I had to cling on to. But what is true is not always what is fact. What is genuine is not always what is real.

I was instantly condemned by my father; that was the last time we would ever speak. My parents' relationship disintegrated shortly after; neither of them accepting any responsibility, neither acknowledging the reality of the situation.

But where does reality end and truth begin . . .?

The only lead the police did not pursue involved a woman who claimed that she was given clues about what was about to happen twenty-four hours before it occurred. That she had been visited by a man in her dreams, who presented a very precise set of signals that she believed would uncover the whereabouts of my little sister.

A fraud. An overnight psychic producing false hope that Cathy was still alive.

She was a liar.

She was my mother.

And this is why I hate her.

Twenty-one years on, I still keep a copy of the case file in my top drawer underneath my single malt Scotch. While every atom of my rationality convinces me that Cathy is gone, that my mother's dementia eats away at her sanity a little more with each passing day, I want to believe that I can still find my little sister; that she is still waiting for me.

I can still save her.

London, 4 days ago . . .

Girl 4

❖

It dawned on me recently. It was the day the sun came out.

I'm stuck.

Routine. Endless, laborious, extended routine.

It starts with the sex. We both know what works and what doesn't by now. The idea of spicing anything up just seems like too much effort. So we do the same thing each time. Of course, there are subtle variations, but always the same end result. It's not even a case of being in sync with each other, either. Just a series of predetermined moves that have a tried-and-tested, 100 per cent success rate at achieving the desired goal.

Not that it has anything to do with desire any more.

We always have sex on a Saturday, plus once on a weekday – determined by the work schedule.

Then you realise that you eat your breakfast at the same time every day and, in fact, all your main meals occur at these preordained intervals, and you know without thinking when to take a shower and how many times you go to your Pilates class in a week and which day you shop for food and when your favourite soap opera will dribble its way on to your television and when your car needs more fuel and when you are due to come on to your period and nothing changes.

It got worse the day the sun came out.

I left the house early, because I always like to fill the petrol tank on a Tuesday morning. I put my aluminium coffee cup into the appropriate holder and root through the glove box for a stack of CDs that have been sat in there unused and unloved for months. I see the record company logo and know that I've hit gold. It's my *The Hissing of Summer Lawns* album by Joni Mitchell.

That's how I know it's summer.

That's how I know it's over.

My routine has bled from knowing what I am going to do day-by-day to week-by-week to month-by-month and now I know that, at exactly the same point next year, I will reach into my glove compartment, flick through my CD collection, which will be slightly more scratched than this year, locate my favourite album and cry inside at the futility of my predictable existence.

I need an event. Something to look forward to. Business has hit a plateau; the wedding was perfect, but that was so long ago, more than a year now; and, despite secretly coming off my contraceptive pill, I'm yet to fall pregnant. The monthly disappointment has now been added to my routine.

I exhale heavily and drop the roof on the car, as I always do at this time of year, hoping that someone will notice me.

Yes, I want a change.

Yes, I want to break free from this monotony.

Yes, I require something else in my life.

But not this.

Nobody deserves this.

Eames

When you watch the news on television and a saccharine reporter talks at the camera, while blue lights flash in the background and a house is surrounded by police tape, that's my house.

When an elderly neighbour is interviewed and drops a cliché like, 'He always seemed so normal. He was such a nice guy.' That's me they are talking about.

When a small crowd forms and people look shocked, because the guy who mowed their lawn last week or helped carry their heavy shopping bags on Saturday or fed their cat while they were away on holiday last summer has been killing woman after woman for the last thirty years, my entire life. That's me too.

Except that nobody in my idyllic Hampstead street has a clue what I do.

I've had affairs with several women in the area, whose husbands put work before their wives, and I've been with a couple of their daughters too. Just think how sick they'll feel when I finally get caught.

Think how relieved they'll feel that I didn't shoot them in the mouth. That I didn't suspend them from the ceiling with a high-gauge fishing wire or shoot an arrow through their skull.

Think how dirty they'll feel that they fornicated with a

sociopathic murderer, and how it will be the most alive they have ever felt, that someone like me could give them something so different, dangerous and exciting in their otherwise dreary, robotic lives.

When you see the reporter *go back to the studio*, and the anchor moves straight on to the next story, as if someone like that can't really exist, it's me they're dismissing.

Think how lucky they'll feel that I didn't beat them to death with a rolled up newspaper or balance an apple on their head or spear them through the gut with a scaffolding pole.

But first, I have to get caught.

My first kill came early. Earlier than most.

Mother.

The original.

Girl 0.

They say she pushed too hard, that an embolism popped in her brain, but I like to think I had something to do with it. Of course, I was only around one minute old when it happened, but if I had wanted to come out, if I'd wanted to be born, none of this would have happened. They say that my guilt over this incident manifested itself into my acute claustrophobia. I tell them I don't understand. That all I wanted was to stay in that cramped womb.

My father raised me on a diet of hatred and negligence. He always blamed me for what happened, as he should. I take full credit. But this isn't why I turned out this way. You can't blame Dad. He never physically abused me or threatened me. He rarely raised his voice. He just didn't have the energy for it after Mother died; he just sat in his chair transfixed by something that might lie behind the

TV. A part-time catatonic. A full-time alcoholic. But don't blame Dad. I am what I am.

I hate it when they psychoanalyse an artist's work and say that it must have been because he wasn't hugged as a child or he was beaten or he was a closet homosexual for so many years. I wasn't hugged as a child; that part is true. But my mother was dead and my father was using both of his hands to cling on to her memory. I wasn't abused and I'm certainly not gay. I'm just doing what is natural. Doing what I am told, what I am predisposed to do.

I know the difference between right and wrong.

The first three girls took a lot of planning, but even with my letters, my clues, the tip-offs, only one detective seemed concerned. But they'll start to take me seriously after Girl 4; they won't have a choice.

So I write another letter. I give them the chance to stop me before it happens.

How long will it take them to piece everything together? I give them everything they'll need apart from the name.

Girl 4.

She changes everything.

January

When I get the call I have no idea that it will be Girl 4 they've found.

Why had The Smiling Man not appeared to me the night before? Why was the killer returning after all these months, fourteen to be precise?

Why her?

I arrive at the scene shortly after Detective Sergeant Paulson and Detective Sergeant Murphy. The community theatre-company building has been broken in to and the cleaner has found a body. Paulson and Murphy are here on routine investigation, while I specialise in violent crime. That's why they called me in.

'What have we got, then?' I ask as I get out of the car to find Paulson finishing a cigarette before entering the building. Murphy is talking to the cleaner, who doesn't speak the best English, but manages to blurt out *'floating body'* in between sobs.

'The cleaner says she got here around 6.30 a.m. to clean the place ready for the rehearsal that is due to start here at nine,' Murphy explains as he flips through pages in his notepad. 'She filled the dishwasher so that the coffee cups would be ready to use when they arrived, mopped the toilets then went into the theatre. And found the body.'

'The floating body?' I question with a touch of cynicism in my voice.

It's at this point that Paulson shouts: 'Murphy! Jan! I think you need to take a look at this.'

We step into the darkened doorway that leads into the auditorium, where the local amateur dramatic society put on their sub-standard pantomimes and fumble through iambic pentameter.

Paulson has turned the lights off to recreate the same feeling both he and the cleaner experienced. To give us the full impact.

'Ready?' he asks, with an almost childlike excitement about his demeanour.

We nod in unison.

When he flicks on the lights it only takes a moment for my eyes to adjust to the brightness, but it takes what seems like minutes for my brain to adjust to what I am seeing.

'A floating body,' I repeat to myself, edging cautiously towards the stage.

Stood at the back of the theatre, my eyes adjust their focus to the stage at other end of the room, a beautifully pale brunette is lying face down. Blood from her head and face drips into a perspex box below her; her long hair dangles down in front of her shoulders, her head drooping and concealing her identity.

But she is ten feet in the air and there are no visible signs as to how she appears to be floating above her plastic coffin.

The image is horrifyingly beautiful.

The stage setting around her has been painted to resemble the sky at dusk. A few cotton-wool clouds give the scene a more three-dimensional feel. The dramatics of the whole effect are hardly amateur.

It looks like a perpendicular, levitating crucifixion.

She looks like a fallen angel. Bloodless, yet pure.

We all stand momentarily rooted to the spot in bemusement, part of the performance, a supporting cast to the play unravelling before us. Murphy writes more notes, Paulson lights another cigarette and we stare at the woman as if she is a sculpture, a work of art. In a way she is. This must have taken hours to orchestrate and arrange.

I turn back to look at Paulson, my eyes saying 'What the fuck?' He just shrugs and takes another drag.

As I inch closer something makes a sound that destroys the weird serenity of the scene and startles all three of us. A loud pop followed by the sound of gas leaking from a pipe.

Paulson stops smoking, Murphy stops scribbling and they join me, one at either side of where I stand. Transfixed, we don't take our eyes off the girl as the sound of gas continues, until it becomes apparent that the noise is coming from a hole behind the plastic coffin stationed below the floating corpse.

A dry-ice machine disperses a rising mist that forms tiny water droplets on the naked girl's body, making the image all the more haunting. She is the most stunning corpse I have ever seen.

The paramedics arrive outside, the light from their siren illuminating our room in a blue glow that resonates through the scene before us, the light dissipating through the smoke to create an image of heaven.

The first paramedic steps into the room and immediately reels in shock at what he sees. Tripping back against the wall he inadvertently leans on the switch to turn the lights off, again plunging the room into darkness apart from the ghostly figure above us. I sense the anguish of the detectives on either side of me. The feeling of panic that comes with inexperience. They start to fidget, making me increasingly aware of their confusion. I take control, remaining calm, concentrating my vision on the smoke enveloping this poor victim, the blue light from outside catching the scene in a certain way that allows me to see the thin wires suspending this fragile rag doll above the scene of growing disorder beneath her.

I know it's him.

I know he's back.

I know that this must be Girl 4.

This is not the work of a copycat. It's far too elaborate. The religious imagery doesn't follow his MO, but if I have learned anything from the first three girls it's that his reasons are not motivated by pattern or logic; it's about the performance and aesthetics.

I turn to Murphy. 'Get her down.' He looks back at me, bemused. I stare back, directly into his eyes. 'Now!' I exclaim with authority, and he races over to the steps at the right of the stage.

He closes the lid on the perspex box, sealing the spilled blood in a transparent sarcophagus, and jumps on top so that he can reach the underside of the victim. He looks up at her body to see the thin fishing wire cutting through her skin, but keeping her perfectly balanced so that she appears to the naked, unknowing eye to be floating.

He tilts her head, the first person to see her face, before trailing a finger across her torso to feel where the wires are inserted. She flinches as he does so.

Then she coughs.

She's still alive . . .

I see shock ricochet through Murphy and I feel it jolt through my guts as well. 'Paulson, help me cut her down, for Christ's sake!' Murphy bites out, and we both make a dash to the stage. Paulson jumps on the box and takes a knife to the wires, while Murphy supports the delicate frame of the woman from beneath.

Eventually she is cut free and her head rests on Murphy's shoulder as he carries her down to stage level. The second paramedic has entered with a stretcher and Murphy and Paulson help him to lay the woman down on her back.

The first paramedic, his movements still jerky with shock, straps her in and wraps her cold body in a tinfoil blanket, while his colleague pulls the hair away from her sticky, blood-covered face. Murphy and Paulson seem to have been too preoccupied with releasing her from her treacherous predicament to register anything, and begin deconstructing the scene as per standard procedure.

But I realise immediately.

As the paramedic pulls back the last clump of hair I see her face in all its cut-up beauty and I know her.

Girl 4.

It's Audrey David.

My wife.

Seventeen months
before . . .

January

Blindfolded and tied to a chair.
This is how all the dreams begin.

He slips the black scarf away from my eyes from behind, but still I see nothing. An empty room that seems to stretch for miles. Dark and silent, except for the shuffling feet at the back of my chair. I wait patiently and the music starts.

At first, the sound of static and popping that you only get with vinyl. A muzak version of a song I'm sure I know, but can't quite place.

A tall, athletic man appears in my periphery, seemingly attempting a pseudo-moonwalk; he backs his way around to stand directly in front of where I sit. His age is unclear. Early forties, perhaps. I find it difficult to pinpoint age with black guys. His hair is shaved short; you can tell it is because it has receded on top leaving a horseshoe of grade-one stubble stretching from the top of one ear around to the other side. He is muscular. At a guess I would say between six foot ten and somewhere above seven foot. All in black, he looks like the world's largest nightclub bouncer or bodyguard. But there is a softness to his face. Like he is here to help me.

I trust him.

He doesn't stop moving. All the time shifting from foot

to foot in time with the music. His eyes protrude from his head and stare at me intently but, again, with kindness. Like he knows something that I don't and he wants to tell me.

Bringing his arms into motion he bends over slightly and smiles broadly. He's always smiling. When his lips part to reveal his teeth, the same yellow colour as his eyes, he is biting down on a 9mm bullet.

For maybe ten seconds he is bent down to my eye level, always smiling, always displaying the bullet in his mouth. He holds out an empty hand in front of my face and edges closer towards me. Shaking his arm slightly, another bullet falls from his sleeve into the palm of his hand. He looks at the bullet, then at me, at the bullet again, then at me. Gripping the bullet in his giant fist he moves even closer towards me. He holds his hand up to my face, still smiling, and pushes the bullet into my mouth. I grip it with my teeth just as he does.

He shuffles backwards and stands upright again, still smiling, still showing me his bullet. He looks at me and nods. He holds up one finger, but is then disturbed. To my left, his right, a spotlight hits the floor directly from above. He turns his gaze to the light, back to me, then back to the light. On the wooden floor next to me, below this beam of bright white light, a chair, identical to mine, appears. I look at The Smiling Man; he stares at me for a few seconds then swallows his bullet and rushes at the empty chair.

I wake up sweating in bed next to Audrey.

'Are you all right? What's going on?' she asks in a startled, high-pitched squeal, waking suddenly, ripping off her Sleep-Easy Eye Cover.

'Yes, yes. Don't worry,' I pant. 'It was just a dream. Sorry. Just go back to sleep. It's fine.' I take a sip of my water and lie back down.

Twenty-four hours later, I find Girl 1.

Girl 1

———◆———

Maybe if I'd tried harder at school or taken one of those night classes I'm always looking at. Maybe if I wasn't such a fuck-up. Maybe, if I hadn't just settled for mediocrity, maybe, just maybe, this could have been avoided.

Maybe.

It was a regular Thursday at work. Old people still using a tattered little bank book and queuing for half an hour to take out ten pounds, when it could have been done in thirty seconds at an ATM. Men with two mobile phones, one for business and one for *other business*, waiting in line with large wads of cash to deposit. Youngsters dawdling nervously with a cheque from a grandparent. Glamorous forty-something women with bleach-blonde hair, fake tans, Botox-treated foreheads and no career moving money from their 'allowance' account into the personal savings account that their rich, fat, bloated husband knows nothing about. It's their getaway fund.

I wish I had a getaway fund.

I just free-fall my way through the day, each one the same as the previous, each one a reminder of my failure, each one leading me straight to Eames.

I'm the last cashier to leave the building society today

and it's awkward. A couple of weeks ago, my manager made a pass at me. I was at work early and it was just the two of us. He called me into the office and directly asked whether anything could 'happen' between us. He even made the speech marks with his fingers. It felt dirty. I felt scared. Nobody was due in for another hour, and if he'd wanted to do anything to me right there and then on his oversized mahogany desk there would have been nothing I could have done to stop him.

'To be honest, I don't really feel comfortable talking about this at work.' I winced diplomatically as I turned him down.

'Maybe we could talk about it more *outside* of work,' he pursued, not grasping my sentiment.

'I think I should, maybe, get on with my work now.' I reversed out of the door, never turning my back to this predator in case he pounced.

I could see his face, smiling in triumph. I'm not sure what his agenda was, whether he expected me to jump under his desk and unbutton his trousers so that I could orally please him while he caught up on some e-mails, or whether he just wanted to frighten me, to let me know who was boss.

Either way, with just the two of us in our tiny building society this evening, the atmosphere is far from comfortable.

I cash out the till and nothing is said or implied. It turns out that he wasn't the man I should be wary of.

January

Girl 1 was found in her apartment. Her neighbour heard two gunshots and called it in.

Her flat is minimalist, whether through stylistic choice or monetary hindrance. There aren't many ornaments, the furniture is small and clearly second-hand and everything from the drawers to the bed to the coffee table is modular but well put together. Sturdy. It tells you a lot about a person just to know that they do these small things properly.

She is handcuffed to her bed. One hand, her left, is cuffed to the headboard, while both feet are attached to the other end with black silk handkerchiefs. She is naked and there are no signs of false entry into the apartment.

It's difficult to determine her age as her face has been largely disfigured, but her body would suggest early to mid-thirties.

Without an autopsy and just using evidence from a preliminary examination of the crime scene, I would guess that the cause of death was a single bullet shot to the mouth from a distance of between five and eight feet. Her state would suggest intercourse and the autopsy will back up whether this was consensual or forced. I'd expect alcohol to be present in the bloodstream and possibly drugs.

The bed has been turned upright so that the girl is facing the door. The blood on the mattress and wall suggests that she was in this position when the gun was fired. Teeth fragments pepper the floor around her and some are embedded into the back of her throat. She is blonde, but I'm not sure yet whether this has any significance.

What is left of her face looks sad and exhausted.

The gun lying on the floor near her feet is not the murder weapon. Ballistics will later show that a single bullet was fired from this gun and the prints will match those of the victim. Gunpowder residue will be found on her right hand. The hand that is not cuffed to the bed.

Why would her killer allow her such an opportunity?

Directly opposite the bed a hole can be seen on the far wall where the bullet from this gunshot has been removed.

I make some mental notes on the pertinent aspects of the elaborate scene before me and slowly realise that last night, when I woke up suddenly, I already had all the information I needed.

Girl 1

The sticker on my left breast says 'Dorothy Penn'. I'm aware that it draws attention to one of my best features and cuts down the time of having to answer the arbitrary first question or introduce myself; I only have two minutes with each guy.

The first prospect sits down opposite me. A heavy-set man, greying hair, presentable, with a face that you can tell used to be beautiful when he was younger. But he's very nervous.

He points at my chest. 'Like Sean,' he mumbles, tilting his head down disappointedly.

'Sorry?' I ask, not quite hearing him.

'Sean Penn. The actor,' he clarifies.

'Oh. Yes. We have the same surname.' It's awkward. His name tag says 'Miles Jennings'. I can't think of anyone famous with that surname. We both fumble about in the awkwardness of this opening exchange. 'But we're not related.' I laugh, trying to ease the tension.

But the laugh is awkward too.

It's a long two minutes of staccato conversation and I even start to wish my lecherous boss had kept me on later than he already had. I nearly didn't make it because he was being such an arrogant pig, making me perform a series of inane tasks while he tapped away at his keyboard doing nothing. My punishment for turning him down, perhaps.

Eventually I just grabbed my bag and left, hurrying out the door so as not to give him the opportunity to offer me a lift home.

The bell rings and I put a mental strike through Miles Jennings' name. He was cute, though. A few glasses of wine and I could be lonely enough to take him home for some awkward sex.

All the men stand up and move around one position. The tables are arranged in a horseshoe with the women on the inside and the men shifting around the outside. The moderator/organiser has a desk in between the two ends of the horseshoe so he can acknowledge each man as he passes by on the long walk from one side to the other.

Another loser sits down opposite me. But I suppose we are all losers for having to attend such a soirée in order to meet people. He looks ridiculous. Thick-rimmed glasses and a Hawaiian shirt. Jeans with no belt, dirty trainers and a mobile phone clipped to the top of his faded-denim slacks.

Is this a joke?

He is the personification of geek. It's obvious that he has created this persona to cover up who he really is, or worse, to give himself a personality. I know I hate him already and I take a sly glance to my left to see who is next.

'I used to have a Penn racquet,' he bleats, 'and balls.'

I start to think that these name tags aren't the best idea. I'd rather them fixate on my breasts than open the conversation like this.

'Wow. It must be fate,' I respond, tired and unable to hide the sarcasm.

His tag says 'Dream Man'. What is he trying to hide?

'So, Dorothy. May I call you Dorothy?'

'Well, it is my name.' I feel bad immediately for responding so harshly. It can't be easy for him to come to these things. He's clearly insecure about something despite his bravado.

I try to rally myself, softening my expression and trying to rescue the situation. 'But maybe you could call me Dream Woman.' I laugh and he joins in.

Maybe I judged him too soon. He looks like a clown, but there might be something worth knowing if you can delve a little deeper. Heaven knows what these men think of me when they sit down. Maybe that I look like a tart in this top, because I'm showing a little more skin than is politically correct. Maybe they can tell that I'm not a natural blonde or my hips are too wide, or I look like someone who is boring enough to work in a bank. Maybe.

I feel a little deflated.

Maybe after a few glasses of wine and a tequila or two I would give this guy some pity-sex.

Am I *that* lonely?

'So, Dream Woman, what do you do?'

Oh God. Kill me now.

After the forty minutes have passed we are all supposed to write down the names or numbers of any people that we might like to see again. If there is any male/female correspondence between the numbers, then you are helped to set up a date. I can't think of anyone to select. My candidates were either awkward or dull, or they were a clear misogynist or workaholic or serial dater.

Out of the twenty men that attended, seven of them

wanted to see me again, eight if you include Dream Man, but something tells me that he hedged his bets and wrote everybody down on his form. I didn't write anybody's name on mine. I just signed it, wrote thanks and drew a smiley face.

I'm sitting at the bar on my own sipping at, maybe, my fifth vodka and tonic, when I see a man walk in and sit down by himself six stools down from me. His hair and jacket are a little wet so I guess it must be raining outside.

Another ten minutes pass and he is still sat there, silently sipping at his whisky; we are the only two left in here. I wonder whether I have one more speed date left in me. With alcoholic courage I decide to go over and talk to him. How much worse could mankind get tonight?

'Mind if I join you?' I say in my most sultry, yet non-desperate, voice.

He pulls the stool out next to his, gesturing for me to take a seat, and orders a Dewars on the rocks for himself 'and another vodka for my friend here'.

I accept with a smile, grateful for his charm after the men I've just met.

'Hi, I'm Eames,' he says in an almost whisper that is so sexy I subconsciously spread my legs a little.

'Hi, Eames, I'm Dorothy. Dorothy Penn.' I extend my hand and he kisses it gently. 'Like the actor, or the tennis ball.' I giggle, the alcohol taking effect.

He's so charming, so enigmatic, so charismatic, yet understated. He is so nice to me, so attentive, so dashing.

He is so coming home with me tonight, so tying me to my bed and fucking my brains out, so putting a gun to my face and blowing a hole through my teeth leaving a gaping exit-wound in the back of my head.

I'm so wishing I'd followed through with my idea of giving 'Dream Man' some sympathy sex.

In a couple of hours I'll be dead, but it's difficult to say just how alive I was anyway.

Eames

---❖---

The kill was so easy that it almost wasn't fun.

Dorothy was sweet. Too sweet, perhaps. You could tell that, despite the terribly average hand she had been dealt, she looked for the good in everyone and every situation.

If her boss was harassing her at work it was just because he was under a lot of pressure and needed to blow off some steam. The idiots at speed dating, who were no good for anyone, were just lonely, like her. The serial killer who sat down next to her in an empty bar and bought her drinks at the end of a completely demoralising day was probably just lonely too, or was just a little too carried away with the passion of the evening.

That's not true.

For me, it was a job. I was just doing my job. I transformed an agreeable young girl into a statistic. I turned a nobody into a headline.

When a distasteful text message is sent to you from a friend containing a joke about a woman who has just been gutted, insert my name as her killer. That's my punchline.

Think how lucky you'd feel if I tied you up, but then let you go.

Everybody gets bored. We all need something

stimulating. To put us back on track. Whether you're a salesman who consistently hits target with the same set of accounts for the last God-knows-how-many years, or a lawyer with an unblemished record, or a simple bank cashier with impeccable customer service. We need that new account, or that can't-win case, or companionship when a day's false sincerity has sucked the will from us.

That's what made Girl 1 so easy.

That's what makes them all so fucking easy.

She just wanted someone to look after her, to take care of her. So I bought her drinks, I made her feel protected in an otherwise threatening area of London; I took an interest in her and complimented her ghastly flat. I brought her to shuddering orgasm.

She was delicate and insecure and a truly beautiful person inside and out. She was stunningly beautiful naked with a slim, tight body and breasts that stood up by themselves. Tiny hands and feet and a nearly symmetrical face. It almost felt like a shame to ruin it by breaking her nose and shooting her in the mouth, but it had to be done.

When the dictionary defines a word as *the tendency to derive pleasure, esp. sexual gratification, from inflicting pain, suffering, or humiliation on others*, that word is me.

I slit a tramp's throat once because he asked me for money and I'd just lost some playing poker that night. Once, I waited a week to follow the woman who had scratched my car at the supermarket car park. I tailed her back to her house and stamped on her head in the kitchen until she stopped twitching. She had only managed to unpack the dairy products and some tinned goods.

Despite the ease at which I pulled this off, the

gratification is still there. But there isn't really time to rest and enjoy the euphoria that always follows a good kill, the high you get with knowing that you have achieved your objective, that it's been a good day at the office.

I have things to prepare.

Carla Moretti must be dead in a month.

Girl 4

❖

When I wake up, January's not there. His side of the covers hasn't even moved. I should be worried, but I'm not. He's done this before.

I wrap my robe around me and head downstairs.

It feels a little colder in the house this morning and I'm not sure that this thin silk gown is serving any function other than protecting my modesty while making me look good. It's a big house and takes a while to warm up, so there's not much point in turning the heating on, because it will still be cold when I leave for work.

The paper has arrived on time, as it always does. I pick it up and take it into the kitchen I designed myself, stroking the granite work surfaces as I make my way towards the extravagant, American-style fridge freezer. I'm reassured by the quality around me; top of the range, high spec: only the best.

Throwing the broadsheet down on the polished glass breakfast table, I grab grapefruit juice and milk from the fridge before making myself a small bowl of muesli.

I sit at the table, alone, and turn over the paper.

The front page tells me exactly why January still hasn't come back. It says that a woman from East London has been tied to a bed and shot in the face. It tells me that the police are following leads to apprehend the killer. It says

34

that this was a heinous act of unprovoked violence by a psychotic individual with a taste for drama.

I suppose that's exactly what it looks like.

The paper errs on the side of sympathy towards the woman, but I'm sure this will dissipate in a few days when they uncover that she used to take drugs or abandoned a child when she was young or worked in pornography in the early nineties or something.

It's not the best way to wake up in the morning, but it is the frightening world that we live in and I'm just happy to know that January is safe.

I don't want to look at the article any more; it's too depressing, too frightening.

I take another spoonful of cereal and grab one of my bridal magazines from the stack that lives on the breakfast table. I know that this will be another consuming case for January and that I'll just end up planning everything on my own, but it's probably best that way: I'm in control of everything. He won't know the size of the guest list, who is coming, where the venue is, what food I have selected for everybody, the wine, the music, the possibilities for the honeymoon. All he cares about at the moment is that we have a free bar for the guests. He doesn't need to worry, though; it's me that's paying for it anyway.

I dog-ear a few pages that have inspired me for table decorations, place my bowl and glass in the dishwasher and head back upstairs to shower and get ready for work. I've already stopped thinking about poor Dorothy Penn, left on display like a mutilated rag doll. The whole sorry tale belongs to a totally different world than the one I live in.

I'm thinking about the seating plan for the wedding in

just three months' time, and about the more pressing issue of my 10.30 meeting with De Vere.

I'm not thinking that the word 'unprovoked' in the newspaper article suggests that this could have been anyone that I was reading about: a friend, a relative, me. So, while January submerges himself in this case, I allow myself to be consumed with what is real: planning our wedding and earning the money to pay for it.

I try to call Jan once I'm dressed, but I know he won't pick up. I hang up instead of leaving a voicemail. I drop him a text just in case he has spared a thought for me: 'Hey, babe, I saw the paper. I figure you are busy. I have pilates tonight but let me know when you think you'll be home. Love you. A xx'. I know he won't text me back for a couple of hours, so I throw my phone into my bag, fill my aluminium cup with a strong, bold Sumatran coffee and head out to my car.

The ground is damp from the rain last night and the sky is that typical English grey that they probably have a Pantone for. I hope that the caffeine picks me up for this meeting because, so far, my morning has not put me in the right frame of mind to negotiate a prestigious new recruitment contract.

I sink into the custom-leather seat of my brand-new Mini Cooper S, Racing Green, of course. It's the perfect car for me; all the charm of the original British design, but now with the build quality you only get with German engineering. I turn the ignition with one hand, the car purring into life as I swivel the air dial with my other hand, circulating heat around the interior. I give it a minute to warm up, then edge out into the main road, preparing myself for another morning of London rush-hour traffic.

That's not going to help my mood.

Girl 1

---+---

I've had a lot to drink. I'd already had three or four vodkas before I plucked up the courage to approach Eames and take full advantage of his benevolent inebriation. It doesn't feel like he is trying to get me drunk, though. He doesn't need to. I'd sleep with him after a cup of Earl Grey tea.

He's not tall, but also not what you would call short. Maybe six foot. Six foot one, perhaps. Dark hair, maybe dyed. There's a brooding look about him that I'm sure most women would find sexy as hell; dark around the eyes, like he hasn't slept in days. A defined jaw bone and brow, with a two-day stubble. He is either a weathered, thirty-two-year-old man or a forty-year-old man that looks great for his age.

For the life of me I can't remember what colour his eyes are, despite staring into them for most of the evening.

It's not the best description. Certainly nothing that would help Detective Inspector January David with his investigation. But I had been drinking, and he did drug me.

And I am lonely.

And this is the problem.

I don't ask myself what a great-looking man with a smart dress-sense and pleasant, giving personality is doing in a dingy pub next to Mile End Tube station on a Wednesday night. Why would this seemingly successful man stumble on this place and pick someone like me, a lowly cashier from a small building society on the Roman Road, living on my own and resorting to speed dating to meet people?

The loneliness had killed me long before I spent the night with Eames.

'Do you want to come back to mine for some . . .' I pause slightly.

'Coffee?' he says, with a smile that just lights up his whole face and makes me feel safe, that I am doing the right thing.

'Well, I was going to say wine, but I'm sure we could pick up some coffee at the petrol station on the way back.' I laugh and put my hand on his knee. He doesn't even flinch.

'Wine would be great.' He puts his hand on mine. 'Don't you have to get up early for work, then?' he asks, as if he doesn't know. As if he didn't know exactly where I worked. As if our meeting was complete coincidence. As if I wasn't chosen specifically to be the opening chapter to his diabolical scam.

'It's not even midnight yet.' I stand up and start to put my arms into the sleeves of my coat. He stands and helps me with the second arm. The one he wants to handcuff to my bed. I feel like I am ticking off the qualities I seek in my mind. Then he pays for all our drinks and I know he is definitely going to hold the door open for me.

The air from outside hits me like a brick in the face, and I suddenly feel more wobbly and frivolous than I had inside. Eames takes me by the arm and steadies me.

'So, which way are we going?' he asks, as if he doesn't know exactly where I live. As if he's never seen my street or watched me walk through my front door.

'Follow my lead,' I slur, trying to sound like I am still in control.

We turn left out of the pub. There are still plenty of people out and about despite it being a weeknight. There's a bingo hall across the other side of the road and the Tube keeps a steady flow of people down this street. I'm aware of the growing number of Somalians that have moved into the area over the last few years. I feel like a minority, and some parts really aren't pleasant for me to walk around at this time of night. It's fine right here, because it's a busy crossroads; and anyway I feel perfectly content because I have Eames for protection tonight.

I'm under the spell of forced serendipity.

We head towards the crossing. I prefer it here at night because you can't see as much. Those horrible primary-coloured flats they built in the distance, the way they painted the bridge over the road, the filth on the streets. The construction all around that they are hoping to finish in time for the Olympics; it all takes away the character of the East End that my parents and grandparents hold in such high regard.

I see the partially lit taxi-rank cabins and ethnic eateries with signs that flicker in neon saying things like 'Chin Garde', because some of the bulbs have blown. It's tacky but at least it's real.

The beeping from the crossing pierces louder than usual, and we pick up the pace to a brisk jog to make it through both sets in time. On the other side I need to stop, because I'm a little out of breath and I don't want to throw up. Eames pulls me around so that I am facing him and leans in for a kiss. Nothing sexual, but enough to be exciting.

'Sorry, I just thought it might be a good idea to get that out of the way now so that it isn't awkward later.' He smiles at me again and I melt. I forget that I'm still trying to catch my breath; I forget that I'm lonely.

We continue to walk arm in arm. It's about ten minutes to my flat from here. We pass the petrol station to our left and opt out of the coffee; by now we both know exactly why we are going home together.

We hit another pub at the corner of Arbery Road called the Queen Victoria. It sounds unreal, but has been here longer than any British soap opera trying to depict our local community. He suggests that we step in for a quick drink before the final stretch. The lights are still on inside; I can see the green light-shade lit up over the pool table through the frosted window. I can hear the crack of balls hitting each other and men laughing. But the door is locked. Eames rattles it and we wait, but nobody comes to let us in.

'Looks like we'll just have to power through, I guess.' He pulls me into his hip with his strong arms and we continue to walk.

I live at the bottom of this road in a ground-floor maisonette. It's not much, but I can afford it on my wage and I keep it nice for when people come over. My mum says it looks like the top floor of Ikea. I buy all my stuff from there. It's got colour and personality and even though a lot of people buy lots of things from there I buy *everything* from there. I like the price and I enjoy putting it together myself.

My living room is modelled on the *Affordable and*

Complete design. So I have the Grevback TV bench and matching bookcase, the Klingsboro side table that I use as a coffee table, the Rejolit pendant lampshade – one of those spherical wrinkled paper shades that cost less than three quid, but look more expensive if you accessorise correctly. I have an Extorp sofa, in white, opposite the TV and have added a splash of colour with the Klinteby rug and the Hallaryyd print hanging on the wall to the left of the sofa – on the opposite wall to the bookcase. It does look a little like you see it in the showroom, but who doesn't love the way they present it all in those spaces? I'm proud of my home.

We get to the bottom of the road and cross over at the corner near the primary school playground. My flat is straight opposite. Number 126, almost in the centre of a long row of terraced houses. Eames lets go of me while I fumble in my bag for the keys.

I open the door on to a communal hallway that both my upstairs neighbour and I use to get to our front doors. I mouth 'Ssshhh' to Eames by putting a finger over my lips. I don't turn the light on in the hall, but inch my way towards my door, almost tiptoeing.

Finally, we enter my flat and I flick on the light.

There is a narrow corridor that leads to the other end of the house and my bathroom and bedroom. You can also get to the garden, but it's not really worth the trouble; it's totally concrete and about as narrow as the corridor. I send Eames in that direction to use the toilet, while I head left into the kitchen to open some wine.

My kitchen is still a work in progress, because I really don't have enough money to completely refurbish it, but I did splash out on the Oxscår mixer tap and I have accessorised with the Grundtal series of products. I love the way my herbs and knives are magnetised to the wall. It will take me a while to save up for the work-top and cabinets, but I have nearly £500 put away so I'm a fifth of the way to my perfect kitchen.

I take a bottle of Merlot from the rack and open it. I don't know too much about wine, but I hear that Merlot is supposed to be nice and it tastes OK to me. Eames comes back to the kitchen.

'I like what you have done in there. Really made use of the space.' He takes his glass of wine. 'Thanks. Cheers.' We clink glasses and sip our drinks.

'The trick is to get smaller units to give the illusion of space,' I exclaim triumphantly. I'm oozing with pride. He wanders into the living room, which leads off from the kitchen.

'Wow. It looks like a showroom,' he says, amazed.

'Thank you very much.' I take this as a compliment, whether he meant it as one or not.

He sits down on the sofa and continues to peruse the room from there, sipping at his wine while he does so.

I never stop to ask myself why a seemingly wealthy man would feel so comfortable in my tiny Scandinavian-inspired flat full of not-real wood and massively reproduced art. Why would this intelligent, clearly well-educated, ruggedly handsome creature waste his time walking through the dimly lit streets of Bow with a working-class nobody like me, who has shelves full of books she has never even attempted to read?

It doesn't cross my mind to question it.

He continues to slouch on my sofa as if he lives here, while I stand in the doorway, leaning to one side with my glass in my right hand, attempting to look elegant yet

42

sexy, hoping that the light from the kitchen behind is catching my curves in the right way.

'Can I top you up?' I ask as he devours the last gulp of his wine.

'Oh, don't worry, I'll do it.' He stands up and walks into the kitchen. He only just squeezes through the doorway without quite touching me and grabs my glass, even though it still has some wine in it. He takes it over to the counter and fills both glasses almost to the brim.

Handing mine back to me he says, 'Maybe you can show me the rest of the house that I haven't seen.'

Without saying anything I grab his free hand with mine and lead him to the back of the flat where my bedroom is.

It's based on the *Perfectly Cosy* design. I have the Malm drawers with smoky glass top, matching Pax wardrobe with two very special drawers that display all my shoes beautifully. I have the Jorun Rug and Stave mirror, but opted for the Hemnes bed frame because I thought it looked more *New England*; plus, it has a slatted headboard so that I can be handcuffed to the bed easily. It's very clean with clear lines and it's bright enough during the day, despite the wall that goes all the way around my concrete garden blocking out most of the sun.

I look at Eames. 'Soooo . . .' I say, inviting him to finish my sentence, and he does.

'This is where the magic happens.'

January

A t this point, I don't know that this is the start of a spate of serial killings, so I have to treat it as an isolated incident. The papers are labelling it as unprovoked, but it seems to me that it was most certainly planned. All the details from the scene itself point towards it being a very thought-out process. It's not a simple culling of an innocent girl, my gut tells me that much. This feels bigger than that. There's something we are not seeing.

The obvious place to start is her work. Acts of passion are not just limited to home life; they can, and often do, extend to the workplace. As she lived alone in her modular heaven I decide to take a trip to the building society that she worked at and question her boss and her colleagues to find out more about her as a person. So far all I know is that she was thirty-five, had no debts apart from her mortgage, paid all her bills on time, had savings of around £500 and a bookcase full of books, but only the Jane Austen novels seem to have any wear on the spine.

The market is on down the Roman Road today, so there is no way of getting my battered old Mondeo down there. I park near to Dorothy's flat, scraping the kerb as I back into a gap left by a much smaller vehicle, and take a five-minute walk to the building society where she worked.

As I get out of the car I see kids on the opposite side of the road with their faces pressed up against the green school fencing, staring at the house surrounded by police tape, some laughing at my parking skills. It saddens me to know that they have to live in this sort of world and that it has to have an impact on them. I think they should be aware of the dangers out there, but it has to be presented to them in the right way. It's a problem close to my heart, though I don't discuss the reasons why at work. My history; my business.

If only Dorothy had been a little more aware, a little more cautious.

I round the corner into the colourful current of people heading to the market to get their cheap fruit and knocked-off clothing. The independent shops are clearly thriving; whether it's a newsagent or launderette or an amusement arcade or café, the global chains don't appear to have infected this end of the street. I allow the flow of people to guide me into the bottleneck of the market entrance. I hear the locals refer to it simply as *The Roman*.

There is a real sense of energy and vibrancy. Traders trying to make themselves heard over the bustle, shouting out prices and weights, exaggerating the word 'pound' wherever possible. The Indian traders are a little more reserved, delicately hanging out their faux gold jewellery and batteries, clipping their luminous price tags to the frames of their stalls. People just getting on with their lives, some unaware of the horror that lurks within their proud community. Most, undaunted by the events of last night, desensitised to the reality of such a crime.

Just over halfway down the road I can see the sign of the building society above one of the clothing stalls. I manage to squeeze through and get to the pavement on the other side, where I can enter the building. It's relatively empty. There are two cashiers on duty, but only one elderly lady with a trolley handing her bank book over to the woman on the right. I move straight over to her colleague on the left.

'Good morning, sir. How can I help you?' the woman behind the glass asks me as if nothing important happened today. She looks about fifty-five. Way too much make-up, like she should be selling perfume in a department store. Her hair is a wiry blonde. The kind of blonde you get when you dye grey hair. It's not a dirty blonde; it's almost like a dead blonde. Like someone turned down the contrast on her hair. It's only accentuated by the brightness of her face. But she seems pleasant.

'I'm Detective Inspector January David.' I show her my ID. 'I'd like to speak with the manager, please.' She looks anxious, taken aback. It's funny how people's body language changes as soon as you tell them that you work for the police. They immediately start to look guilty about something, even if they haven't done anything wrong. It's the ones who don't look guilty that I worry about.

She walks off behind a wall and reappears about thirty seconds later. 'Sorry about that, Detective Inspector. Mr Price will be with you shortly. If you'd like to take a seat he won't be long.' She smiles nervously at me, as though she has been embezzling money for years.

I take a seat at one of the desks on the other side of the room.

Four minutes later, a man appears through a code-locked door and makes his way over to where I am sitting. He is in a grey suit that he clearly bought from the market. The trousers are too high in the leg, so I can see his socks, and the jacket is far too big for his frame. Like the school blazer your parents bought you on your first day that they hoped you would grow into in about four years; that way they didn't have to keep forking out each year during a child's growth period.

His hair is thinning and his face is round with all the features crammed into a small space in the middle. His fake tan makes him look a little dirty. He's around five foot eight with a very slim build; his oversized suit jacket only exaggerates this effect as he drowns in the vast extent of shiny, cheap fabric.

He strides towards me with authority, straightening his half-Windsor knotted tie as he approaches. He stretches out a hand. 'Detective Inspector, sorry to keep you waiting, but we have had one of our girls not turn up this morning and it has been a little manic.' His voice is quite nasal and irritating.

'Dorothy Penn?' I ask.

'Well . . . yes. How did you . . .?' he stutters. I can't stand stutterers, they waste valuable time.

I stand up and grab him by the arm. 'Look, Mr Price. Can we go into your office please? I'm not here to discuss my mortgage.'

I know it's not the correct way to behave and any normal person would have shrugged me off or threatened me with a lawsuit for assault, but experience tells you who will just take this and help you with your enquiries. I think he was still in shock.

He leads me through the coded door. I see that the lock has five vertical buttons and the code he taps in is top button, middle button, bottom button, turn. I would wager that the password on his computer is 'password'. In the back of my mind I start to question just how secure my money is with my bank.

He tells me to take a seat and perches himself behind his oversized desk. I question him about the last time he saw Dorothy, what his relationship with her was like, has he noticed anything different about her lately. He tells me how reliable she is, how she is always early for work and how impeccable her service is. He tells me that his relationship with her is purely professional and that he respects her and her work ethic, as do all her colleagues. This sounds a little rehearsed to me, but he is still talking about her as if she is alive.

He tells me that she is pretty constant. Consistently energetic and friendly. He can't think of any time in recent weeks where she has broken this seamless persona of contentedness.

When somebody dies you often find that nobody wants to say anything against their character. It's the same with murderers. They are always someone you thought was an upstanding citizen. Someone like you. It can make it difficult to extract information sometimes, but a good investigator trusts their instincts and I know that he is not being totally forthcoming.

'Thanks for your help, Mr Price. I think that will do for now, but I may have to return at some point to just clear a few things up.' I scribble in my notebook and I can see him wipe a bead of sweat away from his temple. I know that he didn't do it, but he isn't telling me everything. 'I would like to speak to your staff, though. So I'll need to use your office for the next half an hour.'

'That's fine.' He squirms. 'I'll send Patsy through first.'

I flick my personal mobile on while I wait and see that I have a missed call from Audrey and a message about her Pilates class. She does like to act normal in these situations but, often, it's a little too normal. You have to acknowledge that these events are real otherwise you put yourself at risk every time you leave the house.

I text her: 'Not sure when I'll be home but I will be back this evening at some point.' I forget to put the kiss at the end and I know she'll read into that.

The door edges open cautiously and a wiry nest of tangled hair appears through the gap.

'Come in, Patsy, please,' I say in a deliberately non-intimidating tone.

Once I have her settled it's difficult to shut her up. She echoes Price's sentiments regarding Dorothy's character and appears deeply upset at the news of her death. She tells me that Dorothy had an experience on the Number 5 bus a couple of weeks ago.

'There are a lot of Muslims in the area now. It's really not that safe for anyone. It's tough for the West Indians who have been here for a generation or so now, but I'm sure you are aware of some of the killings in Bethnal Green.' She has that faux racism that you get with a certain generation who aren't completely ignorant about different cultures, but their upbringing was a lot less tolerant than we see now and you have to accept much of what they say because they don't know any better. 'Dorothy was on the Number 5 bus a couple of weeks back. She said that a small Muslim boy was sat with his mother making pig noises at an elderly white lady. The mother was embarrassed and kept telling the child to be quiet, but he continued to taunt the old woman. Dorothy tried to intervene, saying how unacceptable she found his actions. She wasn't really streetwise, you know? These things happen nowadays and you have to just let them go. But she was just too nice to do that, I think.'

My gut tells me this story doesn't have any bearing on Dorothy's death. I don't believe that this was an act of revenge or a racist attack. It was premeditated sadism for some other reason. But I thank Patsy for her help all the same.

I interview the other bank cashier, but glean very little from this. My trip this morning has merely confirmed that Dorothy was a nice, normal girl, living her life, doing her job, building her home. So far, I reflect ruefully, my basic police work is leading me very slowly down a path of no discovery.

If I could just give in to the idea, I'd realise that The Smiling Man was telling me exactly how and where the murder would take place and who was committing this atrocity.

If I could let myself believe.

But I can't.

I can catch him and I can do it my way.

Girl 4

———✦———

Ibuilt this company with little more than a small loan from my father. So, when the De Vere contract negotiations were being finalised, I wanted to be as involved as I could. Not because I want to take the credit for someone else's work, or because I find it hard to relinquish control and trust my staff to do their job, but simply because new account acquisitions still give me the buzz I used to feel when we were going through our growth stage.

I've reached the top and most days feel like maintenance. It's less proactive than it used to be. Being involved in these meetings stops me from stagnating.

That's why I do it.

This account will not be worth as much to us as some of the blue-chip companies that we deal with, but it harks back to our humble beginnings seven years ago when we concentrated on hospitality positions and sales roles. This is our bread and butter, our run-rate business. AU Recruitment represents some of the largest banks in the world and we provide high-calibre candidates for executive positions in IT and FMCG. We recruit ferociously in the capital, but have expanded with offices in Nottingham, Bristol and Glasgow over the last couple of years.

It's a multi-million pound company that I started. I am the managing director and I own the majority of shares. Big enough to handle, small enough to care. That's our motto. But I'm a little bored of it now; although I'm not sure bored is the right word.

At least I have the wedding to plan. Something to look forward to. Something else that I can build from scratch. This company was once a thing that hindered my relationships with men. It was the most important thing in life. It had to be. Other men have suffered as a consequence, men I would not like to see again and would not like to see me. My priorities are changing, though, and I know that January's are too. We're different people.

The meeting concludes, we shake hands and it's official. AU Recruitment will handle all the recruitment needs for De Vere, from the pot-wash to the chefs to the hotel management team. The buzz I get is short-lived, but I feel pleased for Michelle, who brought this account to us, and she completely deserves her new-business commission this month for her effort alone.

I take the stairs up to my office, while Michelle takes the client down in the lift. I can't understand why people use a lift if they are only going up or down one flight of stairs. They say obesity is the biggest killer in the country, but I think it's laziness.

I push through the door on to the sales floor where my reps are busy with prospects and arranging candidate interviews. It is totally open-plan; everyone has a flat-screen monitor and desktop computer that is no older than three years. This is a peak time of day for outgoing calls and the hubbub in front of me suggests that they are all doing what they should be doing, rather than surfing the Internet or updating something on a social net-working site.

As I walk through the aisle to my office at the other end of the room, some people look towards me and smile, some keep their head buried and some just continue with their good work. I tell my assistant to go out and buy a bottle of champagne for Michelle, then sit down at my desk to check my e-mails.

The first mail I open is from a company called Guy's Works. They organise fireworks displays for special events. They offer me three packages for the wedding. The bronze will last for seven minutes and will cost £850. Silver will last for twelve minutes and costs £1,500, but does include some spectacular elements that a bronze package will not cover, such as whistle and flash candles. Gold is £3,000 for eighteen minutes and the platinum package is really reserved for large corporate events. It costs £7,250 and lasts for twenty minutes. Although it's only two minutes longer than the Gold package, it does include a Cracking Star and Brocade Shells salute at the start. There are special effects mines, a barrage of aerial bursting shells, rockets that fly over a thousand feet high with an emphatic finale bouquet of five hundred separate projectiles being launched and firing on five separate levels. It finishes with a titanic burst of shells. For an extra £250 I can have something that lights up with our initials inside a heart.

I respond saying that I will take the Platinum Package and give the initials for inside the heart. The wedding is three months away, so this should give them more than enough time to arrange. It's my treat for Jan. He doesn't know it yet, but he will love it.

I've had a free rein on the organisation of the day. Jan

trusts me to get on with it. He doesn't care about the fine details, just that I am happy and that the day proceeds as I have always imagined it. It is my money that is paying for it, after all. I deserve the ideal, from this relationship, from this day, and I'll do whatever it takes to have it. So I bought the Vera Wang Fairy Princess ivory organza cut-petal bodice gown with vanilla grosgrain sash, we will toast with Drappier Carte d'Or Brut Champagne 1986, and we shall have a meant-for-corporate fireworks display in the evening.

It will be perfect.

Once I have finished the joy of confirming final wedding details I sit back into my chair, slouching, and stare at the bold font that jumps off the screen telling me that I have over eighty e-mails that are work related. I swivel around in my chair a few times to kill a couple of seconds. I see that January has messaged me back when I switch my phone on. I knew that he would be all right and was just bogged down with the case, but it wouldn't have hurt him to put a kiss at the end of the text. It's only one extra button.

I look back on the first half of my day and it's difficult to pick a highlight.

Eames

—✦—

When someone says that 'Satan gets into people and makes them do things they don't want to,' that's not me.

That's just an excuse. I want to do it.

When someone cries, 'Forgive me Lord for I know not what I do,' that's weakness. That's a lie. That really isn't me at all. I know what I do.

When I read in the newspaper that a woman has been cuffed to a bed and shot in the face at point-blank range, that she was possibly raped, that this was a random, mindless act of a deranged sociopath, I can't believe that they are referring to me.

I have never raped anyone. I couldn't do that to someone. To say that this was random or mindless is a gross insult to the effort it took to plan such an accomplished piece of art. I chose Dorothy Penn from a long list. I stalked her. I got to know her before we had even met. It had to be her for a reason.

To look at that crime scene and suggest that any of it was arbitrary or casual, that it was performed without method or conscious decision, is only an indication of their stupidity.

*

I do not kill children.

I do not rape women.

I do not beat up pensioners.

Every kill has its reason. Whether the reason is that your mother tried to expel you from the warm protection of her womb or that she just had the wrong name. Whether you want to give death some meaning, you feel like you are helping somebody in the long run or that you believe it to be the ultimate act of creation. Killing is always about love.

The papers, the police, they don't understand this yet. Until they do, they are never going to catch me.

Until they notice me for what I am doing, they are misdirected.

So I write them a letter.

January

Paulson asks me if I mind having strippers.

'Don't ask me that. If you don't ask me then I won't know, will I? That way, if I have a lap dance, it's not a pre-meditated lap dance.' I tut and shake my head at him.

'Oh. Right, boss. Got it.' He winks and taps the side of his nose a couple of times to signify that we have an understanding.

Paulson is a fantastic investigator. He's around the same age as me, mid-thirties, but a little more rotund. His metabolism is middle-aged, but his diet is that of a fully active child. He isn't fully active, though.

Sitting with a muffin and coffee while he pukes out the answers to the *Financial Times* crossword is a common sight if you manage to get into work as early as Paulson. And, if you can stay up as late as he does, sat at a desk with a chocolate bar and a coffee, playing poker online for sums of money a policeman should never see unless confiscating for evidence, is where you'll find him. His gamer tag is P4U750N. It's also the number plate on his car.

He has been investigated internally due to the lifestyle he can afford on the wage we receive. But he is smart. If there is a puzzle, he will solve it. He's also as honest as they come and he works here because he wants to, not because he has to. I suppose we have that in common.

'Look, man, it's not for almost three months yet. I'll leave it to you two savages to organise. Surprise me.'

'Surprise you with strippers?' He smiles as he says it in his mischievous, childlike manner and I laugh.

'Whatever you want.' I give in. He offers me a giant cookie from his bag of five.

I start to think about Dorothy and how after only a week, the regular police teams seem to have moved on and things are getting *back to normal*. A stabbing here and there, some shoplifting, domestic disturbances, and colleagues already have things to occupy their minds away from the misery that we live and work in. But I specialise in violent crime and there are no breaks. It's always real and always in the forefront of your mind. I take this personally and I can't just forget.

These are the cases that have to get solved.

Eames sent a note a couple of days ago, but it never got to me. They thought it was a crank. It has been filed away and I don't know what it says.

I have some new information, though. Dorothy's upstairs neighbour, the person who called in after hearing the gunshots, saw the perpetrator, albeit from behind and above as she looked out of her window, but we can confirm that it is a man of around six foot in height with dark hair. Not a lot to go on, but she also heard them come home and said that it was about ninety minutes before the first shot. She did not hear a vehicle, so we can assume that they walked back from wherever they met. This narrows it down to a few pubs and clubs in the local area. We can also confidently surmise that she invited her killer into her house and that the sex was consensual.

Her colleagues, family and neighbours had not spoken to her about a man in her life, so, although they want to think the best of her, it is likely she picked him up on the night of the murder. That this was a one-night stand. Her family protest that she was not that kind of girl and I am sensitive to that, but this proves to be a vital piece of information.

Murphy comes into the office with a piece of paper in his hand.

'Here you go, Jan.' He hands me the document. 'This is the list of all eight men who expressed an interest in Dorothy at the speed dating that night. All their addresses are there too.'

'Cheers, Murph. This is great. Good work.' It's normal work really, but I'm hoping he will respond to some positive reinforcement. I take the sheet from his hands and start looking down the names for something I might recognise. Miles Jennings, Philip Bailey, nobody stands out.

'Maybe what you need is a list of the people that *weren't* interested in her,' Paulson chips in with his problem-solving hat on. 'Women can be brutal,' he adds, taking a bite of his third giant cookie. 'You upset the wrong kind of lonely gimp that goes speed dating to meet girls . . .' He trails off knowingly.

He might have a point and, even though I am the lead investigator, I will always listen to him, because he really does think outside the box. I'm not quite investigate-by-numbers, but I am methodical and precise and thorough. My *something extra* is my gut. I have strong, sensitive feelings towards events and incidents and suspects, and I'm usually right on the money. This approach means that, with every day that passes, I am wasting time and more girls will die.

Folding the list, I put it into the inside pocket of my suit jacket. I'll start to work on this tomorrow. Right now I have to get home.

'Off already, Jan?' Paulson asks. 'Not like you.'

'Yeah, I'm cooking Audrey dinner tonight. I haven't seen her much over the last week, so I thought I'd try to make it up to her.' I slip my arms through the sleeves of my coat.

'Oh you old romantic, you,' Paulson says. He and Murphy laugh, both a little jealous that I actually have someone to go home to. 'Don't worry about the send-off, I'll sort out the . . . er . . . entertainment.' They both laugh again.

'Cheers, fellas. See you later.' I walk out the door as they start to conspire about exotic dancers, whipped cream and baby oil.

Eames

———◆———

Weeks before the event, I go over every little detail. Nothing can go wrong. I'm not supposed to get caught yet. I've been watching Carla for weeks, so I know her routine. I know her route to work, which bus she takes, who she meets with in the evening, where she lives, what meals she tends to order in a restaurant. Two days ago I sat at the table behind her in a coffee house. She ordered a cappuccino with plenty of chocolate on top and an almond biscotti. I watched her suck the foam off the end of the biscuit and got aroused. I saw her enter the Embassy Theatre, which is just across the road from the Hampstead Theatre. Both are locations where an agent can spot the latest up-and-coming talent from the Central School for Speech and Drama. Two hours later I watched her emerge from her short course in business.

I made a note of the location as a possibility for my fourth girl. That is going to be something special.

But now I must put all my efforts into the beautiful Miss Moretti.

I sit outside the Tube at Swiss Cottage. I can't go into the Underground on account of my claustrophobia. Think how easy it should be to get away from me in London.

I sit on the steps of Station House in Swiss Terrace and collect myself. I have a notebook and camera, so I can plot any possible routes that I might need to take in order to not be detected. It is fairly simple, though; people are so self-involved that they barely notice me. They don't see that I follow them and appear in their favourite hang-out spots. It doesn't matter how old they are, their class or their profession; people are generally selfish and only see what they want to see.

As I walk out on to Finchley Road I turn left. A middle-aged man jogs towards me. He has a beard and is wearing a California University hooded sweatshirt and baseball cap. He nods at me in acknowledgement and I feel uneasy. I want to go unnoticed. If even one person can pick me out in a line-up it can complicate things. Even without the UCLA sweatshirt, I'd reckon he must be American; the English are not that sociable to passing strangers. Still, he must jog this route often, so I have plenty of opportunity to erase this problem if I return at some point in the future.

I watch him run to see if he turns off on to another road. He keeps going. Past the cinema, past the high-rise flats and off into the smog, as if trying to run to the point of perspective.

I continue down this grey, dilapidated street. It's like walking through Shepherd's Bush with all the colour and vibrancy washed out. The only excitement comes when a fire engine tries to squeeze through some traffic and a coach beeps at an elderly lady who is illegally parked outside the bank.

It just all seems a little out of date.

There is an element of multicultural influence. On the other side of the road I see a string of restaurants, Hungarian food, Chinese, Indian, Thai, even an Istanbul Supermarket where Carla bought some houmous last

Tuesday. Above the shops are flats partially covered in graffiti. *Stop! RTW* it says right at the top. I wonder how they get up that high and go unnoticed. Further along it says *Run Tings Wisely*. Not *things*. It gives some indication of the artist's background.

I have to make sure that I can pick her up in one night, otherwise it gets too complicated. If she talks about me to even one person, it establishes a trail. Currently, I am debating between the lacklustre market in the square that bisects the theatres and appears to only sell home-made food, and the new library, which has a rather impressive climbing wall attached to it.

I know the area now. I know that The North Star pub is out of bounds. They would remember someone who had never been in there before. I should expect this from any establishment that proudly displays the flag of St George in the majority of its windows.

I cross to the other side of the road. Two elderly people walk past me arm in arm and it does fill me with warmth to see their enduring love. As they level with me the man turns his head to the side and spits on the pavement. I picture myself cutting out his tongue and treating him like the animal he is.

Shaking with outrage I take the next turning on the left just to get off the same street as that man. I'm confronted with a rather steep hill that I hope will drain some energy and calm me down. Halfway up I see two builders hanging over a balcony eating crisps instead of doing whatever they have been hired to do. At the top is a school, South Hampstead High School. It has the same green fencing as the school near to Dorothy's flat.

A road sweeper is sat on the bench outside eating a sausage roll and sweating. While I don't want to be noticed, the man gives me a sense of unease and I want him to understand that I have seen him, that I know his face and that I suspect him to be a predator of some kind.

When a paedophiliac road sweeper is found bloody and beaten outside a school playground, but doesn't want to press charges, even though he could identify his attacker, for fear of incriminating himself in some way, that's me that saved your child.

Suddenly I decide to follow a brown sign that says FREUD MUSEUM. I can disappear there for a short time before I allow my mind to race, before my passion gets in the way of my long-term goal. I'm interested in psychology, I have to be in this line of work. And it will just keep me out of the way of things for a while.

Ensure I don't kill a child molester or cut a pensioner's throat.

The houses are quite grand along this tree-lined street. Large red-brick town houses that wouldn't look out of place on a university campus. Cars are parked along both sides of the road; and I can tell that canvassers have already been down here this morning as each vehicle has a pink flyer advertising dry-cleaning services in the local area.

I'm looking for Number 20. Apparently that's where the museum is, but all the numbers on my side of the road are odd.

I cross over where a lorry full of bricks is trying to back out of a driveway. The building in front of me has a large blue oval plaque on the front face that says *Sigmund Freud, Founder of Psychoanalysis, lived here 1938–39.* Another plate tells me that his sister also lived here at one time. The wooden frame in front of me tells me that it is shut. It doesn't open until twelve o'clock.

I want to hit something.

I want to cut something open.

I make my way back down the road and see that the dubious road sweeper is still outside the school. He looks at me and smiles, nodding towards me like the American jogger. There are too many people around for me to do anything, but I'll remember his nefarious brow.

Frustrated, I power back down the hill, my mind filled with venomous thoughts, my nostrils flaring as I exhale heavily, my hand gripping the rail with a force that turns my knuckles white. I continue my power walk around the corner, a mist clouding my vision, and collide with Carla Moretti, knocking a pile of what I recognise as business books from her hands.

'Oh God, I'm so sorry. Are you all right?' I ask, bending down to pick up her books, wondering if I've ruined everything.

'Don't worry,' she reassures me, 'it's fine. It happens.' I hand her books back. 'Thank you,' she says pleasantly and smiles at me with her bright blue eyes.

It's at this point that I decide on the library over the market. The library is where I will meet her before I take her out, before we eat, before we drink, before we fuck, before I pierce some of her vital organs with the white heat of a sharp arrowhead, before I take the final shot that cuts through her brain, splitting her skull and putting her to rest.

She continues her journey, worrying about her course-work, not realising that in three weeks she'll be dead and everything she is working towards is a waste of fucking time.

Girl 4

—◆—

When I get home I can smell the food. It's nice to see Jan this evening and he is making the effort by cooking me dinner. We haven't had sex this week, so tonight should cover off our weeknight session. Even though I know it's coming, I'm looking forward to it, to the closeness.

'Hello-oo?' I say, walking into the hallway, taking off my coat and placing my keys on the antique drawers. January emerges from the kitchen wearing a stained apron and carrying a bottle of beer. As dishevelled as always, January is one of the only men I've met who can look scruffy in a tuxedo.

'Evening,' he says taking a quick swig from his bottle. I walk over and kiss him, tasting the lager on his breath; he's definitely had more than one while creating his culinary delight. 'How was work?'

'Boring. Same old. You know.' I drone out my answer to show that I don't really care to talk about how unfulfilling my position at the head of a large recruiting firm has become. At the same time, I always find it difficult to reciprocate the interest. How can I ask him how his day went? He does something real. Real people die and he strives for a sense of justice in a world that he genuinely believes can be better than it is, while everyone around him succumbs to the notion that we're all doomed. 'You must be glad it's the weekend now.' I know it's a stupid thing to say because he still works over the weekend, but I just don't know how to talk about some random girl who is stupid enough to take a stranger home to have sex and ends up dead.

'I'm just glad we get to see each other tonight.' He takes another gulp of his drink and heads into the kitchen and I follow.

The table is laid with place mats and cutlery. It's lit by three church candles and there is a bottle of red wine that Jan has left to breathe in the centre next to my stack of wedding magazines.

'Oh, Jan, this is lovely,' I gush sincerely.

'Well, take a seat, dinner is nearly ready.' He pulls my chair out for me and grabs the bottle of wine. 'Here's a drink, and I have left the magazines here so that we can talk about the wedding a little more.'

It just fills me with love to have him home and here like this. I taste the wine and watch him over the top of my glass as he stirs some meatballs on the stove. I feel lucky. Although I am having a slight crisis at work and a lot of my day is filled with things I'd rather not discuss, it all drifts to insignificance when I remember what I do have. The fact that his job is so demanding, yet he still comes home at the end of the week and does something like this. I might earn a hell of a lot more money than he does, but he still provides. He still protects. He still takes care of his family.

We eat dinner, which is delicious. We flick through magazines and discuss the wedding. I tell him about the cakes and the dresses, and how the venue has enough rooms for all of our guests to stay over with us and have breakfast the day after. He shows a genuine interest in everything and even some excitement.

We end up in the bedroom and January fucks me like he's never fucked before. It's not quite enough, though. An anti-climax. I can't lie to myself about the disappointment.

Just another unfulfilling moment in my life that detracts from all the hard work in the moments that went before it.

January

———◆———

I don't know why it ended like that. Where did it come from?

Cooking my speciality meatballs takes some finesse and patience. Grating the lemon zest, chopping the herbs, cracking the eggs, adding the parmesan, the seasoning, the nutmeg, rolling these ingredients and the meat into perfect balls, then leaving them in the refrigerator to cool for thirty minutes, while I polish off two bottles of Budweiser. Only after this time can you add the balls to the delicately sweet tomato sauce that has been simmering for twenty minutes – that's another beer – and leave to bubble away until Audrey puts her key in the door a further forty minutes after that.

'Hello-oo?' she enquires from the other room, waiting for me to answer. I take my beer with me and go to meet her. It's good to see her face. Audrey has a great face to look at. It's smooth; she buys all the products on the market to guarantee this, and sticks to a carefully regimented routine to achieve such moisturised skin. Her eyebrows are thin and perfectly shaped, her hair is very dark with a natural curl in places, and she wears a red lipstick that, combined with the colour of her hair, makes her complexion seem whiter, purer somehow.

The sight of her is always a breath of fresh air for me

69

after seeing Paulson's inflated cheeks and five o'clock shadow, or an innocent girl's mangled head from a knife attack or gunshot wound or bruised by a fire extinguisher crashing down on her skull until almost flat, brains coming out of her ears.

It helps to see Audrey.

She's my safety net.

So what possessed me to end the night like this?

The meal went well. I'd prepared it to be romantic. I know when she is feeling neglected, and I know I have been guilty of that recently, because I feel so invested in this case. So I put some candles on the table, dimmed the lights and opened a bottle of wine from the cellar.

We talked and talked, about the wedding, about cakes and food and guests and nothing that seems real, just Audrey's perfect little fairy tale that she is willing to throw her money at. I managed to feign some interest and make suggestions that might imply that I give a shit about what the flowers are or the colour of the cravats.

I muddle through.

Drinking more.

Faking more.

Pretending that we don't live in a world of filth and murder and degenerate selfishness and somehow, at the end of the night, I end up in bed, with Audrey, trying to fuck the life out of her.

The sex started how it always does, kissing, gradually taking each other's clothing off and leaving it on the floor in a pile at the bottom of the bed. We roll around on top of the covers for a while, ensuring we give enough attention to all the parts of the body that we should. When we make our way under our king-size covers I work my way down to orally please Audrey. She grips my head with her thighs and pulls at the top of my hair like she usually does. She writhes and bucks and sometimes suffocates me, but I continue regardless.

The next thing, I am inside her, my arms gripping her thighs, pulling her into me.

I look down at Audrey with her eyes closed and her tongue forcing its way through her teeth as she pants. I close my own eyes and tilt my head up to the ceiling.

I see Dorothy Penn's naked body in my head.

I see a bullet moving in slow motion towards her beautiful face.

I start to pump harder and harder, not realising how uncomfortable this is for Audrey.

I see another girl. Younger this time. She has red marks on her wrists and ankles.

I see The Smiling Man charging at me.

I open my eyes and my hands are around Audrey's throat while I jackhammer away, but I can't stop. Faster and faster I move, putting more and more weight around my fiancée's neck, but she seems to like it, so I continue.

Faster and faster until I climax and release my grip. Audrey swipes my arms away weakly and I collapse on the bed next to her.

It scares me that I could do something like that and that Audrey seemed to enjoy it.

We both lay there, sweating and breathing heavily, not saying anything. What does The Smiling Man want? Who was the girl? Why am I picturing dead women while I try to make love to my future wife?

Audrey rolls over on her side and dozes off but, now, I'm afraid to fall asleep.

Girl 2

———◆———

They say I have a problem with authority; that I'm tough to handle. That I take female independence to the next level.

That I'm feminist with a vengeance.

And it's just not true.

I really don't care about any of that equal opportunities bullshit that a gaggle of women burned their underwear for decades ago. I don't care about a bunch of spotty, talentless teenagers who blew the right guy to get a break in the music industry and now preach about women's rights and roles in contemporary society.

I don't care about any of that.

I just want to be treated with respect, like any other human, and these middle-management schmucks with their colourful shirts that look like deckchairs, including the archetypal single breast pocket, their diamond cufflinks and their gel-soaked receding hairline, are everything I hate about hierarchy and the class system we have in this country.

That's why I'm taking these laborious business classes once a week.

The classes are the reason that I am going out and drinking alone once a week. The rest of the time I'm in the library trying to better myself. I'd use the Internet at home, but I can't afford the connection fees.

I have the dedication when I put my mind to something. I just don't have the direction. I'm sure after the course I'll have a set of skills that will mean I could have my own business, be my own boss, but I don't know what I'd be the boss of. I'm hoping that if I keep reading it will come to me.

Besides, I'm twenty-six. Who really knows what they want to do with their life at twenty-six? I just know that when I find it, it will be worth the wait.

So I'm waiting.

It'll happen, I tell myself.

Something will happen.

January

━━━◆━━━

I haven't slept all weekend.

I've been drinking Scotch and swallowing caffeine pills and it seems to be doing the trick. I'm up to date on my paperwork and I have an agenda for this week. I'm going to talk to the men on the list that Murphy looked into for me; the men at the speed-dating event that Dorothy attended before she was killed. Right now it's my only lead.

The first on the list is Miles Jennings, a forty-year-old risk assessor, single, no kids, no previous marriage, no personality.

No way he did it.

I decide that I'll start with the second on the list. Philip Bailey. Apparently he referred to himself as Dream Man, according to Murphy's notes. Thirty-six, unemployed, single. It seems obvious to say that a list of people from a speed-dating event are single, but 30 per cent of people who go to things like this or indulge in those dating websites are married or in a relationship. I find it hard to believe that this is the only way people can meet each other these days. Our grandparents never had the Internet and they seemed to do pretty well. Most of them had to cope with war too.

People today don't know how easy they have it.

I knock on his door. He lives in a high-rise block on the eighth floor. He opens the door in a dressing gown that doesn't look like it has seen any soap powder for a couple of years. He is holding a bowl of cereal in one hand and takes a spoonful before greeting me.

'I'm Detective Inspector David.' I show him my ID. 'I'm here to talk to Philip Bailey.' He gulps down the spoonful of Rice Krispies he shovelled in a second before.

'Er, I'm Philip Bailey, sir. What can I help you with?' He seems startled and can't fix his gaze on me, constantly looking out into the distance over my shoulder.

'Just a few questions,' I say. 'Mind if I come in?' And I start to step past his front door and into the flat. He mumbles something that I understand as a confirmation that I can enter.

The place is a mess. Wet towels hung over the back of the sofa, empty ready-meal containers on the floor and in the sink. Circuit boards and hard drives and other computer innards decorate the flat surfaces of most of the rooms.

'A PC fan, I see.' I try to make some small talk with him to begin with to show that I'm not here in a threatening way. He does seem nervous, but not nervous enough for me to dismiss him as a possible suspect just yet.

'Well, yeah. I suppose. It's kinda what I do. Or did, before they made cuts.' He hangs his head, as though he just told me his puppy has died or something.

'So you're currently unemployed?' I ask, already knowing the answer.

'Well, technically, yes.' He looks embarrassed. 'But I'm not signing on or anything. I'm not really looking for work at the moment, you see. My company gave me a very generous pay-off for time served there, so I'm working on some of my own projects.'

He continues to bore me with stories of modular robots that he hopes will somehow help the world. In my job I can't afford to stereotype, but examining his surroundings, the way he lives, his interests, it could be fair to say that he is exactly the kind of person you might expect to see at a speed-dating event. Inside I sigh, because I know that I have to see another seven of these misfits today.

'Are you familiar with a Ms Dorothy Penn?' I ask, closely observing his body language as I do so.

'Er, no. I can't say I know anyone by that name.' He seems genuine. He doesn't fidget or shuffle in his seat; it's like her name just failed to compute or fell out of his head somewhere along the way.

'Well, according to my records here' – I pull the sheet of paper from my inside pocket – 'you met her at a recent speed-dating event near Mile End Tube station and marked her down as a possible match for you.' I plan to pause, but he jumps right in.

'Oh God, that thing. I put every girl's name down that night. No takers, though,' he says nonchalantly, munching on another spoonful of soggy cereal. 'What did you say her name was?'

'Dorothy,' I repeat, unimpressed.

'Dorothy. Yes. I remember her. Dream Woman.' He chuckles. 'The one that got away.' He juts his bottom lip out to feign sadness and shrugs his shoulders.

'She's dead.'

'What?' He raises his voice and drops his spoon into the bowl in an almost cartoon way.

'Later that same night she was taken back to her flat and shot in the face. I need to know exactly what you did after the event ended.' I'm being deliberately shocking and graphic to see how he handles the news.

He handles it by crying.

I wasn't expecting that.

'Can you tell me what you did when you had finished at the speed dating?' I continue with my investigation. I don't have time for this. I haven't been asleep for three days. I need to keep working.

'She was so lovely,' he blubbers, sniffing heavily.

'I'm sure that's the case, Mr Bailey, but I need you to answer my question.'

'She was the only one who really gave me a chance at that thing. They were all so cold and dismissive. I mean, God, they're all in the same boat as I am otherwise they wouldn't be there, right?'

'Look, Mr Bailey . . .'

'I came straight home. I walked. I needed to clear my head from another night of rejection. OK?' He seems quite agitated, like he is annoyed that I have made him admit what a loser he is. Then he divulges that he came home and masturbated aggressively several times to try and make himself feel better.

But it just made him feel worse.

'I woke up the next morning, on the sofa, my stomach covered in a disgusting crust, the DVD player stuck on the scene selection screen of *Fist Fuckers 4* and I have been in the flat since then working on my designs for my latest module. I don't have anyone that can corroborate that story, though, because it's a pretty solitary activity.' He's visibly narked, but I haven't pulled this information from him. He gave it up like I was his therapist or something.

I write down *Fist Fuckers 4* in my notebook.

'OK, Mr Bailey. I think that's quite enough information.' I tell him that I will keep all the information he has given me, but that I might be back again, so he is not to go anywhere.

Something tells me that he will continue his agoraphobic lifestyle until the money runs out.

I leave him weeping into his bowl, wiping his eyes with the putrid dressing gown he lives in like some kind of cut-price Hugh Hefner.

Once I am in the sanctity of the lift, I swallow two more caffeine pills, loosen the knot of my tie a little further and look at the next name on the list.

Girl 2

I'm scored on the amount of calls I make per day.

If I make sixty calls in a day, I get paid a paltry hourly wage. If I crack eighty, it goes up a little and, if I manage to make one hundred, then I might hit the £8 per hour mark.

I do the bare minimum.

Surely I should be tasked on the quality of the call rather than the quantity made.

I can do fifty calls by lunchtime. That way I can read throughout the afternoon and I only have to make two and a half calls per hour to ensure that I get paid.

I knew this strategy wouldn't last for ever.

They're on to me.

In our team meeting today my team leader said that some of us are not pulling our weight as much as others and that we now have a team target to hit as well as our individual targets. Apparently it averages out at eighty-two calls per person.

A stretch target, he calls it.

The way I see it, someone is bound to make over a hundred calls, so even with my sixty in the bank, it will average out.

I feel like he is only looking at me throughout the whole thing, though. I'm sure he feels like he is delivering the Gettysburg Address, but he needs to get real. We phone people at the worst time of the day to glean market information from them. Most tell us to fuck off and I don't blame them. In fact, I respect them more for it.

I don't respect my team leader. What kind of a title is that anyway? It's just a role dished out to the automatons who have applied for a full managerial role several times, but really don't have the capacity to organise their own sock drawer let alone preside over ten different individual personalities within a group of employees.

He's an idiot. What does he actually do all day, while I get told to go screw myself by a tenth of the people whose day I interrupt with pointless questions about washing detergent or window frames or water pricing?

Today I make seventy calls by lunchtime. That way I only have to make three per hour in the afternoon to hit my target of eighty-two, the bare minimum. It leaves me time to read my book.

I'll be able to return it tomorrow at this rate.

I only have one lesson and an exam left until I complete my City & Guilds qualification in business management. Then I can really think of getting out of this job. I can start my life.

A real job. A man. A house with a garden that has more than just a five foot by five foot patch of grass with one tree. Nothing special.

Just the bare minimum.

January

I'm physically and emotionally exhausted after talking to everyone on the speed-dating list the last few days. Two men out of the eight had their wives as an alibi for that evening. The rest seemed either too pathetic to think up such a crime or too indolent to put such effort in.

I head back to the office. It's dark in there and nobody is around. A side effect of the caffeine pills is to make me a little sensitive to light, so I don't turn any on and negotiate the way to my desk in near-dark conditions.

Kick-starting my computer I take the bottle of Scotch from my top drawer and swig at it. Before I put it back I catch a glimpse of the paperwork the bottle was resting on. Cathy's case file, several programmes from my father's East-Coast performances in '76 and a picture of Mum I can no longer bear to look at. I force another gulp down. The scalding of the alcohol is a momentary distraction from the consuming misery the thought of my little sister brings. The burn at the back of my throat keeps my eyes open; I've run out of caffeine pills.

I decide that I should type up my notes before going home this evening. It should take a couple of hours and Audrey will be in bed by the time I get back.

I love Audrey. I want to marry her, of course, otherwise I wouldn't have asked her, but I can't talk about the wedding all the time. That's why I am delaying going home to her. There are more important things going on in the world. It has been four weeks since Dorothy Penn was killed and I don't feel any closer to even identifying a motive. I just don't believe that this was random, though.

I push my keyboard forward on the desk so that it rests on the stand of the monitor. I fold my arms, lay them down on the desk and rest my forehead on my left forearm. Exhausted, I fall asleep and, what seems like moments later, I find myself sat on a chair, blindfolded, my arms and legs tied to the seat with twine.

Behind my head I hear a light clicking sound. Each beat in time with the music, which I recognise this time. One finger clicks on the left hand, while two click on the right. It accompanies the initial build-up of music that I hear playing around me. I realise that I can hear the opening of the 'William Tell Overture' with a percussive partnering from the as-yet unseen figure behind me. As it builds to the crescendo, the clicking stops and my blindfold is whipped off the top of my head in one swift movement. Once my eyes have adjusted I see his yellow teeth. The giant grin of The Smiling Man who appeared to me some weeks ago. The location is recurring, but the scene before me is slightly different from before.

He is still dressed all in black. His long black coat over his black shirt that is tucked into black trousers. All I can focus on is his smile as he moves around the area in front of me, gesticulating like a symphony conductor.

He paces around in a circle, waving his arms, all the time smiling, only this time his eyes are closed. They are so bulbous that it seems as though his eyelids were not made for the body they are attached to and leave a partially open slit at the bottom displaying his tawny eyes slightly.

Then he stops.

He turns to me, still with his eyes closed, still smiling, and lifts his arms out to form a large black smiling cross in front of me. As the music begins to build again he rotates his hands over and over. Keeping his wrists still, the fingers move, making larger circles in time with the orchestra. As the cymbal crashes his hands delve directly into his pockets. He pulls his left hand out, holding two fingers up towards me. His right emerges with an apple, which he takes a bite of with his large, dirty gravestone teeth then discards.

Moving in time to the music he reaches inside his coat with his right hand and produces a bow; his left hand digs around in the other side and he pulls out four arrows.

I try to wriggle out of the bind I am in, but the twine cuts deeper into my skin, grazing and burning a red line around my wrists and ankles.

He dances towards me. With every languid step he takes I grow slightly more bemused. Is he going to put a bullet in my mouth again?

He bends over at the waist so that his face is at the same height as mine, his closed eyes somehow peering into mine. It distracts me. Instead of looking at his smile I am drawn to his eyelids and the small strip of dull light that squeezes its way out just below the lashes.

And suddenly I feel the pain.

The slicing stab into my intercostal muscles that feels as though somebody has broken two of my ribs and left a lit match in the gap between them. Then the same in my shoulder, one in my stomach and one in my thigh. When he stands up I see the blood dripping from all four arrows in his hand. He looks at my face, then at the arrows, then at my wounds, and back to my face, all with his eyes closed. His left hand moves towards my face and I flinch slightly. He didn't hurt me before. I woke up in time. But this time I do not see him as an ally.

He takes the blindfold and places it over my eyes. Once this is firmly in place, he opens his own.

He drags his feet a little and I can just about hear his footsteps moving backwards in time with the music. I panic and begin to lose my breath quite drastically. He edges back further and further until I hear him crash through what sounds like a large pane of glass and it startles me back to consciousness.

I sit up sharply at my desk with a large intake of air, patting my chest and stomach with my hands to reassure myself that the wounds are no longer there. Luckily nobody is around and the building is quiet, apart from the low hum of the hard drives whizzing around in the server room.

All the information I need to help save Carla Moretti is there, but I don't use it and, at this same time tomorrow, Eames would have claimed another victim.

Eames

—✦—

Question: What do you think when you see a pretty woman walking down the street?

Answer: One side of me says, I'd like to talk to her, date her. The other side of me says, I wonder how her head would look on a stick?

When you see a quote like this, where some idiot serial killer displays a distinct lack of control, that's not me.

When a tabloid newspaper gives infamy to my work by labelling me the Zone-2 Killer or the Suburban Slayer, please understand, this is not what I wanted.

I have killed in passion or the heat of the moment, but everyone makes mistakes in their early career. Perhaps I was eager to get ahead. Maybe I was an overachiever. But now it's different. I have to kill Carla Moretti.

And it has to be tonight.

I wait in the library with a pile of books on business. On top I have one called *Good Small Business Guide: How to Start and Grow Your Own Business*. I know she will be in here today. She is in every other day. She never takes more than two days to get through a book, even non-fiction. I've been a member at this library for one month now. On the days that Carla doesn't come in, I swap my books. This way I have an eclectic reading list and it

85

doesn't look as though I joined recently, hired some books on business and then killed a woman studying the same subject. I will continue to take books out for the next couple of months too. In two days I will walk past Detective Inspector January David as he talks to one of the librarians. This will be more rewarding than the kill itself.

Tomorrow there will be one less person calling your house to discuss the property market. One less interruption through dinner or your favourite soap opera.

In two days she will be replaced and the cycle of aggravating commerce will continue; she will be forgotten by the end of the month, because she is nothing special.

She's expendable.

What people don't realise is that we all are.

January

———◆———

Iknow that the location of this murder is in a completely different part of London. I understand that the way they died is not the same, but I know that this is the same killer.

The same elaborate scene. The comparable set of circumstances.

Somehow, whoever did this is making a rather large city very small indeed.

I feel it closing in on me.

Again, the victim's hands and feet are bound, this time with a robust twine. She is naked and standing. I suspect that she has had sex and that it was, again, consensual. I would also suspect the same drug found in Dorothy Penn's system in the toxicology report.

She is blindfolded and attached to a pole.

Her kitchen and living room are open-plan and essentially both rooms operate in the same living space. The work surface separates the two rooms with one edge protruding over the cabinets. Underneath it, there is a rubbish bin; on top are three jars. One containing coffee, one holding tea bags and one full of sugar. At the end of this surface a thick metal pole runs from the floor, through the worktop and up to the ceiling. Carla's feet are tied up below the work surface and her hands are tied above it. There is a bruise on her lumbar region, suggesting there was a struggle while in this position.

She is another beautiful young girl – I would say mid-twenties – cut down in her prime due to a lack of awareness. Because she didn't live in the real world. I look at her limp body hanging from the pole and I should feel shocked. I should have some kind of compassionate, human reaction. But, at first, I feel nothing. Eventually, all I feel is disappointment.

I see the blood that has trickled down her arm from her shoulder, the wound on her thigh that stained the carpet, the hole in her ribs that just missed her stomach but collapsed her left lung, and the clean shot through the skull that separates her brain into an equal left and right side. I wonder whether these were deliberately placed in these positions.

But these were not made with a gun like the Dorothy Penn incident. These are made with arrows.

Like the arrows that The Smiling Man showed me.

Like the arrows he used to stab my body in exactly the same positions that Carla has been pierced.

My gut is telling me that this is not a coincidence, but my head tells me to think realistically.

I'm not psychic.

I don't have a helper from another realm aiding my investigations.

I'm not insane.

'Fuck me, Jan. Not another speed-date massacre,' Paulson says insensitively from behind me.

He does have a brilliant mind and it's good to know that someone else agrees with me that this is the same killer as before, but he lacks a certain social grace; a skill that is difficult to develop in a virtual world of late-night gambling and a sequestered existence of crossword-solving.

'Jesus, Paulson. Come on, she's a fucking person, what are you doing?' I protest.

'Sorry Jan, I just thought –'

'– You just thought what?' I interrupt.

'Well, I just thought that there might be a link. You know?' For a big man he can certainly recoil into a timid child quickly.

'You see it too, eh?' I ask.

'Well, it's not exactly the same, but there is a similarity that you'd have to be blind to miss. I can look deeper into the speed-dating angle for you with Murphy, if you want. Might be a lead.'

'Thanks, Paulson. Let me know what you dig up.' He exits the scene and I am left to continue piecing together fragments of nothing.

I worry. I don't want to give this killer any credibility. I don't want Paulson calling him the Speed-Date Slicer or the Press naming him the Maisonette Murderer. Don't give them infamy. It's exactly what they want.

I can't fathom a link between the two murders at the moment. Both girls voluntarily had intercourse with the killer, safe sex too. Both were tied up and killed in a standing position. One was shot rather accurately in the face, through the mouth to be precise, the other with an arrow through the skull. Will the next girl be stabbed in the head? Will there be another girl? How are these girls linked? I press my fingertips hard into my temples to block everything out, to focus on my thoughts. I feel my pulse quicken as my theories and assessments spark across my nerve endings looking for an answer.

Carla's flat has a feel of student accommodation. A *Betty Blue* film poster above the sofa attached to the wall with Blu-tack rather than being hung in a frame. Her TV is a portable 15″ with a built-in video player on a cheap pine TV stand. A few videos scattered underneath include *Pretty in Pink, Sixteen Candles* and *St Elmo's Fire*. Hideous films, in my opinion, and I wonder whether the *Betty Blue* poster is just for show.

I find several textbooks relating to starting your own business and small business accounting, all of which are borrowed from the local library. Looking around the living area, it is sparse. She owns hardly anything.

What could this girl have possibly done to incite such violence and recrimination?

The blood pool below her feet contains several white chunks less than a quarter of an inch in width; also, a liquid of some kind sits on top, not mixing with the blood. I find several more spots around the body that are similar. A flash goes off behind me as photographs are taken of the scene.

Test results will later show traces of apple juice and chunks of Granny Smith. It helps me put together exactly what happened here tonight. I just don't know why.

Girl 2

When I arrive for work in the morning, my team leader is writing on a whiteboard. It's a table with everyone's name on and the amount of calls they did yesterday. At the top, of course, is Kiss-Arse Chris Barker with well over a hundred calls.

It's clear that everyone put in the extra push yesterday, but at the bottom of the pile is my name, Carla Moretti, exactly eighty-two calls. I see the despair in the team-leader's face as I sit down at my desk. In a way, I win.

Chris Barker is given the latest iPod by our revered leader. For every call over one hundred, we were given a raffle ticket. This morning a ticket was drawn and the corresponding number won the prize. Of course it was Kiss-Arse; he owned the most tickets. He had the best chance of winning. I suppose he deserved it, though.

I feel pretty proud of myself for the way I handled the patronising middle-management motivational talk yesterday, but it's at this moment that I decide things are going to change. From today, this moment, my life is going to be different.

I have an idea.

I have some direction.

For me, online is the way to go with business these days. It's cost-effective, you can run it from home and it's an easy start-up. I just need a computer and an Internet connection.

Imagine an online raffle. For example, I buy the latest iPod for £125. I put this online on my iRaffle website. Each ticket is bought for £1 and I sell two hundred of them. Someone could win a brand-new MP3 player for £1. It's not like bidding loads of money on eBay for second-hand goods. These are brand-new, boxed, mint-condition products. I would make £75 on an iPod alone – minus the cost of delivery. This would only be the start. Eventually the number of raffles going on at one time would increase. The prizes could be smaller or they could be larger.

Imagine I buy a car or a house and raffle it. I would eventually need to hire staff and I would treat them a hell of a lot better than I get treated here.

I decide that I need to get a book on e-commerce from the library this evening and something on setting up a website for beginners, and maybe another book on accounting.

Before that, I make one hundred and seventy-five calls, a new record. I need to earn the extra money to buy a laptop and get connected. If I can win my first raffle prizes somewhere along the way and make pure profit on these items, then everything will kick off with some momentum.

I'm excited. I even smile at one point.

This is definitely a new beginning for me.

After work I go to the library feeling buoyant. Inspired, even.

Like nothing can go wrong.

But I'm about to bump into Eames again. Just like I did a couple of weeks ago, only this time I think he could be the man I am interested in, that all the pieces of my life are suddenly falling into place. But he doesn't want to help me set up my business; he doesn't even think that my online raffle idea can work due to certain legal restrictions – especially on the larger items. He doesn't tell me this, though. He tells me everything I want to hear, makes me feel what I want to be feeling and then he fucking kills me.

I couldn't be more dead.

'We must stop meeting like this,' he says, cheesily, as he turns suddenly, knocking my books out of my hand, and the top one from his own pile. But it's just the kind of line I can fall for in this mood.

'I'm sorry?' I respond with a question in my tone.

'The other day. On the street. We bumped into each other.' He pauses. 'Oh God, you don't remember. I'm sorry.' He bends down and picks up my books, fumbling around, embarrassed.

'Oh yes. Of course. I remember. Are you stalking me?' I joke. 'Thinking of starting a small business, I see.' Without realising how flirtatious I am being, I hand him back his book that fell. Something about growing your own business.

He laughs, 'Oh no, no, no. I'm a lecturer. I'm just putting together a reading list for my students. I've never read this, so I thought I'd work my way through it before adding it to their ever-growing catalogue.' He smiles and I'm immediately set at ease.

I start to think about fate. Whether my idea came to me today and then some mystical force brought this beautiful, intelligent man here to help me. That I am, perhaps, supposed to talk to this man in order to gain some information.

93

A sense of gratification and intrigue washes over me, displacing my usual nihilistic outlook on the world and life in general. I allow myself to become vulnerable, forgetting the stories that terrified me in the newspaper only weeks before.

Maybe I deserve this.

'Well, I'd love to pick your brains some time. I'm a business student myself and I'm just researching an idea I have for an online enterprise.'

'That's very wise of you to research it. Too many people just jump in feet first without fully getting to grips with all aspects of running a business. Look, I mean, how does now sound? We can grab a quick coffee and go over your ideas, if you want. I can give you some pointers.' He seems genuine, but I'm a little apprehensive. 'It's the least I can do for ploughing into you all week.' He laughs at himself for his apparent myopia.

And I agree to let him shoot an arrow through my brain.

Girl 4

❖

It's not cold feet, just speculation. I'm wondering how life will be. We are getting married in a month's time and, again, January hasn't come home. No call. No text. No smoke signal or carrier pigeon. Nothing. I don't need to wait until I see the newspaper in the morning, though; I know another girl has died. There is a pattern to it all now.

That doesn't stop me worrying, though.

The house phone rings. It must be January, I think to myself, so I leave it for a while, my way of punishing him. I have an authentic classic candlestick phone in the hallway downstairs made by Automatic Electric and Kellogg in 1919. I think it adds character and individuality; Jan thinks it's ghastly. We have a similar model in the bedroom on Jan's bedside table, but this phone is a little more discreet and modern.

'Hello?' I pick the phone up after the fifth ring and try to make myself sound slightly groggy, so it sounds as though I have only just woken up without even questioning why my fiancé is, at best, sporadically sharing my bed.

Nothing.

'Hello?' I say again, this time a little more high-pitched and alert.

Nothing.

Silence.

'Who is this?' I ask sternly, realising that Janaury hasn't thought that I may be worried and he should call, but nothing comes back. Not even heavy breathing, but I know someone is on the other end.

'Look, can I help you? Who are you looking for?' This is the third time this has happened in the last month. It's not always at this time of day, but it always has the same outcome.

'If you're not going to speak then please stop calling here, OK?' I hang up, slamming the receiver down a little harder than I should. 'Prick,' I say to myself.

I wait, staring at the phone for ten, maybe twenty seconds, then pick it back up again. I turn the dial: *1 . . . 4 . . . 7 . . . 1*, and wait.

A woman's voice intones, 'You were called today at 8.32. The caller withheld their number.'

I slam the receiver down again, frightened. I decide not to tell January. He's got enough to worry about with the high-profile case he is working on, but it does leave me shaken.

As I shower and get changed for work I'm startled by every sound, even the ordinary everyday noises the house makes and which I normally don't notice, my brain usually buffering them into white noise. As more ice drops down from the top of the fridge freezer ready to be dispensed as perfectly formed cubes when I need a cold drink, I jump and my flesh goose-pimples. As a bee flies into the bedroom window making the slightest tapping noise, I panic slightly, because my top is obscuring my vision as I pull it on over my head and I feel momentarily trapped, blindly vulnerable.

Heading down to the kitchen cautiously, I smell the piping hot black coffee that is waiting for me, thanks to the timer mechanism on the machine that I set to pour each morning at the same time. I fill my aluminium travel mug and decide that I'll just grab some breakfast out, either on the way to work or at work. I just need to leave the house.

Normally I start the car and let it sit for a minute or so while I gather myself, but today I wrench the ignition, slot it into first gear and dart out of the drive. I turn the radio up so high that any other noise in the world is cancelled out. By the time I hit the traffic and take my first mouthful of sweet espresso roast I forget about my strange morning and go back to being mad with January.

I'll punish him for forgetting about me again.

January

⬥

Paulson and Murphy haven't come back to me with anything more on the speed-dating angle. After going down this avenue for quite a while, I'm concluding that I don't think the link can really be anything as crass at that. This killer feels he has too much class. He thinks he is smarter than the police, smarter than me.

I mentally run through the facts, methodically picking over the precise details known to me. I know that both crimes were committed by a left-handed person. The bullet wound in Dorothy's face showed this, and the angle at which the arrows entered Carla's body suggests that they were fired by a left-handed person who was trying to disguise this fact. Forensics are suggesting that he may have turned his back on the victim and fired the arrows over his shoulder. This would account for the stray arrows that punctured the lower lobe of her left lung, pierced her left anterior deltoid muscle and wedged themselves in her sartorius, narrowly missing her profunda femoris.

Initially I thought that these arrows were deliberately aimed at these spots for dramatic effect. I thought that perhaps he wanted to keep her alive a little longer, to torture her. But he didn't, he just missed.

In my mind, the picture is clear.

He picked up an impressionable young girl, went back to her modest, rented flat, had sexual intercourse with her, tied her to a pole in the kitchen and sadistically attempted to shoot an apple off the top of her head with a bow and arrow.

The *how* is simple. The *why* is puzzling.

It isn't the same as Dorothy Penn, apart from its elaborate concept. I almost want him to kill again so that I have more information. I'm astonished at this thought, realising my obsession is growing stronger, that my motivation runs deeper, that my desperation can be consuming.

I think about The Smiling Man. His almost-closed eyelids, his arrows, the '*William Tell* Overture' and that smile, that constant smile.

I think about the first time he visited me, and, for the first time in a long while, I think about my mother and tell myself I'm nothing like her.

Subconsciously I start to open my top drawer and reach for the Scotch. It's only 10 a.m. Murphy slithers into the office and his presence pulls me back to reality.

'Morning, Jan.' He sighs in my direction.

'Morning, Murph. Anything?' I ask, hoping he can shed even a glint of light on the case, pushing the drawer closed softly as I speak.

He perches himself on the corner of my desk as though the eight-foot walk from the doorway was a half-marathon. 'Nothing on the speed-dating. This girl . . .' I see his mind ticking over.

'Carla.'

'Yes, Carla. Carla Moretti,' he clarifies. 'She wasn't a member of any of these dating websites. She didn't even have an Internet connection. That isn't the link between these girls.'

'Then what is?' I ask almost rhetorically, knowing what the answer will be.

'That, we don't know.'

'Yet.'

'Yet. What we do know is that she was an average worker at a call centre. Nothing special. Nothing memorable. Except for the fact that she broke the call record the day she died.'

'That could be significant,' I say out loud, thinking I'd said it in my head. I tend to do this when I have had little sleep. Sometimes it's the other way round: I think I have said something out loud, but it only echoes as inner monologue.

'Yeah maybe,' he adds, unenthused at a possible break-through. 'She lived alone, she was taking a night course in business studies at the Embassy Theatre in Swiss Cottage and was a regular at the library nearby. She was in there all the time, apparently.'

'This is all good, Murph. Useful groundwork to dig into. Anything else I should know?' I ask, aware of the likely response.

'Not really.' He closes his notebook and lethargically slots it back into his pocket.

'Where is Paulson?'

'He's looking into any possible links between the two girls, too. Whether their paths have crossed. You know? He thinks it's a maths problem.' He smiles. I don't.

'OK. Good.' I switch my computer screen off and straighten my shirt out. 'You take the theatre. Find out who was in her class, what they thought of her, get Paulson on it with you, maybe her peers or mates or

whatever can give more insight. I'm going to the library.'
I exhale heavily, preparing myself for the long day ahead.
'We've gotta catch this fucker, Murph.' I'm not sure if I
sound determined or desperate; I'm not even sure what I
feel. I'm frustrated with the case, exasperated by the lack
of evidence, tired of achieving nothing.

I'm also somewhat perturbed by Murphy's lack of
urgency. He just stands there satisfied that his pathetic
debrief is adequate. It's like he is going through the
motions. Like it's just another case for him; that it carries
the same weight as a domestic violence incident. He's
waiting for me to tell him how to investigate the case,
whereas Paulson takes it upon himself to develop his
own leads and strategies. I almost have to usher Murphy
out the door.

One of the new police constables almost collides with
us in the hallway. He stands before me, slightly out of
breath, his forehead caked in tiny globules of sweat. He
hands me an envelope and says that he has been asked
to run this up to me urgently. I thank him impatiently
and send him brusquely on his way, dismissing him, my
gaze already boring into the packet now clutched in my
hand.

Nervously I lift the flap. It has already been opened
and read by someone before being sent up to me. The
envelope is A5 sized and manilla. In block capital letters
on the front it says DETECTIVES RE: CARLA. I look at
Murphy, wide-eyed, but he just peers over my shoulder
at the envelope, waiting for me to take out whatever is
inside. I can smell the coffee on his breath.

Carefully I lift out the piece of plain white card from
the envelope. It's like a cue card or one of those cards you
see students using to aid with their revision. It is blank on

one side. I turn it over and handwritten on the other side is a short message.

B4 to C3.

I copy the message shakily into my notebook, my hand quivering, my thoughts already racing. Concealing my agitation, I hand the envelope and card to Murphy to take for analysis to look at under their microscopes. I'm sure they will confirm that the slant of the writing and the pressure on the descenders will indicate a left-hander. That, despite the capital *E* looking like a capital *C* with a line through the middle, and even though the curvature would normally indicate a female, this is in fact a male and he is the actual perpetrator of these atrocities. I feel the evil emanate from the page, like I've made contact with malevolence. My body goes cold, but is soon thawed by the adrenalin that courses through me as I transform this incident into a renewed sense of verve.

B4 to C3?

I send Murphy on his way for the second time and head back to my desk. Taking a sheet of paper from the printer, I quickly use my biro to draw an 8 × 8 grid. On the *x* axis I write a letter to correspond with each square, *A* to *H*; on the *y* axis I label each square with a number from one to eight. It's a standard chessboard. I've seen this tactic before. A killer wants to enter into combat with his eventual captor and chess is an expression of his apparent intellectual superiority. But he's never played me before.

B4 to C3. I look down at my roughly drawn grid and try to visualise this game plan. The only pieces that can make that move are a bishop, the queen, the king or a pawn when it takes another pawn. What is he trying to say? That these women are pawns? That he is the king? This message itself gives me very little, apart from confirming that the killer has a certain amount of showmanship. Perhaps he wants to be caught. Maybe this is all part of the process. Or it may have been sent to misdirect us.

But this is his second letter.

I still haven't seen his first.

The one that says C7 to B4. The one that is filed away somewhere.

Of course, it's not chess. For the same reason that he isn't preying on speed-daters. For the same reason that each murder scene is vastly different.

The Smiling Man is telling me how and when.

The killer is telling me where.

In my experience, when solving a crime, the solution is often the simplest possible interpretation. The answer is staring at you. But I can't believe that's true this time. Just as I feel I am getting into his head, he throws something new into the mix.

I decide to continue with my plan and head to the library. In my haste I forget to call Audrey to let her know that I am all right.

Girl 2

———◆———

I've never done anything like this before. My innate misanthropy has always been a stumbling block, if I'm honest. Today is different. A new day. A new me. So, when a charming, attractive stranger offers to take me for a quick coffee and discuss my business plan, of course I accept. It's not like he is a photographer and I am trying to make it as a model. It doesn't feel like he wants me to take my clothes off.

It's innocent. An act of philanthropy.

'Coffee?' I pause slightly as if I am considering it. 'Yeah, OK. Sounds like a plan. Now?' I ask.

'Now is as good a time as any,' he responds. 'Have you checked your books out?'

'No. Not yet.' I look over my shoulder at the counter; there are only two people in the queue.

'I'll wait outside for you. I just need to make a quick call.' He smiles and heads outside, while I queue up to grab the two books I am looking to read over the next couple of days to help me with this new enterprise. I think about the extra £20 I earned today making all those extra calls. Two weeks of that will get me my very own laptop. I can order it online at work; it's cheaper and more convenient than hitting the high street.

I glance back outside through the glass door and see

104

Eames pacing back and forth, absorbed in conversation on his mobile phone. He catches me staring at him and throws a smile at me and waves.

It feels like a good idea. It's broad daylight. What could possibly happen to me in broad daylight?

He doesn't want to get on the Underground; something about terrorism and no escape. We walk. We walk until we hit a Starbucks. It's a fairly safe bet that you'll hit one at some point if you keep going in a straight line. He says he likes to support local businesses when possible, family-run cafés, that sort of thing. I'm a business-woman, nearly, and I support capitalist takeover. It's what I expect to do. When people complain about capitalism I just like to think of it as successful business. Besides, who doesn't love Starbucks? Comfortable chairs, high-quality food and beverages, well-trained staff. Even when there is a procession of twenty people before you all waiting for a cappuccino and a panini, you know that the turnaround is efficient and the quality never diminishes.

People pay for quality. They pay for the lifestyle.

This is where I always go anyway. But, of course, he knows this. He's seen me in here sucking on biscotti and licking my lips at espresso chocolate brownies. He already knows everything I have been twittering on about as we walk down the Finchley Road. He's bored. I just think he is a great listener; that we are connecting on more than just an academic level.

I've really fucked up this time.

Eames

—◆—

Carla was nothing compared to Dorothy. Not in the bedroom, not as a person. Part of the thrill of killing is the remorse that you should feel for taking a life. But Carla wasn't worth a second thought.

She almost wasn't worth the effort. And now she will be recorded for eternity as a composite piece of my installation, my art.

And I feel sick about it.

We walk and walk until we finally come across her favourite coffee chain. I've done the route before, several times, while researching the area and how she lives her life, her routine, but this feels longer than usual. She isn't talking *to* me, she is talking *at* me.

I feign interest, pretending I know the names and theories she is referencing, looking her straight in the eyes. I imagine the arrow slicing through her thick skull and I'm overcome with a comforting sense of warmth, the peace that comes with knowing you have rid the world of something worthless.

But this isn't what I want.

This is much bigger than just one person, bigger than Carla Moretti, bigger than me.

I leave the scene of the crime in a state of ambivalence. Everything went according to plan. I took the correct girl on the night I was supposed to and disposed of her in the way I had imagined, but something is niggling me. I feel that people will view her as the weakest part, that there is a flaw. But I can't do anything about it now, because I have already posted the letter to the police station to arrive in the morning.

I pace down the Finchley Road, my eyes wide and unblinking, the rage building inside me. I think about the jogger that acknowledged me yesterday and pray that he passes me tonight, so that I can drag him on to one of the nearby estates and beat him, maybe break his ankles, maybe stamp on his neck, collapsing his oesophagus and watching him as he chokes out. But that isn't me any more. I'm better than that.

I need some release.

As I cross the road an ambulance speeds through the traffic lights, its lights revolving, the siren blaring. I wonder if this has been called out for Carla. They're too late to do anything now. It gives me some respite to believe this is true.

Walking into the lobby of the hotel I steer my gaze away from the concierge, so as not to enter into a dialogue. I am meeting one of my women here tonight. I set something like this up after every murder. One of the women desperate to have an affair, to feel like she is getting one up on her husband for flying to Europe for a meeting or staying behind with his secretary. I didn't feel the need to show up after Dorothy, but tonight is different.

She is already in the room when I get there, lying on the bed with a glass of red wine in her hand. I wonder whether she strategically laid herself in the position as she heard the key-card in the door.

I don't speak to her. I don't want to speak to her. She stands as I walk over to her. Knocking the wine glass out of her hand across the room, I pull her face into mine and kiss her aggressively. I want to put her feet on my shoulders and my hands around her throat, but I can't because her husband would notice if I left bruising.

I grab a clump of hair on the back of her head and twist her face away from mine, and push her down on to the bed so that she is lying on her stomach. She pretends to fight against this movement, but I know it's what she wants. Still holding the hair tightly in my fist I use my other hand to hitch up her skirt at the back. I rip her tights as I force them down and feel her underwear stretch as I do the same again.

She turns her head to the side, saying, 'Yes. Yes. That's it. Come on.'

I lean my weight slightly on her head, so that she can see my face as I enter her from behind. I pound her roughly and she makes almost a grunting noise as I do so. I yank her hair back as I get closer to finishing, arching her back, causing her some pain.

At the climax I fall on to her, lying on her back, my full weight crushing down on her. I keep her hair in my hand, but release the grip slightly as we both lie there breathing heavily.

It helped. This is how killing usually feels to me, but Carla let me down.

I roll over, gathering my thoughts. I have a job to get on with now. Carla is finished.

Amy is next.

B4 to C3.

January

———◆———

I'm worried. What if the killer *is* smarter than the police, smarter than me? What if he is one step ahead right now? What if he is already planning his next victim, while we run around call centres and libraries trying to grab anything that can help us link these two girls together?

There is definitely something about this library, though. I feel it when I walk in.

It's busy for an early morning weekday. There are several colleges and schools in the area and I can see a lot of the tables are filled with gaggles of twenty-somethings cramming for exams or researching for theses. There are elderly people in here, sifting through reference books on the local area and how it looked for previous generations. A bohemian male in his thirties is flicking through the CDs that are available to rent out.

I haven't set foot in a library for years. I wasn't really sure that many still existed with the ever-presence of information available on the Internet. They have that here too on 22" flat-screen monitors all along one wall. Available to the public for a small charge, so the sign informs me.

I see two younger children giggling at a page in one of the biology textbooks, then one of the librarians taking it out of their hands and shooing them on. Despite the gravity of my mission, I smile to myself at their innocence.

The whole scene appears to be nothing out of the ordinary, but I have a feeling of unease about this place. Like I am the only person in here who feels cold. I can't place what's giving me this sense of disquiet, but I can't shake the sensation.

The woman in charge at the main desk paradoxically looks approachable yet stern. Petite would probably be how I'd describe her, if I were taking notes. Mousey, perhaps. She has bright blonde hair that is verging on looking albino, especially with her pale face. She has an angular chin that finishes in an almost-point and pronounced cheekbones that would make her look more like an Eastern European model if she were taller, with darker hair and a tan. I can't decide whether she is pretty or hideous. It's an odd cusp to sit on.

'Good morning, I was wondering whether you could help,' I greet her in an almost whisper in an attempt to conform to what I remember as common library etiquette.

'Yeeeees,' she drawls, sounding like she is asking a question. 'What can I help you with, sir?' She looks up from her papers, eyeing me speculatively with her near-turquoise eyes.

I flick a hasty glance over my shoulder to see who might be watching me, then dip my left hand into the inside pocket of my suit jacket and produce my ID. I lean across the desk further so that I can speak even quieter, but she will still be able to hear me.

'I'm Detective Inspector David and I need to ask you some questions.' She looks instantly terrified. I watch her expression freeze. 'You are not in trouble in any way,' I add quickly. 'I was just hoping that you could help me with some enquiries.'

I feel I'm choosing my words carefully today, being overly cautious. I haven't slept for over thirty hours now and my paranoia about saying something out loud that I meant to keep in my head is overwhelming. The chill of this building is making me feel like I am being watched or somebody is listening in on what I say. Unconsciously I rub my arm, wondering if it's just me who feels the coolness in the air.

'OK, Detective . . .' She pauses.

'David. Detective David.' I try to reassure her further with my tone.

'Detective David, what would you like to know?'

I show her a picture of Carla Moretti and ask whether she recognises her at all.

'I was told that she comes in here quite a bit,' I encourage her.

'Well, we have a lot of people come through the door each day, Detective David,' she states obviously, emphasising my name as though I am an intolerable schoolchild, clearly trying to regain the authority that I never tried to take from her in the first place. 'But yes, I recognise her. She is often in here, taking books out, going online, but I couldn't tell you her name.'

'Carla Moretti. Her name was Carla Moretti,' I jump in, trying to elicit a response, hoping she hasn't picked up on the fact that I referred to her in the past tense. My brain is tired. I wouldn't normally make a slip like that.

She starts tapping away at the keyboard in front of her, phonetically spelling the name out loud as she types. 'Car-La Mo . . . is that one *r* or two?' she asks.

'One *r*, two *t*s.'

'Ah-ha.' She beams shortly after pressing ENTER. 'Here it is. Carla Moretti. Two books taken out yesterday at 15.28. *The Best Small Business Accounts Book (Blue Version) for Non-VAT Registered Businesses* and, let me see . . .' She scrolls down the page a little. 'Right, yes, *Cyber Gold: A Guidebook on How to Start Your Own Home-Based Internet Business*, build an E-Commerce website, blah blah blah. Does that help at all? Does it mean anything?' She seems suddenly eager to please.

I already knew which books Carla had taken out, because they were in her apartment. The dates that they were due back were stamped in the front, so I also knew they were recently borrowed. I'm not really sure what I hoped to glean from this visit. It might be another dead end. My instincts are telling me something different, though.

'What about Dorothy Penn?' I ask. A shot in the dark really, but I'll try almost anything at the moment.

'Two *ns*?'

'Yes,' I answer shortly.

She types in the name. I wait, expecting yet another dead end.

'Here we go . . .' Her voice trails off a little as she taps a few more keys. 'Dorothy Penn. She hasn't been in for a few weeks. Do you want to know which books she took out?'

'No, thank you. I need an address. Would you print off her details for me, please?' My tone is deliberately brazen. I know that she won't; that I can't really ask for her to do this.

'Well . . . I'm not really sure that I should be giving out personal information.' She winces, suddenly retreating behind library policy. But I can tell that she wants to help if she can.

'I could come back in an hour and have your computer confiscated as part of an official investigation, but that would really be wasting time in an important case where time is a luxury we simply don't have,' I lie. I couldn't do this. But I adopt my most self-important tone, hoping I can scare her enough into just giving up the information.

'I don't know . . . maybe you should . . .' Her indecisiveness is irritating. I cut her short.

'Look, I don't need her full address, I just need to know which borough she lives in.'

She clicks the mouse twice.

'Camden,' she says briskly.

'Camden?'

'Yes. That's where you are right now, Detective David. Most of our patrons are from this area.'

I'm getting sick of her constantly repeating my name. I'm trying to keep a low profile and she is alerting people within a twenty-foot radius that I work for the police.

'How old is she?' I snap back, losing patience now.

A couple of clicks later, 'She is sixty-four years old.'

'FUCK!' I exclaim, slamming my fist down on her desk. Somehow, the library seems to become quieter when I do this. It must be the lack of sleep; it's making me sloppy.

'Detective David,' she trills in apparent disgust. Now she feels she has the right to talk to me like I am an insolent teenager. As she says my name out loud for the umpteenth time, I instantly goose-pimple. Partly through sudden embarrassment, partly through the inexplicable sensation of being in this building.

I don't know why I am finding being in here so unsettling.

I don't know that one of the patrons in the library, one

of the plethora of people who can hear my conversation, is Eames.

And now he knows who I am.

What I look like.

He can make this personal.

And I don't have a clue who, why or when he will strike next.

'Please keep your voice down,' the librarian tells me, ever so slightly raising her own, all helpfulness now dissolved.

Her manner has ceased to irritate me, though. I just feel deflated. If I don't come up with something concrete soon I could be pulled on to another case, because this one is a little too resource-heavy. I have Paulson and Murphy devoting their time to it, both experienced investigators, and I won't get away with that for much longer unless we start producing results. My Chief Inspector is already on my back for a progress report and I can't afford an unsolved case on my record.

Everything seems to lead me to a dead end.

I let my gaze wander unfocused around the room, trying to dredge up fresh ideas. Suddenly I register strategically positioned cameras and something clicks in my brain. Noticing the direction of my stare the librarian informs me almost proudly that the CCTV cameras inside are a deterrent. To put off prospective book thieves in the aisles. They are actually only operational in the evenings when the library is closed, she adds prissily after I probe further.

I feel like someone has kicked me between the legs.

All of a sudden, I shudder and go cold. The hair on my arms stands to attention. I inhale deeply and it's as if I am sucking icicles into my lungs. I cough heavily as if I am choking, as if my head has been held under water. I splutter for twenty seconds, bending at my waist, grabbing at my throat.

Eventually I manage to straighten my body. The coughing finishes, the tickle in my throat has disappeared and I am left staring at the perplexed librarian through watery eyes. The sensation that has enveloped me since I entered the library has now dissipated and my head has cleared.

Eames is gone. The darkness is gone. All that's left is me.

Eames

I am not a man of God. Neither do I subscribe to anything Satanic or occult. That would be far too obvious. When someone gets caught for doing the things I do, the things I love to do, I find it irritating that they blame some higher power. When they say they could feel Satan working within them or the voice of God was trying to speak through them it makes me sick. If there is a God why would he try to speak through someone who takes a ten-year-old girl from the front of her house, crushes her skull by beating down on her with a brick, leaves her for a couple of days and then returns to rape her? Why would 'God' do that?

Why would God allow me to be born, yet kill off my innocent mother for doing something so natural?

Why would Satan want me as competition?

If something on high is watching down over us, then why would they allow me to be standing at the opposite side of the counter to the detective who is working on my case? How is it fair that I know exactly what he looks like and that his name was revealed to me over and over and over again?

Detective Inspector January David.

I repeat it several times out loud, slowly, each time emphasising a different word.

I can still see his face. He looked weathered and tired. What once may have been a defined chin is starting to sag. Groomed stubble has turned to a neglected fuzz. Hair greying prematurely. His shirt was creased and his top button undone, so that his tie could hang low so as not to constrict his neck. He looked so like a fucking detective I don't understand why he bothered to try and hide it. A scruffy, unshaven, haggard man, fishing around the library, looking for clues that will help him locate a killer. A killer that is stood only ten feet away from him as he persists with routine questioning that will only lead him to yet another dead end. Another bowl of nothing.

Is this really the man that will eventually catch me and stop me from doing the things I do, the things I love to do?

He still has no idea who I am or why I am doing this. But I know him now. I know more than him.

Inspector David.

Detective Inspector January David.

How much do you really care?

Girl 2

—◆—

Iorder a grande, dry cappuccino with an extra shot of espresso. Dry means that it is mostly foam. A regular cappuccino would have half-warm milk and half-foam added to the single shot of espresso, but this is almost entirely fluffy, bubbly milk scooped on top of my coffee. I enjoy sprinkling it with chocolate and eating it with one of the environmentally friendly, and cost effective, wooden stirrers that they so thoughtfully provide. When the chocolate sprinkles have been eaten, I can top them up, because I still have plenty of foam left. It's a real guilty pleasure. I take a chocolate brownie to nibble on afterwards too.

Eames orders his own and pays for both. He opts for an Americano, black, Espresso Roast, and goes with the barista's suggestion for something sweet, taking a section of the apple and cinnamon slice. Then we sit down at a table for two. I take the comfortable purple bucket sofa, while he sits the other side on the wooden chair.

'That looks pretty extravagant,' he says to me, pointing his stirrer at the perfect dome of foam rising out of the mug.

'It's just a cappuccino,' I say. 'Having it this way is a bit of an indulgence for me. A pat on the back for a good day.' I dip my splint of wood into the drink, slicing off a section that is covered in chocolate, and slowly lick it. Eames watches as I do this, as if it is something rather suggestive, sexual even. I use the tip of my finger to wipe at the corners of my mouth, unconsciously teasing his fantasies a little more.

I'm waiting for him to bring up the business discussion. It feels rude to instigate it; after all, he is giving me his time and expertise for free. So I waffle on about nothing, about work and how I would like to work for myself one day and, eventually, he gets it.

'I mean, I really hate the call centre, but it is a means to an end. You know?'

He nods, swigging at his cheap coffee and eyeing up his food.

'I just need to get enough together for my own laptop and things can get under way. Sure, at first I'll still have to keep the call centre thing going, but by next year I might only need a part-time job or a temp thing. You never really know, though, do you? Sometimes these things work and sometimes they fall flat on their face.' It feels like I am putting most of the work into the conversation, while he just scoffs and agrees with me, but if he is agreeing then maybe I am on the right track.

I stop talking and take another couple of swipes at my drink. Perhaps I can force him into talking through my silence.

'So, what is this idea of yours, then?' he asks, after watching my tongue work its way a few inches up the stirrer.

'Well . . .' I sit up straight on my chair. It's so comfortable that I tend to slouch, and his posture, on the less comfortable wooden equivalent, is making me feel smaller than I actually am. I straighten my skirt out with both hands and start to deliver my pitch.

I explain *iRaffle* from the beginning. How I intend to start with smaller items and work my way up to the kind of gadgets and luxury products that people only dream about. I say that people could end up winning a car or a house for only £1; that the odds would be better than the lottery and the initial lay-down wouldn't be high, but marketing could cost money; relying on word of mouth is not always the quickest and most efficient way of getting a message out to the masses.

He looks interested. Like he is mulling over the finer details in his mind.

He isn't.

He is picturing what I might look like naked. What expressions I might have while grinding away on top of him, while he lies on his back, his hands on my thighs, helping me to crash down harder with every thrusting motion.

He pictures me bleeding from my forehead. The blood trickling down my nose and on to my naked breasts. He thinks about gripping my wrists and pinning me to my bed, sweating as he moves in and out of me, waiting for the drugs to kick in and knock me out.

And then he says, 'Wow. That sounds like a fabulous idea. You have clearly thought it through. I'm very impressed.' He's placating me. He only really caught enough information to get him through in between thoughts of my upcoming demise.

He smiles at me and I feel myself go weak.

He's an older, attractive man who, on the surface, appears to have genuine interest in me and my ideas. It's days like this that I wonder whether there is someone looking down on me from above. Perhaps fate and faith have collided.

'Do you want to . . .?' I pause. I feel a little invincible today, like everything is going according to a pre-ordained plan, that everything I do, every decision I make is the right one.

What an idiot.

'Want to . . .?'

'Er, go for a drink, some dinner or something. We can talk some more.' Asking the question takes me back to feeling like a child. Innocent, unaware, unafraid of rejection.

It's not Eames' fault. I pursued him. I voluntarily drank the wine and flirted. I asked him back to my flat knowing that I could get him into bed if I offered myself to him. I wanted to seduce an older, more experienced man. In a way I wanted to thank him for all his advice and companionship, the way he listened to me, and it felt like the right thing to do the whole time.

After the sex, when I wake up in the kitchen, this is the first time I know anything is wrong.

January

◆

The library has given me nothing. I step outside through the glass door and get slapped in the face by the cold breeze of the polluted city air. Looking back over my shoulder I see the spectre-like figure of the unhelpful librarian as she stamps another book, living her life as though her most reliable patron dying will mean nothing to how the place will operate.

I call Paulson and tell him that I want him to meet me back at the station in an hour with Murphy. I don't ask him how investigations are going at Carla's workplace, because I don't think I can take it if he tells me that they are turning up nothing. I can't hear that there is no suspect or that nothing is suggesting any correlation between Dorothy and Carla.

Did these girls know each other?

How are they linked and who links them?

'OK, Jan, we'll be done and back in an hour,' Paulson says and I almost detect a hint of enthusiasm in his voice, like he has uncovered something pertinent to the case, but still I refrain from allowing myself to believe.

'That's great. I'll grab the coffees and some lunch. We can talk it through when you and Murph get back.' I force myself to sound more relaxed than I feel. I think it's good to keep it informal on occasions; if you think about the job constantly it can get to you.

I can't switch off, but I need my team to be operating to the best of their ability if we are going to solve this. Even if I can't let myself kick back, I need them to a little.

'How was it at the library?'

I dismiss him straight away. 'We'll chat in an hour. See you then.' And I press the red button to hang up.

It's grey out, the grey that is almost blindingly white. I squint, sigh and rub my eyes. I need to sleep. I need a drink.

The journey back is fraught with the usual endless stream of incompetent drivers and overcrowding of public transport blocking my view. I start to empathise with Audrey about her commute every morning. And I realise that I haven't spoken to Audrey, again. I don't need the hassle of her being upset with me like before. I can't keep coming home from work, exhausted, and cook her dinner, while listening to more drivel about the wedding preparations.

I take my mobile out and quick-dial Audrey. At the speed I'm travelling through the centre of London, you could hardly class it as driving, so I ignore the law about not using a mobile phone while in control of a vehicle.

She lets it ring seven times before she picks up.

'Hello?' she says coldly. She knows it's me: my name flashes up on her screen.

'Hi. It's me.' Sheepishly, I wait for her to respond to this, but the pause turns uncomfortable and I am forced to continue my grovelling. 'Have you seen the papers this morning?' Still no answer. 'Another girl . . . look . . . I was working all night . . . another girl was killed.' I wait. 'I'm sorry, I should have called, I know.' I don't know how she manages to reduce me to such a quivering, passive, embryonic version of myself sometimes, but I just can't bear to hurt her, to hurt any woman.

I think about Cathy. I hear her voice calling for me to play with her that last time. I relive the moment I stepped outside to find she was gone.

There is another short pause, then the sound of a car horn behind me startles me back to reality. 'Audrey, I'm sorry. OK?' I raise my voice a little as the adrenalin starts to propel through my veins as a result of the car behind scaring me into motion. I tuck the headset under my cheek with my shoulder, freeing my left hand to change into second gear.

Finally she speaks.

'It's fine, Jan.' I'm relieved that this is now a two-way conversation and that she is calling me Jan rather than January. I know her guard is down now. 'I just want to know that you are safe. What would I do if you didn't call one night and everything wasn't all right?'

'I know. I know.' I look in my rear-view mirror and the driver behind is shaking his head in my direction to show his disgust that I am not paying full attention, because I am on the phone. Luckily I am in an unmarked car.

'Will you be home for dinner tonight?' she asks, knowing that I have to say yes. 'It's OK if you're not, I just need to know either way.' Now I have to. When she says that *it's OK* or that she *doesn't mind*, that means that it definitely isn't OK and she certainly does mind.

'Yes, yes. I'll be home at the normal time. Can we order in, though? I haven't been to sleep for nearly two days and I don't think I have the energy to cook.'

'Of course. I'll pick up some wine on the way and we can have a lazy one this evening, eh?' I sense the affection in her voice and I'm relieved. She is understanding of the demands of my job and I love her for that. It is my fault that I get caught up in these cases and block everything else out.

'Sounds perfect,' I say, a little breathy, but not too much that it comes across cheesy.

'Great. I'll see you later then. Love you.'

'Love you too.' And I mean it.

I hang up the phone and throw it on to the passenger seat. I manage to overtake the bus in front as it pulls over to pick up more passengers. The traffic is a little clearer, but I know some other roads that will get me back in a quicker time. I turn down a back road and pull over. In the glovebox is a hip flask. I pull it out and unscrew the pewter cap. Looking over my shoulder and in all of my mirrors I see that nobody is around. I slouch down in my seat and take a large gulp that burns the back of my throat, making me cough, and thins the saliva in my mouth.

I close my eyes for just a second and see a huge yellow smile. It scares me back to life.

This is why I am afraid to sleep. I can't prevent The Smiling Man from visiting me there. I have to stay awake to keep him at bay.

I throw the flask back into the glove compartment and slam it shut. Shaking my head, I slap both my cheeks hard to keep myself alert and pull off into the road, hoping I make it back to the station in one piece.

Girl 4

———✦———

I let the phone ring seven times. To punish him. Make him sweat a little.

I don't care that he has to work late sometimes. He is out there saving people's lives and bringing criminals to justice, but he needs to know that I am the most important person in the world to him now. I'm about to become his wife. He needs to let me know that he is safe. That he cares. That he isn't like all the other men.

So that's why I make him wait, to play the game. His job is infinitely more rewarding and important than mine, in the broader sense of human worth, but if I am learning to balance my home and work life, then he should also be able to.

'Hello?' I say, as if I don't know that it is January or have forgotten who he is. I just saw his name and picture flash on my phone as he called. My tone immediately alerts him to the fact that I am not in the best mood, something I would not have been able to convey as implicitly had he chickened out and sent a text, like he did when the first girl died.

'Hi, it's me.' I can feel him testing the water here, but my best option is to remain quiet until he just apologises. The silence will make him feel uncomfortable. He starts to mumble something about the case and another girl and working late and, eventually, he says sorry. And this is enough for me.

I can't wait to be Mrs David.

I am dying to walk down the aisle with hundreds of people looking at only me in my beautiful dress.

I want to say *I do*.

I want to look January in the eyes and know that I am the most important person in the world to him, because we are alive and together. I want him to know that nothing will come between us and I will never hurt him, that everything I do is for him and him for me.

We both deserve happiness. To start a new life putting everything behind us.

Arguing is a waste of time. But the beauty of even having a minor altercation with January is that he always likes to make it up to me.

When the last girl died he came home early the next day and cooked me dinner. We talked through the final stages of the wedding and then we made love. Well, that's how it was to begin with.

He started very tenderly, like he always does, ensuring that I am pleased before he even contemplates his own gratification, but part-way through, he turned. I don't know what caused it, but it was like someone else was on top of me. It was a lot rougher, his eyes glazed over before shutting completely and it was as if he was in the zone, in a sexual trance, or something. He pinned my hands down with one of his and gripped hold of my left breast with the other hand. He pushed himself up to the tips of his toes in order to get the best leverage and maximum amount of force to pound himself inside me, the loud repetition of the slapping noise caused as we came together each time not fazing him. Then, still holding my hands and gripping my breast harder and more painfully, he brought himself up to his knees and made shorter, sharper movements, in and out, in and out, faster and faster. His hands came up to my throat, gradually gripping tighter and tighter with every other thrust, the pressure on my neck and the force between my legs culminating into a thunder somewhere near my diaphragm.

I felt like the next step was going to be him striking me around the face as he climaxed.

But he didn't.

That was a shame.

Because I think I would have liked it. I deserve that. I need that.

And he hasn't done it since. He won't even mention what happened that night, because he feels ashamed or weak or disgusted.

We've hardly even had sex since then, and when we did it was lethargic and tender and average.

So, if I can give him the impression that I am more annoyed with him than I actually am, then he just might hold me down or choke me or slap me a couple of times.

That would be exciting.

To remind us we're alive.

January

❖

I have three coffees ready. Straight black with no sugar for me; Paulson has a little milk and two sugars, Murphy goes for a latte. Each one representing our personalities, I muse. Murphy's is a little weak, mine is somewhat intense and Paulson's is calculated to a steady equilibrium of sweet and bitter. Stereotypically, I have a bag of six doughnuts for us to share, plus some sandwiches and crisps.

I inwardly debate making my coffee more Irish with the Scotch in my top drawer, but Murphy and Paulson arrive in time to stop me doing that.

'Afternoon, Jan,' Paulson says as he enters, holding the door open for Murphy.

'Hey, Jan,' says Murphy in a slightly less respectful-of-your-superior way. But this is supposed to be informal, I remind myself. I let it slide.

'All right, lads. Food is scattered around the table, help yourself. Grab your coffees.'

They both grab their coffee before plunging into the food. Paulson sips his straight away through the small hole in the lid, while Murphy takes his lid off and inhales like a cartoon character before blowing over the top to cool it down.

Everyone grabs some food and sits down around my desk.

'So, Jan,' Paulson blurts out with half a jam doughnut still in his mouth, 'any luck at the library?'

I explain to him that the link between the two dead girls is still proving elusive. That at one point I thought they might both belong to that same library, but it turned out to be a pensioner with a late fee. Murphy chuckles. I let them know that we are dealing with someone who can cover their tracks extremely well and that we need to cling on to any thread of evidence that we find.

'Are you sure that these two girls are even linked?' Murphy asks.

'I know they are, Murph.' I look him dead in the face to show that I am serious.

'It's just that the scenes were so different and they are both in completely different parts of the city . . .' He trails off as he takes a bite from a BLT sandwich.

'It doesn't matter about that, Murph,' Paulson chips in, 'it's the elaborate nature of the scenes that links them. That's his hallmark. Right, Jan?'

'Right,' I confirm, wondering whether Murphy really wants to be a part of this case. Perhaps it's a little over his head. He is still doing his job, though. He's not a thinker like Paulson, but he's not an automaton either, and every team needs someone who will just get on with what is asked of them. It can be frustrating at times, though.

'Okaaaaay,' he drawls, not truly understanding.

'I can feel it,' I tell them. 'It's the same guy. These are not random kills. They take an extreme amount of planning. It's as if he appears from nowhere, takes these girls, kills them without anybody close to the victim having an idea of his existence, and then disappears without leaving a plausible motive.'

'He's like a fucking ghost,' adds Paulson.

'These women have both had sex consensually with the guy, though, right?' Murphy asks.

'Yep. That's the terrifying thing, Murph. It's in the papers. Everybody knows what is going on, but people aren't scared enough to think that it will affect them. These aren't prostitutes that he is killing. These aren't unattractive, desperate women.' I go on to lecture that every woman is at risk and to take a man home on the first night if you live alone is unquestionably ignorant. I'm not usually preachy; this case is just starting to feel like a personal crusade for me. It feels like Cathy all over again, but this time I'm in a position to do something about it.

Paulson explains to me that Carla's colleagues generally thought of her as a bit of a loner. That she wouldn't get involved in company functions, and would often spend her lunch hour with her head in a book or taking advantage of her Internet access at work. Her boss said that she only really offered the bare minimum, but despite her tendency to remain separate from her colleagues she wasn't a freak or unconfident. In fact, quite the opposite. She was articulate and unafraid to voice her opinion. She would do the bare amount of work needed, but knew that there was nothing they could do about that because she was solid and reliable.

'The only anomaly was that, as Murph got from her boss, she managed to set a new call record the day she died. Her boss said that it could have annoyed one particular member of the team, because he always got the top stats every day,' Paulson explains.

'Yeah, I thought that could be significant, but there is no way anyone could have planned this in an afternoon, right?'

'Exactly. Besides, we checked and the guy has a solid alibi for that evening.'

I can't hide my frustration.

'So, basically, we have fuck all.' I turn my head to the side so that I am not looking at either of them and rest my chin in my hand, leaning my elbow on the desk.

There's a short silence, then Paulson speaks up. 'We have the note,' he says matter-of-factly.

Another silence.

'Murph told me that the killer sent a note to the station.' He looks at Murphy as if he didn't mean to get him into trouble. I puzzle over why it had slipped my mind to tell Paulson. I had intended to, of course. 'Sounds like a chess move to me.' He bites into a sandwich, as if it is the full stop that punctuates his sentence.

'That's exactly what I thought. I just don't know what it could mean without more information, though. What do you think, Murph?' I want to test him. He won't think unless you ask.

'Er . . .' He pauses as if something is going around in his mind. 'Yeah. Yeah. You're probably right. A chess move. Could be a chess move.' He stares at me, waiting for some kind of acknowledgement that his response is acceptable.

'So, I think we've established that it could be a chess move, then.' I shake my head slightly to accentuate my sarcasm. 'We can't just sit around and wait for another girl to turn up dead, so that we can get another note and start piecing this all together, though.' I push back into my chair and stare up at the ceiling. The only sound in the room for the next minute is the rustling of crisp packets as my crack team finishes their lunch.

'Unless . . .' I trail off.

'Unless what?' Paulson scratches, sitting to attention.

'. . . there's already another note.' My eyes widen as I transmit my thoughts.

And then Murphy speaks.

'Wait a second.' I nod in his direction, signalling for him to finish my thought out loud. 'If these two murders really are linked, then we are missing something.' He looks at me, then at Paulson, waiting for us to chime in. 'Another note,' he says in a slightly higher pitch. 'If this is the same killer, then maybe he would have sent a note to the station after the first girl was killed . . .'

'Bloody hell, Murph.' I laugh. 'I think you've got it.' It seems so obvious. We have been thinking too laterally, giving the killer too much credit maybe, but the answer was right in front of our faces.

'. . . and,' he continues unexpectedly, 'because we didn't necessarily realise that this was a spate of murders by the same perpetrator, the note may not have been taken that seriously, because it's so cryptic. But it will be filed somewhere, surely.' He looks to me for the answer.

'Of course it will, Murph. We file everything.' I see the pride rise in him, brightening his face, and he even allows himself a smile, as if he believes he came up with the idea. 'Paulson, get downstairs and find that first note. This could be the key.'

He jumps to attention and wipes the crumbs that have landed on his shirt on to the floor. Without saying a word he turns and heads out the door, never looking back at us, waddling his large frame as fast as he can towards a piece of information that we have frustratingly always had in our possession and could start to unlock the mysteries that this case holds.

I follow suit in the excitement. Taking half the sandwich and stuffing it into my mouth in one swift, monstrous movement, I stand up and head over to the whiteboard, chewing with my mouth open along the way.

Murphy remains seated, as though he has done his good deed for the day. He sits there like a child, tipping the last few crisp crumbs into his mouth directly from the packet.

I take one of the blue markers and start to write on the board. It has run out or dried up. I grab the green one next to it. This, too, seems to be faulty. Throwing them both on the floor is Murphy's cue to help in some way. He roots around some papers on the desk and pulls out a black marker, which he tests on the end of his finger to ensure it is working. It is.

He throws it across the room to me and I start to write on the board.

I draw two 8 × 8 squares to represent chessboards. Above each board I write one of the victim's names. The first is Dorothy Penn, the second is Carla Moretti. Below Carla's board I write the message from the note, *B4 to C3*. I then draw an arrow from B4 to C3 on the grid. It feels like this takes me around ten seconds, but in actuality it is much longer and, by the time I put the lid back on the pen, Paulson rounds the doorframe panting with a piece of white card in his hand.

Girl 3

—◆—

I read about him. About the terrible things he did to those girls. How he seduced them and then tied them up before he killed them, but I refuse to live my life in fear. You can't just stop.

You can't give up.

Just because a bomb goes off in the Underground it can't stop you from travelling around on the Tube. Just because one boyfriend cheats on you, you don't swear off men completely. And just because two women were living their lives, as they always did, and were unlucky enough to be selected from the eight million people that live in this city to die at the hands of the latest deranged serial killer to walk our streets, it can't stop you from continuing to treat life as a party, as a glorious experience that you want to squeeze everything out of.

I won't let it.

Eames

—✦—

C an I be forgiven?
Dear God, I know that I have sinned against many people and against you. I need your forgiveness. I believe that Jesus Christ died for me and arose from the dead. I invite him into my life to be my saviour. Thank you for your gift of forgiveness and eternal life.

An oriental woman in her fifties hands me this prayer as I walk away from Shepherd's Bush Market.

The back of the leaflet tells me that she is part of the Oasis International Church. They have an Arabic/English service on a Sunday at 5.30 p.m.

I don't fucking care.

I don't care for their preaching.

I don't care for them stuffing this literature into my hand when I am trying to gather information on the surroundings for my next kill.

I don't care for anyone who thrusts their beliefs on to others who haven't asked to enter into that discussion.

The front of the leaflet shows a white female looking off into the distance in contemplation, her chin in her hands. Beside her, a man sits with his back against the wall, his hand on his head in despair. Below the scene are the words *Can I be FORGIVEN?*

I don't care for forgiveness.

Aggressively I screw the leaflet into a small ball and clench it in my fist in annoyance. I look back at the elderly lady inflicting this tripe she calls literature on to anyone that passes her by. I wait. Stood in the centre of the path with people from all cultures squeezing past and tutting obviously in my direction.

I want her to see me, to see my eyes. To know that I am picturing her tied to a chair with her hands on a desk in front of her. I want her to know that I could hammer a large nail through the back of each of her wrists, so that they are securely fastened to the wood in front of her. I want her to realise that I could break her fingers one by one, that I could sit a stack of her leaflets on the desk in front of her and feed them to her slowly and after every time I break another finger, every time I force her to swallow her propaganda, I will ask her if she forgives me.

If she says yes, I will continue to line her stomach with this pathetic biblical filth.

If she says no, if she caves and admits that these words mean nothing, it doesn't matter to me. I will keep feeding and breaking and asking for her forgiveness. And I will do this every day until she is dead. I have the patience.

I want her to look into my eyes and know this.

But she doesn't. Then a woman nudges the side of my knee with her pram and shocks me back to reality. I blink a few times then close my eyes, while taking a deep breath. I turn and head off towards the green. Away from this distraction.

Carla is still on my mind, I want to make sure that I get this one right. I want it to be undeniable that my next girl is the one I should use. She has been selected and I know how she must die, but I need to be certain.

I have to be patient.

January

'I've got it,' Paulson says as he enters our room. He's sweating, which is something he does a lot as a consequence of his lifestyle. He stops in the doorway and buckles slightly at the waist, resting his left hand on his knee and catching his breath. All the time holding the letter in his right hand high above his head, as if he is under water and saving it from impending peril.

'Fuck, Paulson. Get a grip.' I fiddle with the marker, taking the lid off, putting it back on. Taking it off, putting it back on.

'All right, Jan,' he pants, 'I haven't even read it myself, yet.'

Seeing him struggle for air is infuriating. Having an active mind does not mean you can neglect your physical health. I pace over to him and snatch the envelope from his hand. The envelope was opened when it was originally delivered, so I only need to pull out the flap that has been tucked inside.

The card is the same as the one we received for Carla. I extract it slowly. It's almost exciting; I see my hand shaking, but this might be because I need the Scotch in my drawer. Carefully I grab the top of the card, only using the tips of my fingers. As it emerges I see the black ink and the same rounded handwriting as was inscribed on the other card. I read the message in my head once, then out loud.

C7 to B4.

'C7 to B4,' I say aloud for Paulson and Murphy's benefit.

'Another move?' Murphy asks.

I move over to the whiteboard. In the space below Dorothy's chessboard diagram I write C7 to B4, then pause to look back over my shoulder at Paulson and Murphy. I see them literally edging forward in antici-pation. I turn back to the board and plot an arrow for these directions.

I feel the mood in the room fall flat.

We all rock back on our heels. Stunned.

It doesn't make sense. No chess piece can make that move from C7 to B4 in one move alone. I feel like I've been punched in the stomach and hang my head in disappointment. I know I need to compose myself, to be a leader, but everyone has their breaking point.

'So it's not chess.' Murphy's idiotic, ill-timed, comedy rhetoric is one thing too many for me to handle after all the setbacks and the lack of sleep, and I overreact.

I take the lid off the pen again and start to scribble erratically over the diagrams, growling as I do so. Then I raise my voice.

'No, Murph, it's not . . . fucking . . . chess.' I say each of the last three words with a pause in between so that I have time to grit my teeth and scribble further, trying to keep my frustration in check. As I curse, I press the pen down on the board too hard and the nib disappears inside the plastic tubing, making a scratching noise against the board.

I continue to scratch against the grid, despite the pen

now being broken and I repeat, 'It's not fucking chess,' then I whip around and throw the marker viciously, striking Murphy in the chest. It wasn't on purpose, but it looks that way and I can't back away from that, otherwise I come across as weak. They are both dumbfounded by my overreaction. I don't know what to tell them.

That we can't give up? That I won't give up just because of a few setbacks. I won't be lazy like the police that stopped looking for Cathy. I won't let my superiors convince me that this case is not important, that it's over. I won't allow another girl to vanish like my sister and I won't let another family live the rest of their lives feeling the way that I always do. But we have nothing.

Nothing.

Right now, in the depths of this despondency, I think the only way we can get a handle on this is to wait for him to kill again.

We need another girl to die.

Girl 4

When I get home January is sat alone on the Chunky Arm Cuddler in vintage shabby natural leather that I ordered for us to snuggle up on and watch films together. There are three oak blocks next to the chair that I never really had use for, but thought they looked bulky and interesting. It looks as though January is using them to store his empty wine bottles on. There are two empty bottles on the lowest block, a Tempranillo and a Merlot, and a half-empty bottle on the highest, Shiraz.

It's affecting him.

'You're late.' His voice is croaky, like he has just woken up, but that's not the case. It's because he is drowsy. Two days without a minute of sleep, running on adrenalin and disappointment, drinking to fight the effects of his body trying to shut down.

'I had some things to finish in the office and I stopped off on the way home to pick up some wine.' I look over at the oak blocks to see that the bottom of the Shiraz has stained the wood. 'But I see you have already done that.' He looks at me with bleary eyes, then over at his stash and chuckles with a slight snort. I can see he's finding it difficult to keep his eyes open.

'Have you eaten?'

He shakes his head.

'Do you want to?'

He shrugs his shoulders.

I wonder whether I pushed him too far on the phone earlier. Maybe I sent him over the edge. Maybe this is all my fault.

'OK. Stay here. I'll be back in a second. Try to stay awake. I haven't seen you properly for days.' I leave him to wallow on the seat built for two that he is managing to completely occupy, sandwiched between his own self-loathing and pity.

In the kitchen I pull open the drawer where the bottle opener lives. January has put it back in there, at least, but has left the cork from the Shiraz attached to the cork-screw. I pull it out of the drawer and slam it shut. But it doesn't slam, because I had all the drawers and cupboards fitted with a hydraulic system that slows them down an inch before they impact to keep them silent.

I unscrew the cork with my hand and dispose of it properly, then open my own bottle – a Pinot Noir from Mount Difficulty. Normally I would let it breathe for a minimum of thirty minutes, but I don't have the time tonight as I'm playing catch-up with my fiancé. Leaving the bottle on the work surface, I move over to the refrigerator. Opening the large door, which is roughly my height, I'm hit by a refreshing gust that cools my temper. On one of the shelves inside the door sits the remnants of a bottle of Cloudy Bay that I almost worked through the other night. I take it out and lift the bottle to my lips. So uncouth, so unlike me, but I down the last sixth of the bottle in record time. It hurts my teeth. But I feel I have given the Pinot some respect by at least letting it sit there for even a short while.

When I re-enter the living room, Jan is leaning over the side of the chair looking intently at the tallest block. He is unaware that I am watching him from the doorway. I see him lick the end of his index finger then rub it ferociously on the burgundy ring that has already soaked into the oak.

'Leave it, Jan.' He jumps at the unexpected sound of my voice and swivels around until he is facing forward again.

'Sorry, babe. I didn't think.' He looks so innocent as he says this. So subdued.

'Don't worry about it. It's just a piece of wood.' I bought it from a website that seemed ethically sound and they promised that all of their wooden furniture comes from a sustainable source. I think it was around £79, so not that expensive. Expensive for a coaster, sure, but replaceable.

'How was your day?' he asks, not really caring. Just going through the motions.

'Same as ever. You know?' He doesn't know. I'm not sure he really understands what I do each day as the head of the company. 'Business is steady, nothing to worry about.' He nods and stiffens his lips in approval.

'Good. Good.'

I don't know whether or not to ask him about his day, because clearly it isn't going well; the litres of wine tell me that much. 'Apparently the hen night is all set. I just need to bring a party frock and a sense of fun.' I smile as I say this and take a gulp of the Pinot Noir.

But first I take a sniff. Blackberries and dark cherry. The taste is underpinned by a spice I can't quite identify, but I'm definitely getting liquorice. It's exactly what I need.

'I'm worried about what Paulson has planned.' It looks as though I have escaped the depressing work talk. 'I said no strippers, but he says that a stag night without strippers is like vodka and tonic with lemon. Wrong.' He shrugs.

'I don't care if there are strippers there, Jan.'

I do.

I don't agree that this is the last night of freedom. We've been together for the last two years; that isn't freedom, that's togetherness, monogamy. So, to go out and let a half-naked whore writhe about on a part of your body that, technically, only two people in the world should be seeing or touching, is unacceptable. How would he feel if I decided to be 'free' with a male stripper or escort?

'It's the last night that I will allow you to be anywhere near a stripper, so you might as well enjoy it.' I don't know why I said that. Maybe there has been too much confrontation today. Maybe I'll save it for some time in the future.

'Well, I don't want one. Just a few beers, a few laughs, tell some old stories, hammer out some clichés about married life. Nothing major.'

'I'll drink to that,' I say, raising my glass to toast. January finishes the last mouthful and turns back to the blocks he has ruined, to refill. As he turns his back on me I empty my glass of its contents straight down my throat. There's so much in there that it takes me two gulps. The second gulp is harder to take than the first. As he turns back to me I am pouring more wine into my bulbous glass and walking over to where he is sitting.

I can easily fit on to the chair with Jan, it's the reason I bought the thing in the first place, but I don't want to invade his space just yet; he clearly needs it. So I perch myself on the floor next to the seat, not quite kneeling. I rest my weight against the leather and put my left hand on his thigh. We touch glasses to toast the end of another difficult day and say nothing as we sip our chosen inebriant, looking each other in the eyes, knowing exactly where this is leading.

For a while we sit in silence. I lean my back against the sofa, my legs stretched out in front of me, slightly resting my side against Jan's leg. My arm covers his thigh and I stroke him lightly as we both stare through the wall opposite. I imagine myself walking towards January at the altar, him smiling back at me slightly nervous. Jan is doing the same, but his thoughts are not on the important day that is less than three weeks away now, but on his sister and the two girls that have been so inventively culled over the last months.

He moves his glass into his left hand and strokes the back of my head sensually with the other. It's so relaxing and I tilt my head up to the ceiling in half-ecstasy to show my gratitude.

I leave my head where it is, my eyes closed, feeling January's strong masculine hands massaging my head; it's heavenly. Even though my eyes are closed I still sense him as he draws ever closer. Leaning down, he kisses me softly on the lips. I open my eyes to see him above me, his weathered face and bloodshot brown eyes peering intently into mine.

'I love you, Audrey,' he says meaningfully, and I believe him.

I take my hand off his thigh and grab a handful of hair on the back of his head to pull him back in and kiss again, this time with a little more vigour.

As our heads move apart I give him a smile and push his chest up, so that he is back in a seated position. All in one movement I manage to stand up and corkscrew myself around to end up straddling him. I lean over and place my glass on the stained wooden block, pushing my breasts into his chest as I do so. I grab the back of his hair again and yank his head back against the shabby brown leather. Playfully, I grip his bottom lip in my teeth and pull at it slightly, while also moving my hips subtly back and forth.

Then I stop, look him directly in his weary eyes and say, 'Yeah, me too.' Then I kiss him one more time before I take control of everything.

Eames

———◆———

I don't know whether it's pride or self-promotion.
Maybe eighty out of the one hundred people that
leave the building are wearing their company lanyard
around their neck. You can tell which ones do this
through necessity or ease of use and which ones feel it is
a status symbol.

I've seen people walking to the Tube in Shepherd's
Bush wearing them. I've noticed them at King's Cross
trying to look important, like they matter.

Amy leaves the BBC building and puts hers straight
into her bag. I watch her do this from the grassy area
where so many of them congregate for lunch to talk about
work even more. To jabber on about contracts and rights
and talent and nothing that is important.

I can sit here behind a book on my own and nobody
will notice me or converse with me, because it would
mean that they might have to stop talking about themselves for a second.

Amy has vibrancy. She stands out from the drones that
are too afraid to admit they have nothing in their lives
apart from their work, and they hate their work.

I see her take the time to talk to another girl in sign
language.

And I know that she is worthy.

147

I hear her talking about a hangover, as if it is as normal as eating cereal.

And I know that I can kill her.

She listens to what people have to say and appears enthusiastic about everything.

To take the life of someone who truly appreciates what they have, someone who understands the privilege of existence, is far more rewarding; it feels like an achievement.

When someone is convicted of a crime and they confess to preying on the weak, harmless and unsuspecting, that's not me. That's indolence. For some, death is a privilege; those that I do not kill are already dead, living in their personal hell.

Weak and harmless is simple. There is no reason for it.

For Amy, her death should be the greatest thrill of all. For both of us.

I wait until she passes me on the path that bisects the two green areas populated by asymmetrical haircuts and designer stubble and protruding lanyards and ego. She is with two work colleagues, one male and one female. They look to be heading out for lunch.

I wait until they are through the first crossing, then I stand, locate the bobbing blonde head of the effervescent Miss Mullica and begin my stalk, throwing my book into the first rubbish bin I see.

I assume they are heading towards the market, because there really isn't much in the area apart from White City Tube station, some flats opposite that appear to have perpetual scaffolding attached and the official BBC car park. A building site on the left will house a large shopping centre in the next few years, making the A40 even harder to negotiate during rush hour and weekends.

Along Uxbridge Street there are plenty of eateries that accommodate the plethora of diverse cultures that make Shepherd's Bush what it is. It reminds me of the Swiss Cottage area that Carla was from, only this has so much more colour. But even a serial killer has to be aware that this is not the safest area of London to be in.

The first hundred yards of the street are filled with chain eateries, but past the market are places like Pizza Corner, Chicken Cottage and House of Pies. For the more adventurous there are Indian, Thai, Vietnamese and Caribbean restaurants. There are Polish delis and large independent Asian supermarkets, but Amy, the same as last week, has walked the mile from her desk to the market in order to buy Palestinian falafel.

While most would make an event out of this, perhaps saving this as an end-of-week treat or something to break up a laborious Monday, Amy is different. I've seen her here on Thursdays mainly, the occasional Tuesday and seldom on Wednesday. She just does it because she likes it. Just from watching her I can see that nobody could make her do something that she didn't want to.

This is the challenge.

This is my thrill.

This is what sets me apart from the impulsive, sexually minded, cross-dressing, habitual killers that have come before me.

I have class. An agenda.

My résumé would list my abilities as *organised* and *determined to drive a project through to its conclusion, working under pressure to defined deadlines and targets, a proactive worker with a mind on achieving the final goal*.

I also have *a lifetime of experience in this industry*.

I see Amy through the window of the falafel shop

laughing with the owner, pointing at her work friends. I see how she commands attention with her presence. She doesn't seek it, she just has charisma. I can imagine her in bed with me. I can see her on top of me, below me, on the floor in front of me, her hands tied to her feet, her back arching as I watch the last bit of breath leave her body, her sound muffled, her tears silent.

Carla nearly ruined everything.

Amy will be my redemption.

I can't wait to fucking ruin her.

January

---✦---

A udrey is gone.
　　Even though we are getting married in just over a
couple of weeks, I feel a little used. Like it was a one-night
stand. As though she was just getting something out of
her system.

I can feel those bottles of wine creeping up on me,
ready to assault my senses, for the numbness to wear off
and the pain to ensue.

The bed covers are sticking to me. My body is damp
with a clammy sensation that feels as though I am
sweating alcohol, like my system is attempting to expel
all the poisons inside me in any way it can.

I feel like water will help. Two pints of water. Or a glass
of Scotch to take the edge off.

As I try to sit up I feel the blood either rushing to my
head or away from my brain. Either way, it makes me
dizzy; it temporarily paralyses my intentions and my
head falls back on to the pillow. Even that hurts.

As I stretch my arms up behind my head I brush the
top of Audrey's top pillow with my forearm. She has left
a note on there for me to find when I wake up.

*Didn't want to wake you. You seemed so peaceful. Thanks
for being there last night. It meant a lot. I love you. A x.*

Thanks for being there?

I have no idea what she means.

I remember being at work. I remember that our break-through on the killer's chess moves came to an abrupt halt when we realised we had it all wrong. I remember losing it, scribbling on the whiteboard, breaking the pen, punching the whiteboard and scaring my team. I remember coming home and drinking wine; a lot of wine.

Then I lose some time.

This is the problem with sleep deprivation: things don't always happen as you remember them. Sometimes it's difficult to differentiate between something that happened while you were asleep or whether it happened while you were awake.

Audrey ravaged me, that's for sure.

It wasn't rape, because I wanted it, in a way. But it wasn't far off.

As I put my hands behind my head and start to recall the events of last night I feel a patch of baldness. Maybe two inches in diameter where a clump of hair is missing.

I remember Audrey straddling me on her favourite Chunky Cuddler sofa. I had to do nothing apart from sit there and take it. I remember her holding my head back, so that I was always looking up towards the ceiling, occasionally seeing her big dark eyes bounce into view. I remember the climax where she gripped the clump of hair on the back of my head harder, twisting it with each pelvic thrust and then ripping it out at the final moment before collapsing on me, her head resting on my shoulder, breathing heavily, kissing my neck lightly.

I didn't feel the pain at that point; it wasn't until a few minutes later that it dawned on me.

Thanks for being there?

If that's what she meant by *being there*, then I'll be there for her every night – minus the hair removal.

It makes me wonder about her. It's not cold feet and I'm not questioning our relationship, it's just that, when something happens that you've never seen before it makes you ask questions. We've been together for a couple of years now and we've lived together almost as long as that, but do we know each other that well?

Do we really need to know *everything*?

Is constant discovery the secret to a long relationship, or is full disclosure the key?

This is the first time that I have ever considered bunking off for a day. But I won't be one of those people. I can't let this go. It's true that we don't have much information to go on, but we are detectives, we need to hunt it down, to detect. We need to pick ourselves up and realise that there are two families out there who have lost someone in cruel, extraordinary circumstances. We are their only hope for possible closure.

Paulson was visibly stunned by my outburst yesterday, so I need to get into the station and make things right. Keep spirits up. Motivate. Get this investigation back on track.

I just don't know where to start.

I'm another step behind.

Girl 3

I don't know what I want to be. Do I have to know that right now? Can't I just live a little? Can't I just be alive? Taste the world before the pressures of life force me into conforming to the conventional wants and needs of the human race.

I'm twenty-five. I don't want to be married or have a kid or be sucked into a mortgage-repayment scheme until I retire. I don't want a career.

When did it stop being acceptable to have a job and a roof over my head and a few quid in my pocket?

My job is menial. Not everyone working for the BBC has a glamorous role. There are people behind the talent, there are people that liaise with the people behind the talent, there are underlings who have meetings about the liaisons and then, about seven people below that, you get the person who has a perpetual stack of papers to work through that never get archived properly, are usually misplaced and never actually read anyway. That's what I do, and it's just too boring to explain any further.

When I'm out and a man asks me what I do for a living – a fairly frequent ice-breaker – I just tell them that I work for the BBC, and swig some of my drink. It's usually enough to impress. If they persist and ask me exactly what it is, I simply say 'Legal stuff, bit dull.' Then I ask them something about themselves. People always want to talk about themselves more than they want to talk about you.

Eames doesn't ask me to go into detail. He already knows what I do. And he doesn't care.

I'm not against a relationship, but I don't feel the need to be in one; that can take over your life. I enjoy sex. Of course it can be meaningful, but it can also just be fun. I've slept with four different men this year and I have been safe with all of them. Three were actually fun and none was close to meaningful.

Until Eames.

He ticks all three boxes.

He will be my fifth, my last.

Dad inscribes my epitaph with words like *devoted daughter, fun-loving* and *kind-hearted*. What it should say is *Here lies Amy Mullica, no career, no mortgage, no husband, no children, no idea.*

January

———◆———

This time I wake up and I'm not tied to a chair. But everything else is the same.

The blindfold, the shuffling feet, the muzak.

I can smell smoke. A lot of smoke. It's not the smell you get when a building or a tree is on fire, it is infused with nicotine; I can taste it.

I wait patiently on the floor. My arms have been wrenched backwards, my legs bending at the knees and hinging at the waste, so that my hands can be tied tightly to my ankles behind my back. It stretches my chest and my thighs to an uncomfortable ache. They burn.

In the darkness I hear The Smiling Man behind me, shifting his feet, side to side like a metronome keeping perfect time with music and slowing my heart rate as I concentrate on that beat to keep myself calm.

I don't want to see his smiling face. Not after the last time.

I follow the sound of his footsteps as he circles me once, then again, and then for a third time in slow, calculated movements. With my eyes closed under the blindfold I sense the walls closing in, the smoke getting thicker, and it becomes difficult to control my breathing.

The shuffling sound as he drags his feet around the dusty wooden floor I find myself lying on grows around me, in front of me, behind me, surrounding me. Like an army.

And then, as he always does, he rips off my blindfold wildly, yanking my head forward as it catches on my hair.

I blink several times, looking around for The Smiling Man, but the smoke obscures my vision and my eyes start to water. Then I see it. Through the dense smoke, large yellow gravestones make their way towards me. His smile.

He looks down at me through the smoke; his eyes are open this time and he moves them slowly around the awkward circle that my body shape is making. He starts at my face, looking into my eyes, smiling at me in my discomfort, then he moves anti-clockwise around the rest of me. Down to my right shoulder, along the arm to my hands, to the cable that binds them together, to the next cable that attaches them to my ankles. He then works that icy gaze around my legs up to my waist, my stretched chest, to my neck, the only part of my body that has a free range of movement, and back to my eyes.

He bends at the waist to bring his face close to mine, his bulbous eyes almost touching mine.

I don't move.

I can't move.

Then he pulls his head back by about ten inches, so he is no longer a blur to me. I look away from those eyes and back to his smile. The small gaps in his teeth seem to be seeping. I focus on them and between each tooth a small puff of smoke is being secreted slowly. It's not through him breathing. I'm not even sure if he does breathe. But he doesn't break that smile. That smoking smile.

Then he moves closer to my face and blows a plume of smoke through his nose directly into my eyes.

I hear his feet shuffle away quickly, so that he can take his position ten feet away to deliver his cryptic message to me, but when I regain my vision it is very different.

A ring of smoke hovers at about eight feet in the air, just above The Smiling Man's head, but behind him I see more. More Smiling Men. Hundreds of them. I manage to swivel around in a complete circle, digging my hip into the ground and spinning like a human dreidel.

I am surrounded by exact replicas of The Smiling Man. There must be five hundred of them, easily.

I spin around fully back to my starting position, where my Smiling Man is standing. He starts to click his fingers, in time with the music, a perfect 4/4. I watch his hands, but can still make out the large grin through the smoke. From nowhere, a cigarette appears in his right hand and the right hand of every Smiling Man around me.

He continues to click with his left hand, until, after eight clicks, a lighter appears. It then appears in the hands of all the men.

In unison they all flick the lighter, so that a small flame shoots up. They leave it burning for another four beats, then place the cigarette end into the flame and light it. Four beats later they place the cigarettes into their mouths, clench their fists around the lighter then, four beats later, open their hand to reveal that it has disappeared. They recommence their clicking.

On every fourth click The Smiling Man takes a small step towards where I lie, uncomfortable, crying from the smoke, blinking hard so that I can try to decipher what is happening to me. Why they are doing this to me.

After ten steps he arrives above me again, this time with a lit cigarette in his mouth, wedged into the corner so he can still smile that smile at me. He bends down, looking as if he wants to help me, but he doesn't.

He takes the cigarette out of his mouth and places it into mine, like he did with the bullet. I'm too afraid, too intrigued not to cooperate.

He moves back to where he started.

Another Smiling Man comes forward from the crowd. He does the same. Moving cautiously towards me in time with his brethren's clicks, he drops down and places another cigarette in my mouth. I now have two cigarettes in there.

Then three, then four, then twenty.

And I just take it. The more that come to me, the more my mouth is stretched, the harder it is to push them out, the tougher it is to breathe normally. The smoke burns my nostrils as I expel it out through my nose with every exhalation.

Once a Smiling Man has passed on his cancer stick to me, he rejoins the crowd of doppelgängers and resumes the click; the beat that seems to be counting down the seconds of life in me.

The smoke is rising from my mouth and stifling my vision, so I try to inhale and exhale quicker to keep it out of my eyes, trading blindness for hyperventilation.

And then they stop.

I see my Smiling Man turning round and round on the spot, his left foot staying on the floor, his right guiding him in circles. He moves so fast and the smoke around him causes a fuzz. When he eventually stops he is facing me again, his chin resting on his chest, while he regains balance. Slowly he lifts his smiling head to stare at me intently. I am so focused on his mouth that I haven't noticed the jump cable around his neck. Grabbing the large bulldog clips at either end he makes his way towards where I lie, crumpled and ageing quickly on the gritty floorboards.

With each pace he swings the cable around like a lasso. Every movement measured to inflict an incremental rise in terror. As he gets to me I look up at him with a plea for mercy in my watering eyes, but he continues with his mission. He clips one end to the wire that is holding my hands shut and connecting them to my ankles. Then, he takes the other end over my left should and wraps it around my neck tightly, but not so tight that I can't breathe. This leaves enough cable length for him to still be able to run some up the side of my face and clip the heavy-duty spikes to my nose, closing my nostrils firmly and cutting through my skin, causing me to bleed over the cigarettes that protrude from my lips.

I start to choke.

There is no way to get rid of the smoke other than to take it into my lungs or attempt to push it out through the microscopic gaps between each tobacco-filled tube. I can't build enough force in my tongue to push them out on to the floor. As I wriggle the restraints become tighter and cut into my skin more and more. I wonder whether I could use this to slit my wrists, so as not to endure this.

Wake up, Jan.

Please wake up!

But I don't. I feel my throat constricting, and start to yank on the cable with my feet hoping that I can break my own neck or strangle myself. The Smiling Man remains over my body, tilting his head to one side, as if I am a cute baby he has seen for the first time. The rest of his identical entourage are still clicking.

A thick saliva builds by my epiglottis and falls down

the back of my throat, but I can't swallow, I can't splutter. I try to expel something, anything, through my nose, but the teeth of the clip cut deeper.

I lose control and start to rock. Taking my eyes off The Smilling Man, my inner panic takes over. I shake my head from side to side, I try to scream but nothing comes out. I attempt anything to kill myself before the fumes take effect.

Suddenly I can't make myself breathe any longer. This must be what it feels like to drown. I look up one last time and The Smiling Man is holding three fingers at me; all his minions copy.

I go to breathe in, but nothing happens and I wake up gasping for oxygen.

'Huuuuuuuuuuuuuuuuuuuuuuugggh!' I sit bolt upright, wheezing like a dog with whooping cough. Audrey is startled and does the same, looking around the room with her night cover over her eyes. She panics.

'What the . . . what's going on?' She starts to feel around the bed and slaps me in the torso. This wakes her up fully and she takes off the mask to find me sweating and panting. 'Jesus, Jan. What is it? Another bad dream?' she asks, putting her hand on my leg reassuringly. It calms me.

'Oh God!' I drop my head and blow air out through my lips, so that I can feel it rush past my nose and momentarily move my hair. 'Sorry.' I exhale again, pleased that I can do so, not taking it for granted. 'I'm sorry.'

'Are you OK?'

'Yes. I'm fine. Just a bit hot, that's all. Go back to sleep. It's fine.' She doesn't say anything, just stretches the elastic and pulls the mask back over her eyes, plunging her once again into darkness. She lies down and taps me a couple of times on the thigh again, as if to say *there, there*.

I push the covers off me completely, letting the air in the room hit the sweat over my body to cool me quicker. There is no way I am going back to sleep now. I'm too afraid. But I have it. The information that tells me another girl is going to be taken in the next twenty-four hours.

But the information is only useful if I accept that this is real.

And I can't do that. Not yet.

I won't become a fool.

I won't become my mother.

Eames

I see Amy walk in to the pub on her own. Her solitude could be misconstrued as desperation.

It's not. It's confidence.

I've been waiting for her.

People seem genuinely glad to see her, the majority of the time. As soon as she enters, a table of people wave in acknowledgement. She makes a signal of tipping an invisible glass to her mouth to ask whether anyone would like a drink while she is at the bar. The overweight Indian girl she has made eye contact with asks around the table of five to see whether anyone needs a refill. Only one person takes up the offer. The girl grabs his almost empty pint glass and wags it from side to side to suggest that one beer is enough. Amy gives a thumbs-up and orders herself two glasses of Sauvignon Blanc – it's happy hour, two-for-one – and a pint of lager for the mystery male.

I know that she hasn't been invited here tonight; she has just turned up. Even if nobody from the BBC building had come here on a Thursday night, it wouldn't bother her. She would have found someone else to talk to, someone else to bond with, someone else that she didn't know. I've seen her do it. I've watched her. It's amazing. She can befriend someone, make them warm to her, trust her, and then she can take them home with her.

I wonder whether she can be recruited. Whether her insatiable lust for life could become a voracious desire for death.

She has the traits that I feel are needed to be successful in my line of work. Only through an undoubted respect for living can you truly comprehend what killing means.

But it is my respect for her that makes her such an unquenchably desirable subject.

This will be my greatest work to date. The realisation of an artistic vision.

When I'm finally caught, when they piece together all the information about these girls, when they ask me why I did it, I will tell them, 'Love. It was about love.'

And art.

Hate rarely entered into it.

I watch as Amy continues her Dionysian conquest, mixing red and white wine, throwing in a mojito when it is somebody else buying the drinks. I see the crowd disperse sporadically. One girl leaves to go home because it is a 'school night'. Amy cringes at the use of this cliché, others acknowledge it for what it is with a pity-chuckle. A couple leave to go and have sex. Soon, the only people left are Amy and the man she bought the initial beer for when she arrived.

Some would worry at this.

I take a sip of my Scotch and look over at him like collateral damage. He is disposable. A pawn. Less than a pawn.

I'm not worried.

This will happen tonight. I have planned it this way, so it will occur as determined.

The next note has been sent to torment January David.

He is no closer to me than he was when I shot Dorothy through her pretty little mouth. No closer to discovering the key to these crimes than he was when the first arrow scorched through Carla's quadriceps.

When a psychoanalyst sits across from a patient and shows them a series of ink blots and that patient sees a uterus or a couple fucking or a pair of breasts, that's not me; that's not what I see.

Think how lucky she'll feel that I brought her to a quivering orgasm before filling her lungs with nicotine-infused smoke. Think how grateful she'll be that I gave her such a vivid taste of life before the muscle cramps started, before the pins and needles set in to her body's extremities, before her brain was starved of oxygen causing her to black out, for ever.

I wait.

I could let her go home with this muscular idiot tonight in his tight green T-shirt, flexing his pectoral muscles, and be completely unfulfilled as his affected-by-steroid-abuse tiny dick slots easily into her, barely touching the sides. She stares up at him, bored, faking a grunt or a moan as he fills his mind with thoughts about how he looks when he tries to fuck. Or, I could wait.

I could wait until his bladder is at bursting point, follow him into the men's room and take him out of the equation there.

That is what I do.

I see him stand up at the table, leaving Amy on her own. He grabs his pint glass and downs the last third of a pint like an animal. As he heads towards the toilets I finish my last mouthful of Scotch, stand up from my stool and follow him in.

He doesn't bother to hold the door open for me as I

come in behind him. This annoys me. If he won't do it in this situation, then he certainly isn't going to do it for a lady like Amy and she deserves better than that.

I follow closely as he heads over to the urinal. Nobody else is in here, which is perfect. He tries to undo his belt as he walks, for efficiency. While he attempts to solve the puzzle of the buckle in his drunken state I take him down. A sharp kick to his lumbar region causes his knees to buckle and thrusts him forward into the urinal, his stomach thumping into the porcelain bowl, winding him and dropping him to the floor with a groan. I ram the heel of my hand into the back of his head, knocking his face into a pile of urinal cakes and stunning him. With one hand under his armpit, the other wringing his gel-drenched hair, I force his face into the cubicle door, flinging it open. All that is left is to drag him into the cubicle and leave him to piss himself. His eyes are open, vision blurred with tears, but he has no control over his bodily functions and cannot move anything apart from his eyelids.

I give him a final shoe to the face, I don't want to damage my hands. Holding the sides of the cubicle for balance, I see his head snap back as he loses consciousness.

I don't let him see me. There's no need to kill him. The humiliation is the reward in this instance. The lock on the door can be opened and locked from the outside with a coin, so I shut him inside for the rest of the night.

Then I wait again.

Watching Amy getting restless. Nobody will discover the pile of meat left to defecate all over the backs of his own legs.

I order another Scotch before making my move.

Girl 3

———◆———

I assume he is taking a little longer in there because he is buying condoms from a machine. A waste of money. I have my own. I've learned my lesson. I was with someone earlier in the year who bought a whisky-flavoured condom packet. The smell alone made me gag. He also wasted money on a tickler in the shape of a fist holding a hammer. Clearly no idea what a woman wants.

After a few minutes I start to consider the fact that he left through a window. Never does it cross my mind that he is covered in his own excrement, locked in a cubicle unable to move anything but his eyelids.

Three more minutes pass and I resign myself to the fact that he has bolted. My only worry is that I have finished my drink, but don't want to go to the bar in case somebody steals my table.

Then he arrives, just in time.

It's Eames.

My one in eight million chance.

He's here to save me.

January

———◆———

This time was different. I saw him. I actually saw him. The Smiling Man, right in front of me.

It wasn't in my dream.

But I couldn't stay. I couldn't wait around for his message.

They had just found Girl 3.

Paulson had stuck to the brief fairly well. We hopped from bar to bar around London as if on a faux Monopoly board, trying to forget for one night about the terrifying things that happen in the capital. For every pint of lager we had some kind of chaser and it was nice that everyone had to drink the same thing. I hated the idea that I would be drunk in an hour, while everyone else was fine and they'd strip me naked and tie me to a lamp post or something just as immature. But it wasn't like that.

We left work out of it.

Mostly.

I couldn't forget about Dorothy or Carla and the image of them when they were found. I couldn't stop going over The Smiling Man in my dream last night and the horrendous ordeal that he put me through. So I took my pager with me. If it is true, if another girl turns up the day after I have a dream about this sinister figure, then I want to be there. I don't care if it is my stag night. I don't care if I am supposed to be getting married tomorrow, I need to be there.

'Ready for this one, Jan?' Paulson says, smiling over his entire bloated face, his cheeks red from excitement and the alcohol he has already consumed. It seems as though none of this has affected him. Like he is drinking pints of lemonade with orange juice chasers.

'What is *this one*?' I ask. There are about fifteen of us out tonight, all from the force. No family. Audrey's father died when she was younger and mine disowned me after Cathy was taken, so it's just people I work with; none of them can really be called friends. I only asked Paulson to be my best man because he's the person I see the most. We work well together and I do like him a lot, but it's not like we went to school together or I knew him growing up. We met here and we share similar values when it comes to the justice system; we share similar interests when it comes to problem solving and detective work. I know he'll do the job well. I think that's why I picked him: competence.

'It's called a ladyboy.' He laughs out loud, unknowingly spitting in my face.

Across the bar there are forty-five glasses lined up. Three drinks for each stag member.

Number one: A pint of lager. Something weak, around 4 per cent proof.

Number two: A gin and tonic with a slice of lemon.

Number three: A glass of Baileys cream liqueur.

'The idea,' he says gleefully, 'is that you have to do it in one.' Everybody looks at him in dismay.

'In one?' Murphy asks in his usual confused tone.

'Well, by *one*, I just mean without a break. So, down the

pint in one, as soon as the glass hits the bar, pick up your G and T and knock that back. When you put that down, drop the Baileys down your gullet. Easy.' He performs a comedy maniacal laugh.

'O-kaaaaaay.' I drag it out to indicate my trepidation about this next event, which Paulson has so lovingly suggested, following his evening's itinerary to the letter.

'We'll go one by one, starting from the left. So, Jan, you will be last. Gives you a little longer to come to terms with it.' He pats me on the back and we all line up at the bar. I'm at the far right; it's like being on death row. I know what's coming, I can see what happens to those that go before me, but there is going to be no last-minute reprieve.

'You ready, Adams?' Paulson shouts down to the other end of the line. He is stood next to me in position fourteen. No doubt to show me exactly how easy it is before he goads me as I struggle with the lager alone.

'Not really,' Adams shouts back nervously.

'GO!' Paulson shouts down to the left to indicate the beginning of this ordeal. Adams struggles with the gassy pint and takes around twenty seconds to finish it, but it still counts as one. Everyone is cheering him on, chanting his name over and over. As he puts down his pint glass he takes a breath. This is not allowed and the mob to his right let him feel their disappointment. Murphy throws a handful of nuts in his direction and others boo him accordingly. He sinks the gin and the Baileys easily, and the second in the queue starts his journey towards total inebriation.

The whole bar has stopped what they are doing and turn in their seats to watch this pathetic spectacle of manliness.

What feels like a long time to the person drinking feels like seconds to me as my impending moment of validation approaches like the arrow to Carla's brain. But, for this short time, I forget about the girls. That is the power of fear.

Glasses of water start to emerge for those who have completed the task. They need it. The combination of Baileys with gin can be lethal. It shouldn't be mixed. It congeals within the stomach and is often regurgitated if overindulged. This can be seen with Dobbs at position four, who is sick into his mouth, but swallows it, and McMahon at position eight, who vomits a little into his own hands.

It gets to Murphy. He drinks half a pint, then stops for a second, the gas filling him up. He burps loudly and completes the rest in swift succession. Paulson is an animal. It's as if he opens his gullet and the liquid vanishes in seconds. He turns and gives me a wink.

A wink that tells me he has been practising this, but also wishes me luck.

I need it.

I try to get the pint down as quickly as possible, knowing that the last two can be tipped in with relative ease. After I swallow the first gulp it gets harder and I slow down, biting down on the glass slightly; I'm worried I might crack it in my mouth. I take a few steady breaths through my nose as I ease on the pace towards the end of the pint.

The gin hurts. I never noticed that mine was the only one with ice in the glass. My teeth ache as I move on to the final creamy liquid, the entire entourage shouting, 'Jan! Jan! Jan! Jan!' Strangers around us joining the chorus. I shudder as I finish, and the saliva in my mouth thins. It's the feeling I always get before I am sick. Paulson grabs my left arm and raises it in the air in triumph, as if this is confirmation that I am indeed 'a man'. My head still hangs down and I exhale heavily, blowing my lips out as I do so.

'Well done, Jan,' he says, still holding my arm in the air, looking around at the adulation, as if I have just won a heavyweight boxing title. 'Ready for the next place?'

'I need water,' I croak at him. 'Get me water.'

He waves at the barmaid and she brings over a pint glass filled with water, ice and a slice of lemon. Paulson hands it to me and says delicately, 'I bet you wish we were going to a strip bar now, eh?' And he laughs at my pain.

'Oh God, yeah. Anything but that again.' And he takes this as confirmation.

He turns his head over his shoulder and shouts, 'Come on, lads, he said yes! Let's go!' And they all crowd around me in a bundle, pushing me out the door.

Forcing me on to the street and towards the club where The Smiling Man is waiting.

Girl 4

Icheck my make-up in the hall mirror before leaving the house, pushing my lips into a kiss, almost making a bright red heart with my lips to accentuate their plumpness and fully appreciate my new lipstick. It works well with my new dress, a Versace, of course. A black, one-shoulder dress, sleek and slim. A stretch-cotton sateen with some wonderful structural detail. I turn to the side on tip-toes to admire the way it promotes my curves.

The phone rings and startles me.

'Hello,' I answer in a pseudo-sexy deep voice, as though I am Marlene Dietrich, joking around, thinking it is one of the girls calling before we go out.

Nothing.

'January?' I ask. I don't know why. He's the first person that comes to mind. He knows we shouldn't be in contact until the wedding tomorrow, so it would be just like him to go against that and call me.

He laughs.

'Jan . . . is that you?'

Silence.

It's happening again. The phone calls. The mysterious silences that are becoming all too frequent. But this time I heard something. A laugh. A man's laugh. When I said

January's name, the person on the other end sniggered. That made it creepier. Maybe it is someone who knows January. Maybe it's because he now knows that January is not here and that I am a woman alone in a large empty house.

But I can't show that I am scared.

'Oh grow up,' I say in the most patronising tone I can deliver. I muster enough courage to add, 'Loser' before I hang up.

I can feel how flustered I am now. It has taken some of the enjoyment out of the night ahead. Just as I feel I have stopped perspiring, before I start to hyperventilate, there is a thunderous rap at the door, which makes me drop my lipstick as I jump.

I watch it roll across the floor, quickly at first then slowing as it approaches the door. As I make my way over to pick it up I lift my heels so that I can ballerina over to where it stopped without my heels making a noise on the floor. As I crouch down subtly to pick it up my knee makes a cracking sound that feels as though it echoes and amplifies through the hallway.

I rise from my squatting position with lipstick in hand, close one eye and use the other to peer through the peephole. A short Asian man with thinning hair is standing on my step looking up, as if admiring the outside of the house. I see the small circular light intermittently flash on the Bluetooth headset protruding from his right ear. In the background beyond the driveway, a Mercedes is parked up, the engine still running, the lights still on. It's the taxi I ordered to take me out to meet the girls.

I open the door and he brings his gaze back down to where I am.

'Hello, miss,' he says politely. 'Taxi service, eight o'clock, Miss Audrey.' He looks me up and down quite obviously, but I feel flattered that he bothered.

'Yes. Thank you. I'll be with you in just a sec.' I smile at him. Partly to let him know I saw him looking me over and partly through relief.

'OK, miss. I'll wait in the car for you.' He turns, giving a nervous wave, and trundles back to the warmth of his driver seat.

I go back to the table in front of the mirror to pick up my clutch bag and have one last look at myself. I feel like I look great, like the only time I will look better is tomorrow in my wedding dress.

I take one last look at the phone before I leave, wondering who keeps calling and saying nothing. Asking myself why they would suddenly laugh at me from the other end.

But this call has nothing to do with me.

The sniggering man at the other end of the line does not want to talk to me.

He is waiting for January.

He has something he wants to say to January.

I leave the light on in the hallway and shut the door behind me, double-locking it before I saunter over to the Mercedes where my appreciative driver is patiently waiting for me, watching me intently as my new dress displays the exact shape of my body beneath.

As I approach he gets out of his seat and opens the back door for me to enter.

'Thank you.' I slink into the opening and perch my bag on my lap.

'You're welcome, miss.' He smiles and closes the door before getting back in himself.

I don't wear my seatbelt, because it could crease me in the wrong places and, even though it is his duty to do so, the taxi driver says nothing to me as he turns around to look through the rear window, while he reverses out of the drive. As a result of my confidence and my obvious success, people are rarely confrontational with me.

This is supposed to be a civilised send-off. Ten girls from the office, out in the West End for a meal and a few bottles of wine. I don't want to go to a club and drink tequila shots from a man's belly button. I don't want a fake-tanned bodybuilder holding a towel up in front of his waist while I kneel in front of him on stage taking him into my mouth. I don't want to wear a plastic tiara, pink feather boa or 'L' plates on my £2,000 dress either.

But, after another call, I don't want to go back to that huge, echoing, empty house and spend the night alone either.

January

———◆———

The place is dark and windowless. There is no sign outside to say what it is called or that it even exists.

Am I asleep?

Is this happening?

The rest of my party usher me down the stairs from the street. It reminds me of an old Chicago speakeasy during prohibition. It's tucked away under a closed shop. I wonder how Paulson would even know about the place. I suppose everyone has a darker side, a secret part to them, but this is particularly seedy and I start to wonder how much I really know about my best man. Everything about it screams exclusivity. I'm surprised there isn't a secret knock.

The door opens on to an area surrounded by heavy purple curtains. They look expensive, like the ones we have in our living room, only ours are a more earthy tone; Audrey tells me that is the fashion right now. Paulson holds me back from moving through the curtains until all fifteen of us are crammed into the small material square and the door is shut behind us.

'Which way do you want to go?' he asks me.

'What?'

'Which way do you want to go?' he repeats. 'Pick a curtain.'

'Is this another trick?' I look around frantically at my options, everyone peering at me, waiting for an answer.

'Which way do you want to . . .?'

'Left,' I say, interrupting. 'Left, for Christ's sake.'

And, like a sinister circus ringmaster, Paulson bows his head to me and motions his hand towards the left curtain saying, 'Ah, they always choose the left.'

I push through the curtain and enter the underbelly of our fine city. The lights are dim and there are large circular booths of black and purple leather scattered around the room. Some have a table in the centre, some have a table with a pole up to the ceiling. Some even have a girl dancing exotically, utilising the pole in her routine.

Before I even manage to take in the black granite bar surface or the roulette tables where you bet on black or purple rather than red or black, I am greeted by a short man with slicked-back dark hair.

'Mr David, I presume.' I look at him quizzically. 'Please follow me, sir. Your area is over here.' I follow him through the club, past the bar and gambling area, the smell of leather only just masking the scent of sweat and other stale bodily fluids, until we enter another area through a larger set of curtains.

A private room.

It follows the same pattern as the room before it, only this table is large enough for all fifteen of us to fit around. The table in the centre has two poles; we have a private bar and gambling area. There is also a small stage area to the left as I walk in. In the far right corner is a doorway covered by curtain and a large bouncer lurks in the shadows concealing his identity, guarding the entrance.

'Please, take a seat, your waitress will be out shortly with your drinks.'

I look at Paulson, my eyes asking him how he pulled this off.

'I play poker in a lot of fucked-up places, Jan.' And he smiles at me, raising both his eyebrows twice in quick succession.

A woman of perfect proportion appears from behind the stage area. She is wearing a pair of purple French knickers and nothing else. Her hair is a dirty blonde with a natural wave. I would place her at twenty-seven years of age. Her breasts would suggest that she has never had enhancement surgery, nor does she need it: a 32C unaffected by gravity. Her legs are lean and long, her arms follow suit and her breastbone is evident, but not indicative of an eating disorder. She is 5' 7", but her heels make her 5' 10". Her face is a symmetrical triangle ending in a perfectly thin rounded chin.

She silences us all with her presence. But she is merely the starter.

Two other beauties appear at her sides. One with dark hair, one with flowing red hair. Each with a small silver tray resting on the hand over their shoulder, each containing a set of champagne glasses. They walk towards us, brunette and redhead with glasses, blonde with three bottles of champagne. All naked apart from the exotic underwear that protects some of their modesty.

Paulson starts to sweat profusely. His face is reddening in anticipation. I can almost hear him salivate.

The next hour goes by in a quiet, seedy way. The women dance around the poles and we watch. They pour us more champagne and we watch. They kiss each other and we watch. We don't even really talk to one another. In fact, it takes several glasses of champagne to realise that nobody wants to be here apart from Paulson. It makes us all feel somewhat uncomfortable. The fact that these girls seem completely at ease is even more unnerving for us. For me, anyway.

I cautiously check my pager. No messages.

Then another girl appears on the stage with a chair and a blindfold, and I am five minutes away from meeting The Smiling Man, from seeing his face in all its exaggerated reality.

It's been twenty-four hours.

Amy, Girl 3, is already dead.

I am beckoned forward with a seductive curling of the finger from the Amazonian vision on the stage. The rabble regresses back to their more base instincts seen earlier in the bar as they push me out of our secluded booth. Paulson taps me on the buttocks in a playful way, as if giving his blessing for me to enjoy the imminent pretend fornication. Dry-humping, they call it.

Warily, I edge closer to the raised area. The exquisite temptress in front of me is pulling me in with her doe eyes and long lashes. I look back at the gaggle of reprobates prodding me forward, secretly wishing they were in my position, their chants fading into a steady hum and then a silence. Turning forward again I suddenly find myself on the stage, where the stunning siren forces me to a stop by placing both hands on my shoulders and lowers me effortlessly to a seated position in the chair.

I feel mesmerised, like in a dream. Like I have no power over what is to happen to me.

I am four minutes from my living nightmare.

Four minutes from the smile.

She circles me like a predator marking its territory. I belong to her now. I am under her spell. She never breaks contact with me, always leaving her index finger touching me, dragging it over my shoulders and chest as she circumnavigates my ever-decreasing world. Sultry and smooth, it relaxes me to begin with.

She stops behind me.

Now touching me with both hands she runs her smooth cold palms from my shoulders down my arms to my wrists. I smell her perfume, floral and acidic; as she crouches the whiff of hairspray makes me clear my throat.

Her touch is soft and sensuous as she ties my wrists together, jerking them at the end as she pulls the fabric tighter.

I sense her stand up again and the sound of her heels as she wheels around to face me increases my anxiety. I look left towards the horde, who cheer me on in a silent, smoky bubble, punching the air and blowing inaudible wolf whistles.

I look back at the denizen of sin before me. The light behind this goddess envelopes her in a calming halo and she bends in front of me, her finger pressed against her pursed lips.

'Sssshh,' she whispers. 'Relax. You're going to enjoy this.'

I feel excited and dirty all at the same time. Audrey was right, this isn't my last night of freedom, so I shouldn't allow this to continue, but the danger of the situation has allure. And I let it happen.

She produces a blindfold from the waistband of her panties and places it gently over my eyes, before stretching the elastic over the back of my head to secure it in place.

I'm plunged into complete darkness, despite the spotlight that now illuminates me from above.

I have three minutes.

The music starts.

She circles me again, this time touching more than just my shoulders and chest, using more than just one finger. She moves round behind me and turns her back to mine. Leaning against the back of the chair she lowers herself slowly, so that the satin skin on the back of her legs grazes my tied hands. She lowers herself further until her bottom just touches my wrists and I can feel the warmth from between her legs. Instinctively, I curl my fingers, touching her where I shouldn't be touching anyone apart from Audrey. She jolts up, feigning surprise, and slaps my hand playfully.

Lowering herself to her knees she licks the tips of my fingers and sucks on the ring finger of my left hand. Then she crawls. With the coiled poise of a jungle cat she eases her way around to my front and perches herself on the floor between my legs.

I can feel her all over me, not quite touching me, but getting close enough to give the sensation. I try to stop myself from getting excited, but she grips my zip in her teeth and teases it downwards. I feel myself getting hard. She pushes her face through the opening and grips my underwear in her mouth, her lips momentarily touching me *there*. She pulls the fabric up through the gap left from my now open zip, then releases it, snapping it back inside making a sharp slapping sound as my underwear cracks against my body. I flinch with the shock, with the excitement, still getting harder, forgetting that fourteen of my friends and colleagues can see me like this.

Is this real?

Am I here?

This isn't me.

Two more minutes.

She straddles me. Her back to my chest, she slowly drops down to my lap, her hair tickling my face as she descends. Sitting on my lap, her thighs taking the strain, so as not to put her full weight down, she tenses and releases her gluteal muscles. Gripping and releasing my girth, baiting it into a standing position. She swivels her hips slowly, revolving in time with the music, which now seems louder. I close my eyes behind the blindfold and tilt my head back, exhaling heavily.

She adds in a controlled bouncing motion for variation.

I'm a statue. I don't want to enjoy this.

Then her entire weight rests on me as she raises her legs up and out into an almost split position. Her hands grab me behind my head, interlocking her fingers for extra support. The bulge in my trousers is now evident and almost protruding from the open zip. She moves back and forth, slowly at first then growing in vigour. She fakes her own pleasure for the onlookers.

Sixty seconds.

She tilts her head back and places her cheek on mine. Grabbing tighter on the back of my head she breathes heavily into my ear, subtly letting out the faint hint of her voice with muted moans. The air from her mouth in my ear is making the hair on my head stand on end, as though someone stepped across my grave. I turn cold.

Thirty-nine seconds.

Thirty-eight.

She releases her right hand and puts it down between her legs. Stroking her breast on the way down.

Thirty-two.

Reaching into my zip she pulls me towards her, so that we touch as she writhes against me.

I want her to stop.

I don't want her to stop.

When a man goes out the night before his wedding and thinks that it is acceptable to pay a whore to do something degrading or to let a woman dry-hump you until you ejaculate into your own underwear, that's not me. That's not who I am.

Twenty-five.

She continues, getting more erratic and out of control.

Then I feel a vibration.

At first I think it might be the finale to her act. That she is involving some kind of toy for final gratification. But it's not that.

My pager.

It clicks me back to real life.

I wriggle slightly.

'Get off,' I say in her ear. But she continues.

I move more frantically, lifting my hips, but she just thinks I am getting excited.

It vibrates again and I shout, 'Get the fuck off me!' And I lift my hips so high that it launches her on to the floor in front of me.

The music stops and everything is completely silent.

Ten seconds.

'Untie me,' I say out loud into the black silence.

Seven seconds.

Silence.

Then just a slight sound. Shuffling feet. Behind me.

Getting closer. As if someone large is shifting from side to side. The sound moves around to the front of me and I feel paralysed.

The blindfold is whipped away from my eyes and the spotlight above blinds me further.

As my eyes adjust I see the silhouette of a large figure before me. Behind, in the haze, the stripper or exotic dancer or whore is lying on the floor rubbing her elbow. To my left, the mob stares on, completely still, stunned. But they are not looking at the tall spectre in front of me. I don't even think they can see him.

The light hits his teeth. Those big yellow teeth that torment my dreams.

The Smiling Man. In front of me. I can't move.

He bends at the waist, like he always does, and looks me straight in the eyes. All the time smiling. I want to look left to see whether Murphy and Paulson can see this, but I'm too afraid after our previous two encounters. But he isn't here to hurt me. Not this time.

He stands erect again, never taking his eyes off me, then begins to wag his finger exaggeratedly at me, shaking his head as he does so.

Like a giant smiling metronome he entrances me, but what is he warning me about? What does this mean?

I feel my hands suddenly free themselves from the binding behind the chair. I bring them slowly round to where they belong and look at the clammy palms in disbelief. When I tilt my gaze back up, he is gone. The dancer storms off behind a curtain and the sound returns to my party.

The pager vibrates again.

I wrench it from my belt and read the message as it scrolls across the miniature screen.

They've found her. Amy Mullica. On the floor of her flat in Shepherd's Bush. Girl 3.

While I have been out galavanting like a hormonal teenager, knocking back shots of God-knows-what and getting lap dances, nobody has been trying to prevent another girl from being slain in another suburb of London.

'What is it, Jan? Are you OK?' Paulson asks, still fulfilling his role as event organiser.

I can't answer him at first. It's all too confusing. Why was he not asking me about The Smiling Man? Why is nobody shocked?

'Jan?' he probes.

'I've . . . I've got to go,' I say under my breath slightly, looking down at the pager.

'What?'

I look up. 'Sorry lads, I really need to go.' And I walk through the curtain to my right, back through the plebeian area of the club. Nobody tries to stop me, nobody even notices me against the backdrop of tits and sweat and £50 roulette chips and champagne and lesbian strip shows and degenerate apathy to the reality that lies outside the exclusivity of this curtained lair of iniquity.

I'm happy to get outside and breathe in the polluted smog that most visitors to the capital complain about. I'm alive. This is reality.

I hail a cab and make my way over to see Amy's crumpled, naked husk of a life contorted on her lounge floor, just as The Smiling Man had told me it would be.

Girl 3

———◆———

When they find me, I'm lying on my side on my dark, dusty, laminate floor. I live right next to a road and the laminate seems to act as a magnet for any microscopic debris that car tyres help to throw up and disperse. No matter how much I sweep it, it's never clean for long. But the faux wood was the allure when looking for a place to rent in this area. Especially after the first three places the estate agent recommended.

My left hip bruises as it digs into the floor, as I try to release myself from Eames' grip. If I'd have taken the place up near the Catholic school, the place that had carpets, I might have got away with just a small carpet burn. But that place was too close to the market. The market scared me when I first came here. It felt enclosed. Like the endless stalls selling saris and fabrics and personalised mobile-phone covers, towering so high that they reached a point in the middle where they met, forming a canopy of technicolour ethnic products I would never have a use for. But I found it intimidating. So much so that I was afraid to venture down an aisle advertising £6 haircuts for men *and* women.

As I got to the end of the market, when I thought I was all the way through, back to safety, a short black guy was shouting at himself about a Chinese family. 'I pay rent.

All their family's here. Call the police! I've had enough of this Chinese shit!' He eventually found a female community warden to vent his distress at. As he powered ahead towards the aggravator, she waddled along, laid back, always six or seven steps behind him. I dropped my pace and slotted in just behind her. That's when I decided to never walk down there alone, but the fact that I felt the need for an escort meant I wanted to live away from here. Farther down the road, where the cultural diversity spreads even more and the floors have less carpet and instead of a little burn on your hip bone, you end up with a black bruise the size of an Olympic discus.

But the bruise is the least of my problems.

I can't swallow. That's another issue.

I haven't been to the dentist in five months. The last time I went was a simple check-up, fundamental in maintaining dental hygiene. The time before, I had a filling in my lower left premolar. It was numbed with a local anaesthetic and a cotton-wool tube was placed in either side of my mouth to soak up any excess saliva. To aid with the fact that my mouth was open wide, preventing me from performing the natural reflex of swallowing, an attractive girl in her early twenties stood on the other side to the middle-aged doctor of teeth with a small tube that sucked the saliva I would usually swallow into the vacuum.

But that doesn't stop you wanting to swallow.

It's a similar situation now.

A brace, usually used by dentists to hold the mouth open when performing a bleaching or whitening, is wedged into my mouth, forcing my jaw apart so far that the corners of my mouth might tear at any point in the next minute.

So not only can I not naturally swallow, but I can't bite down either.

But it's worse than that.

My back hurts.

Nothing to do with the laminate floor, though.

At school, in gymnastics, the girls would demonstrate their flexibility by falling into the crab position. I remember that Kelly could fall backwards from a standing position and place her hands down on the mat to perform the crab. What was even more impressive was that she could then push off with her feet straight into a handstand, then drop her feet back down to the floor to end up in her original start position, only four feet behind where she started.

I couldn't do this.

I had to start from a lying position on my back, bring my hands so that they lay flat on the floor with my fingertips almost touching my shoulders and, essentially, force out a reverse press-up that would end in me holding the crab position for around a maximum of four seconds before collapsing into a heap, resulting in cruel, demoralising laughter from the other girls.

That's what this feels like. Except, the four seconds I could hold the crab has been eight minutes. And instead of pushing up from a lying position or falling into it from a standing position, I am on my side, my hip digging into the floor, forming a very unattractive bruise, my arms and legs stretched beyond their point of elasticity behind me, the ankles bound tightly to my wrists. My stomach is taut with the force of all my limbs extending in a position alien to me since I was twelve years old.

But that's not really anything worth complaining about.

I'm naked, still.

The last thing I remember was being in a position that was almost the complete opposite to this, lying on my back with my knees resting on my breasts and my hands gripping my ankles voluntarily, while Eames pushed himself deeper inside me. I remember us both splayed on the mattress, sweating, panting, not saying anything.

And then I remember waking up, still naked, my arms stretched backwards, tied to my feet, my entire weight balanced on my hip on the dirty fake wood floor that enticed me to this location, with my mouth being held open by a mould that is slightly bigger than my jaw can usually open.

That's nothing, though. It's merely preparation.

I can just see the white paper and brown scraggly wisps of tobacco hanging from the front end below my nose, which blurs and shrinks into a pink triangle as I peer down the length of my septum. The smell is putrid for a non-smoker, but Eames soon helps with that by clamping my nostrils shut with a red jump lead. He wraps the long wire around my neck twice, before clipping the other end to the wire itself so that it remains secure. The initial pain of the clamping detracts from the constriction of my oesophagus with the cable. It feels almost sexual, but the pain is starting to outweigh the pleasure.

I feel blocked. With my nostrils clamped together, the only way I can suck in the polluted London air is through my open mouth. I push my tongue forward and feel the soft filters of what feel like hundreds of cigarettes. The pressure I can generate through my tongue is not strong enough to displace the tightly packed cancer sticks that have been wedged into the hole created by the mouth brace. My tongue isn't long enough either.

Now I panic.

Shaking on my already bruising hip I try to dislodge something, anything. The cable ties cutting through my wrists, the one hundred and fifty-six cigarettes stuffed into my mouth, the industrial bulldog clip clamping my nose. But every time I move I cut deeper into my ankles or the cable tightens around my neck and the hundred-or-so B&H remain fixed.

Eames yanks me by the hand, scraping my hip and sending a jolt of pain through my stomach, which stretches beyond muscular flexion. I stop moving. As a reward, he unclips my nose.

But this comes at a cost.

He tells me to stay still.

'Don't move.'

He whispers it to me, peering deep into my eyes as I lie below him completely at his mercy.

Pulling a lighter from his pocket he tests the flame once. Then he pushes a switch across underneath the flame and flicks his finger to light it again. This time the fire stretches upwards five times higher. It illuminates his mouth from beneath as he smiles broadly, maniacally. All I can see are his teeth and I know that I am going to die. And that all the pain I feel at this moment is nothing compared to the agony I am going to endure when he lights all the cigarettes in my mouth and replaces the clamp, locking the toxic gases into my lungs with no possible way of expelling the poison.

My brain starves.

I stop breathing.

In a couple of hours, Detective January David will arrive, fall to his knees and weep at yet another personal failure.

But, of course, it's much worse than that.

January

———◆———

It has nothing to do with chess. Paulson has the answer, but doesn't realise.

'You don't need to be here.' I've managed to compose myself after my initial breakdown on arrival at the crime scene. In my imagination, the adrenalin released into my bloodstream as the pager vibrated on my hip, as I wrenched myself out of the erotic situation thrust upon me, as I met face-to-face with The Smiling Man from my dreams, was sobering. In reality, I remain a slurring ruin unable to fully function in the capacity that I want to.

'Jan, you shouldn't be here either. Not now.'

Of course, he's right. There is nothing I could have done. We did not have enough information to put any preventative measures in place. We have no idea how Amy is linked to Carla or Dorothy. We've done everything we can.

'It just shows that we can't rest for a single day, Paulson. If we lose focus for even a minute, another body could show up somewhere else.' I'm hoping he's taking me seriously, that he can detect the intent through my bloodshot eyes.

'Well, tomorrow is your wedding day.' He grabs my shoulder firmly to demonstrate his support. 'You can't work tomorrow.'

I try to argue with him, but his tolerance for a debauched night such as this is far more impressive than my own and his eloquence of debate surpasses my weary ramblings.

'How long have you been here?' he asks rhetorically. But I answer.

'Does it matter?'

My petulance wears thin eventually. Paulson manages to subdue me, before taking me away from the scene.

It has nothing to do with chess. He holds the answer in his pocket.

Paulson, like me, has the ability to drink during the day and still have the wits to drive home in the evening without causing havoc. Tonight is a whole other level of drinking. It's the reason I took a cab and the reason that Paulson, eventually, took the Tube to meet me.

The Central Line.

Shepherd's Bush.

C3.

'Let's get a cab back to mine eh?' Paulson takes out a pocket Tube map and thrusts it under my nose, directing my attention to the tangled mess of colour that was his exhausting, irritating journey here. The spectrum of Underground lines blur together and the only thing I can focus on are the numbers around the outside.

'Give me that!' I snatch the map from his grasp, sobering more at my discovery.

On the Tube map, Shepherd's Bush, on the Central Line, is in square C3. I squint to focus on this. The killer's last note said B4 to C3. Paulson looks in square B4 and, sure enough, on the Jubilee Line, Zone 2, is Swiss Cottage. This is where Carla was killed. Dorothy was killed in Mile End. Again on the Central Line, again in

Zone 2. Again it corresponds to his first note, C7 to B4.

He is telling us where he is going to kill.

'So, when we receive his next note, it will give us a grid reference. It doesn't pinpoint a location, but it narrows it down. As long as he stays in Zone 2 we have something to work from. So if the next says C3 to B7 we know that the next murder is supposed to take place in Canonbury, Dalston Kingsland, Hackney or Homerton.' I point at each place name with a proud, sharp finger.

'Wow!' I stretch my hand across my forehead, placing my thumb on my left temple and my middle finger on my right. 'So simple, it's perfect,' I whisper to myself, sounding as though I admire the killer's work.

We have a strong lead now. As long as the note arrives we have so much more to work on. We can catch him. I can feel that now.

Paulson escorts me from the premises and takes me back to his flat. In four hours' time, I am getting married.

Girl 4

❖

In twelve hours, I'll be married. I will be Mrs Audrey David. The thought of that makes me smile. The idea of changing my driving licence, passport, business cards and e-mail signature fills me with dread. There should be a company that you can send everything that needs to be changed to and they sort it, while you get on with your life. I'm not used to taking care of mundane details; I employ a team to do that.

The girls from the office insist on paying for the meal, which is incredibly sweet of them. We talk about marriage and how lucky I am with January and how it is a new phase in my life, and they ask if I am thinking about having children and whether we will move.

I feel blessed to be with January. He is everything I want. I need him.

I agree. This is a new phase in my life. Something I've never done before. It's exciting.

We won't need to move. None of the girls have ever seen my house, but it is big enough to hold the two of us and anyone new that may come along.

I tell them that I haven't really thought about children yet, because I've been so focused on the wedding, but that's a lie. I want them and I want them soon.

There is no doubt in my mind that I will have them

too. When I set my mind to something, I always accomplish it.

The light is still on in the hallway when I return and I am reminded of the phone call. A cold fear washes over me as I turn my key, remembering the sinister chuckle of my tormentor at the other end of the line. I run into the house, heading straight for the phone in the hall. I pick up the receiver and lay it down on the table, then bend down underneath in my designer dress and yank the wire out of the wall, so that I don't have to deal with this.

Tonight is the last night I will have to cope with this on my own. From tomorrow, January, my husband, is my partner and protector.

He makes me feel safe. Secure. Like nothing bad could ever happen to me.

But love is fleeting. It is pain that endures and gives life its meaning.

London, 7 days ago . . .

January

––––◆––––

As expected, a note arrived the day after Amy was found.

C3 to E3.

For weeks after the wedding we increased our presence around Fulham Broadway, Parsons Green and Putney Bridge, but Eames didn't strike. For weeks after that I still patrolled these areas before and after work, despite being assigned to different cases, one of which was another high-profile, year-long investigation. A case I had to solve without the aid of an apparition, without the torment of The Smiling Man, but still, he remained on my mind; this killer remained on my mind.

It has been fourteen months since a murder carrying his hallmark has been discovered.

Fourteen months since the last time The Smiling Man appeared to me.

But the case is still not solved. It isn't over.

I wonder whether the killer is currently serving time for another crime and that is the reason for this quiet period. But that isn't the case at all.

He's planning something.

Something big.

Something personal.

Something memorable.

Married life is the same as my life before I took the vows. Audrey is still working hard and increasing the size of her business; I am still spending too many hours working multiple cases. I still forget to let her know where I am sometimes. We still argue about that and I still have to find new ways to make it up to her. I still use a bottle of Scotch as a paperweight to my sister's case file, and I still look at it every day. It's the same; I just wear a ring now.

For Audrey it's more than that. It's a confirmation of our love and a declaration of our commitment to one another. She has been different since we got married. Her job doesn't appear to get her down as much and arguing is minimal. She has made a change for the better, while I remain largely the same. Perhaps with a renewed sense of calm or completeness. I'm at greater ease with myself. Something has certainly changed in me.

But when I arrive home today, she is sat on the sofa crying.

I stride over to her and sit down next to her, rubbing her back.

'What's wrong? What's happened?' I'm not used to seeing Audrey so vulnerable. I question her as tenderly as possible, fighting the rage inside that I automatically feel when in protective mode.

'He won't leave me alone,' she whimpers.

'Who? Who won't leave you alone?' This crumb of information is enough to release a dose of adrenalin that tenses my arms and chest. I subconsciously make a fist with my free hand.

'I don't know.'

'You don't know who won't leave you alone?' I tighten my fist.

'No. He just phones and doesn't say anything. Once, he laughed when I said your name, but that's it.'

Audrey goes on to explain everything to me. That this has been going on, sporadically, for months. It started just after I took on the case for Dorothy Penn. That she didn't want to involve me, because I was under enough stress at work.

'Babe, I'm your husband and I work for the police, who better to tell?' I stroke her back. She is visibly shaken by the whole thing. I hold back my sense of disappointment that she could not share this with me, but it concerns me to think she could keep something like this secret for so long and I wouldn't notice.

'I know. I know. I'm sorry.'

I tell her that she has nothing to be sorry for. She hasn't done anything wrong. She is the victim in all of this.

As I go out to the kitchen to get Audrey a glass of water I see the wire flailing across the floor in the hallway. She has unplugged the phone to avoid any further upset. I feel saddened. Useless, even. That I haven't been here to protect her. Maybe that I didn't even realise she needed protecting.

I hand her the glass as I return to the living room.

'I'm going to plug the phone back in now,' I tell her.

'No, Jan. Don't. Not yet.' She seems so frightened. I'm torn between anger at the situation and surprise at seeing Audrey so shaken up.

'I'm here now. You don't have to worry,' I try to reassure her. I want her to know that she has nothing to worry about. I won't let anything happen to her. The one woman I absolutely can protect is my wife.

On my hands and knees I crawl under the decorative hall table with the wire in my hand. I lift the white plastic cover to expose the socket and push the connector into the hole.

Within a microsecond a spark ignites and travels up the wire into the phone, making it ring instantly. I bang my head on the underside of the table in shock.

Scrambling to my feet, I stand in front of the mirror and catch sight of my startled expression and dishevelled appearance. Automatically, unthinkingly, I straighten my clothes, trying to work out how to handle this.

I pick up the receiver.

'Hello?'

Silence.

'Who is this?' I ask calmly.

A slight pause then a man's voice says, 'January?'

'Who is this?' I repeat in exactly the same tone.

Again, he asks, 'January?' His voice is tired and strained.

'What do you want?' I lower my voice, speaking through gritted teeth, trying not to let Audrey hear me from the other room.

He pauses again, as if reflecting on the sound of my voice.

'It's time, January.'

This time I wait in silence.

'It's been far too long.'

I start to wonder whether this is the killer. Whether this is his reintroduction into my life. Maybe he feels that fourteen months is too long.

'Talk to your mother.' And then he hangs up.

I'm frozen with shock, too stunned to move. I glance at the mirror again and stare into my own eyes, questioning what I just heard and why it is happening now. Why has he been tormenting Audrey? Why not just ask for me?

Why is my mother suddenly important?

I place the receiver back on to its hook and zombie over to the doorframe that leads to Audrey.

'Jan. Are you all right?' she asks, concerned by my pale, vacant expression and the fact that I haven't blinked. 'Jan,' she says louder to startle me.

'Uh?'

'Did you find out who it was?'

'Er, yeah. Yeah I found out who it was. I know now.' I don't look directly at her as I say this, more like directly through her, up above her, to the right of her, anywhere to avoid eye contact.

'And?' she prompts forcefully, easing herself forward on the sofa, anxiously waiting for me to divulge, wiping the moisture from her cheek with the back of her hand.

My eyes well up and I inhale deeply to prevent the emotion from developing further. Finally, I manage to draw strength from somewhere and look directly into her dark innocent eyes.

'It was my father.'

Eames

When somebody creates three of London's most talked-about murders in decades and then disappears, hiding behind his own legend, that isn't me. I'm not gone. Just think how unlucky they'll feel when they find the fourth girl. Think how sick it will make them to know that I am still one step ahead, that the next to suffer will be the wife of the detective supposedly investigating my case.

Detective Inspector January David. I like to say it out loud.

Think how blessed he will feel to have another chance at catching me.

The first three girls were normal. Regular people doing regular jobs for regular money. Audrey David is not a part of that world. She comes from a different part of the city, an affluent part where a dress that she will only wear once will cost more than all of Dorothy Penn's prized modular furniture.

She belongs to an elite part of society; people who are generally untouchable. That is what I have been missing.

To really have the whole of London in fear, the entire population of the capital, I need an Audrey David and what she represents.

She opens it up. She can make everyone, not just a minority, feel unsafe.

And collective fear can be so destructive.

Girl 4. She changes everything.

She makes it so easy.

Now they will start taking me seriously.

Girl 4

———◆———

When January comes home, I am on the sofa crying, and I've needed to do this for some time. The calls have been more frequent of late. They died out after we were first married, but today just sent me screaming over the edge. I don't like not to be in control.

But the silent calls, the laughing man at the other end of the line, that isn't really what I am upset about; it has just tipped me too far.

Every twenty-eight days for the last seventeen years my body has run like a clock. You could set the time to my periods, they are so regular. I know when it's coming, I know the different feelings I get just before it arrives and I know how I react once it's here. But as the fruitless months continue to pass, it brings with it a growing sense of disappointment and worthlessness.

I want a baby so much.

I didn't expect it to happen straight away, not even in the second month, but after three months of trying I started to add self-loathing and frustration to my usual list of cramps and tender breasts and bad skin.

This month was the worst yet. Because I was late. Because my breasts didn't hurt. Because I allowed myself to believe for just a fraction of a second that I was pregnant. Before it all came crashing down around me today at work.

January stands in the doorway of the living room after putting down the phone. I'm still curled up on the sofa feeling sorry for myself, but he looks dumbfounded. I try to make sense out of it, but he looks right through me.

Then he tells me that the person that has been tormenting me for over a year is his father. The father that abandoned him after his sister disappeared. I'm shocked too. I'm angry. But I can't be like that now. I'm his wife. I have to support him. So when he wants to reminisce about the times when his father was a great dad to him and his sister and his mother would always cook from fresh, or the stories of his father as a funny man, a touring comedian, magician, impersonator, all the stories I have heard before when January has had too much wine and drifts helplessly into sentimentality, I listen and I comfort. I don't pass judgement on his father's apparent psychosis or his commitment to my torture.

It's as if he has forgotten about me. That I was upset when he walked in.

But I have to be the strong one here in this situation.

I can't burden January with my problems and self-pity.

He doesn't even know that I have stopped taking my contraceptive pill.

He has no idea that we are trying for a child.

January

———✦———

Idecide to visit my mother on my own. Audrey offered to come with me, but I think this is something I have to do by myself. It has been too long and I don't know what state of mind she will be in. Will she even recognise me?

I don't even know why I feel the need to obey my father after all this time. I'm like a child that just blindly accepts what my parents say as fact, even though I have considered myself an orphan for the majority of my time on this planet.

I'm scared to meet with her. Especially now. Particularly after my visions of The Smiling Man. Mum might have been the person I was supposed to look after all along. She could be the only one that understands.

What if she does know where Cathy is?

I half expect the building to be grey brick interior with moss growing up the walls and water dripping from overhanging pipes on the ceiling; like a sewer without the aroma, but at a moderate temperature. It doesn't look like that at all.

It resembles a hospital, if hospitals were lemon in colour with a cheap pine dado rail around the centre of every thin wall. It smells like cancer covered with an aloe vera cleansing cream. This isn't the place that people come to die; it's the place they come to decay horrifically before they perish, unrecognisable to their family and themselves.

I walk past a doorway where an elderly woman has become so thin that she does not have the strength to even pull herself out of bed. She looks like a skeletal two hundred year old. Next door, another woman sits in a wheelchair next to an old turntable, listening to the same song over and over again. Her shaking hands adding another scratch to the vinyl each time she resets it back to her favourite song.

It fills me with fear.

I suddenly remember that my Scotch is in the glovebox still.

'If you could just sign in here, sir.' A foreign woman, probably approaching her mid-forties, squeaks at me from behind the counter. She puts a ballpoint pen on top of a folder that contains a quick checklist for me to fill out. Full name, date, car registration, who I am visiting, contact number, time in. Standard.

I jot down the information and sign my name, my hand shaking the entire time. A million thoughts going through my head at once. Cathy, my father, Mum, the three girls that have perished, Audrey's tormenting phone calls and breakdown, The Smiling Man, then Cathy again.

I never stop thinking about her.

'You must be Irene's son,' she says, turning the clipboard round to read my information.

'Er, yes. Irene's son,' I stutter, repeating her words back to her.

'She never stops talking about you, you know?' she goes on.

I don't know what to say to this. I have systematically erased my own mother from my mind for nearly two decades, and she has made sure that, even in her demented state, she reminds herself of me.

I just smile.

'Both of you,' she continues in her ignorance.

I assume that she is talking about Cathy.

My heart aches.

Mum is the same, I'm sure. I'll go in there and she will be talking about my sister like she is still around, like she knows where she is. But as the nurse leads me down a corridor peppered with the infirm, men and women spluttering, singing, shouting at their own imagination, I am led to a room where my mother lies motionless, attached to a machine, tubes and wires resting over her withered body, and I cry.

I lean both of my hands on the door to my mother's tomb and weep out twenty years of tears. With my head resting against the window I see the saline drops fall from my eyes and bounce on the floor below in front of my feet. I inhale loudly and let out more tears. The woman from reception rubs my back in an attempt to comfort me. I can tell it's not the first time she's done this. My annoyance at her tactility breaks me out of my fit.

'You don't have to go in until you are ready.' Her voice is soft and soothing and despite my irritation I appreciate the sentiment.

'I'd like to be left alone, if that's OK,' I request.

'That's fine, dear. You can go in. The doctor will be along in a minute.' She tilts her head to the left and softens her gaze, as if giving me consolation, as if to say 'good luck'.

Then she turns and heads back to the confines of her cubicle at the entrance and my eyes return to the small window which frames the tired shell that used to be my mother.

With one last breath I push through the door.

The room is as pallid as my mother's face. The colour of the walls is difficult to determine. They look peach, but not because of the paint; it's as if there is another colour beneath and the residue on top is formed through years of nicotine abuse. But Mum doesn't smoke.

There is a solitary landscape picture on the left wall and below are nine boxes stacked in blocks of three.

That's it.

The only other thing in here is a bed, a machine monitoring vitals and a decrepit woman with a tube attached to her nostrils. There's not even a chair for a visitor to sit on.

Because she has no visitors.

We have left her here unloved, unwanted.

I cry again. This time silently, not taking my eyes off her.

At this moment she looks beautiful to me. Like she did when I was young.

There are things I want to say to her, but can't quite force out of my mouth.

Then the door opens and the doctor bounds in.

'Ah, Mr David. I'm glad you could make it.' I don't correct the title. It doesn't feel relevant. I'm not here as a copper. He extends his hand to me. I grasp it, shaking it firmly.

'Can you tell me what is going on?'

He explains to me that it was my mother's wish for me to visit her once, before she died. Her mind has been deteriorating over time, but a recent aneurysm has left her incapacitated.

'How recent?' I ask him.

'Two years,' he responds, clinically.

'What the –?' I squeal in a high pitch, turning my face away. 'Two years? She's been like this for two years?'

'Yes. I'm afraid so. But your contact details were not on her forms and we have been liaising with your father during this time.'

He goes on to inform me that the machine she is attached to is keeping her alive and that she doesn't have the mental or physical capacity to do this for herself. He tells me that she maintained her stance on my sister until her ultimate brain malfunction and that the boxes in the corner are full of notepads that she has filled with information over the years and has left to me.

My inheritance.

'What do you mean *left to me*?' I ask, screwing up my face. 'She's not dead.'

'I'm sorry, Mr David, but now that you have visited we have been instructed to turn off the machine that is supporting your mother.'

'What?' I raise my voice. 'Who gave you that permission? I am her next of kin. Surely that decision lies with me.' I feel the blood rush to the surface of my face and the doctor's eyes widen as he recoils.

'I'm sorry, but your father is down as the next of kin and it was his decision to –'

I cut in forcefully, 'No, my parents were divorced. He has no say in this matter.'

'I don't feel comfortable that I should be the one to tell you this, Mr David, but your mother and father were only separated. They were never officially divorced and this leaves your father with the right to choose. I assumed he had spoken to you about it.' He hugs his clipboard for comfort.

I can't speak. I don't want to tell him that the first time I spoke to my father since I was twelve was only a couple of days ago, and that was hardly a two-way conversation. I don't have any time to digest the words that I am hearing.

'When is this happening?' I question.

'Today.'

I gasp, my eyes filling up again. I haven't cried so much in years.

'It is to happen the day that you visit,' he says after a pause, giving me a moment to gather myself. He avoids my eyes, but I see him physically cringe as he tells me his instructions. 'I'll give you some time alone.' He walks out of the room, leaving me standing next to Mum.

I don't know what to do. I feel like I should say something to her. Apologise for abandoning her, for not believing in her, for neglecting her all this time. For letting Dad kill her off. But I don't know if she can even hear me. Surely her brain can't process language. It can't even open her eyelids.

I settle for holding her hand. Her cold, wrinkled hand.

It feels like I stand there for hours, staring at her, crying, gripping her hand, telling her that I'm sorry and that I love her. But the words are only in my head.

Then I feel it.

That same cold I felt in the library. Like I am being watched.

Slowly, I turn my head to look behind me, a human instinct when you think you are being followed. I am not prepared for what I see and my first glimpse literally floors me. I drop down on to the linoleum with a thud, but I don't let go of Mum's hand.

Framed in the small window that gives outsiders a view into the room, I see a smile. A broad, unflinching smile aimed perfectly in my direction. Like the smile that haunts me in my sleep, the teeth are large and yellowing. The same piercing eyes that drain me of courage. But this is not The Smiling Man.

It's Dad.

Gazing in on his work. His sick triumph. He has been keeping Mum on the brink of death for two years, waiting for the perfect time to execute this evil plan. He still feels the hatred for Mum that he did back when Cathy was taken. He still blames me and this is his way of punishing us both. The sadistic joy in his face is evident. He needed to see us both suffer as much as he feels he has suffered.

'You!' I snarl from my place on the floor, spitting out thick saliva as I do so. But I can't move. I'm incapacitated at the vision before me, still smiling, still enjoying my pain.

Finally, as I get angrier, I summon up the strength to struggle to my feet. He still looks at me through the window, smiling at his work. I want to catch him and hold him down on the floor by his neck; I want to ask him why he is doing this to us.

But as I move towards the door, my comatose mother clamps my hand like a vice. I look back at her to see if she is waking up, but there is no movement apart from this insistent grip.

Am I awake?

I turn back to the window, but he is gone.

Mum releases my hand and I run to the door, but when I get outside all I see in the hallway is a man on a Zimmer frame. My father is gone; and soon my mother will leave this life, and all I have is a box of notebooks.

Notebooks full of the ink musings of a mad woman. Mostly about Cathy, some about me. Many about the people she sees in her dreams.

I only flick through them briefly; I'm not ready to dedicate the time to them yet.

Somewhere, hidden deep within the scribbled text, beyond the nonsense and mischief, there are answers. Answers to the abilities that both myself and my mother share.

Answers to the reason for The Smiling Man.

The answer to where I can find my sister.

Girl 4

———✦———

I'm the only one that knows who he is. But I can't tell.

The cuts across my body from the positioning of the wires that held me above the stage in Putney Arts Theatre should be stinging me. I should be in pain, but I'm not. I have drugs to numb that.

The mental strain of such an emotional ordeal should be playing on my mind, but it isn't. I'm still unconscious and I'm not dreaming.

But I survived.

I'm the only one to survive.

But survival means drowsiness from the drugs, tenderness of my wounds, incapacity to converse, to shed light on the situation. I know who Eames is. I've seen him. I've slept with him. It was the greatest sex of my life.

Does January really want me to wake up?

Does he really want me to tell my story?

Does he want everyone to know exactly what happened?

I can't be protected from Eames. Not even here.

Eames

—✦—

I can finish the job. Audrey David getting away is not a problem. I don't have to spend the next months researching for the girls that will follow on from this beautiful display. I have already done that. I've had fourteen months to plan that. They will disappear before Detective Inspector January David even knows it is coming. When he finally catches up, it will be too late: I will have his wife in my hands again.

She will complete the masterpiece.

While he wastes time dwelling over his bride's condition and his macho ego is dented by the knowledge that I fucked his wife and she wanted me to do it, I am ready to execute my next slaughter.

By now, the police should have received my next note.

E3 to D8.

I see the police arrive in their usual conspicuous manner that makes my life so much easier. I sip wine at Smollensky's Bar and Grill, while they roam around the exit to Canary Wharf Tube station not knowing what they are even looking for.

I smile into my glass as I raise it for another sip, but laugh inside at how superior I am to these fools.

I already took Girl 5 from this very spot yesterday evening and I plan to deliver her back here in one day.

But right now, Girl 5 is still alive.

Richard Pendragon is still alive.

January

———◆———

I have always referred to the girls by their number. Dorothy is Girl 1, Carla is Girl 2, and so on. It's important for me to remain professional and distance myself from the cases in this way. I can't refer to Girl 4 as a victim and then call her by my wife's name; I won't be able to cope.

'Nobody talks to her without me present. You hear?' I snort out these orders to Paulson and Murphy and the two guards that I have placed outside Girl 4's door. 'I don't care if the fucking Queen comes in here wanting to deliver a bunch of grapes personally, if I'm not in this hospital at that time, she doesn't go in.' I almost press my nose against the face of one of the guards like an army drill sergeant.

This isn't me.

I don't behave like this.

It's starting again. I won't be able to sleep. But, for the first time, I want to. I want to meet The Smiling Man. I want to be tied to that chair. I want to be blindfolded and abused. I want to find the man that did this to my wife. But I don't know what I'll do when I find him.

'Yes, sir,' the guard says firmly back at me. It's the response I want to hear. I want to know that Audrey is protected. I don't want anyone going in or out of there without me knowing. When she wakes up I want to be the first and only person that she sees.

'What can we do, Jan?' Murphy asks nervously.

'Go home, guys. Get some rest. Tomorrow, the work really starts. There's nothing more we can do tonight.' I look over at Audrey through the glass of the door, so still and pure. 'Go home,' I repeat, and I tap Murphy on the shoulder to let him know that it's all right.

'What are you going to do, Jan?' Paulson asks, genuinely concerned.

'I'm staying with my wife,' I answer, sternly.

Paulson looks at me and deliberates with himself about adding something else. Something like, 'You should rest too, Jan' or 'Don't tire yourself out for tomorrow' or 'Just call if you need anything'. But he doesn't. He can see in the lines of my face that the term 'visiting hours' will certainly not apply to me.

'I'll see you both in the morning. Early,' I say pointedly. And they walk off down the sterile corridor of the hospital ward muttering to each other.

I enter Audrey's room on my own, closing the door behind me, leaving the two guards at either side, rigid and unflinching. It feels like déjà vu. I was only just by my mother's bedside, holding her hand as she lay insensate under a blanket with a clipboard at her feet and a screen to the side of her head displaying information that I didn't understand. As long as the line peaked and troughed then there was little to worry about.

I feel guilty. Like it is my fault for allowing Audrey to get into this situation. I tell her that I am sorry, hoping that she can hear me. I tell her that I will catch the person that did this and make them pay, but her inertia is off-putting.

Leaving her room, I shut the door behind me and bid goodnight to the two guards. 'Thanks, boys. Keep it up. See you in the morning.' And I take the same route as Paulson and Murphy, down the shady corridor where patients are in such a critical condition that a high percentage won't ever recover.

The lift at the end of the hallway takes me down to the ground floor where my car is parked. I lean against the back wall, staring down the long passageway that leads back to my wife, the floating corpse – almost. As the doors move closer together I feel even further removed and alone.

I feel relief as I open the car door and sit down away from the situation, closed off from the real world. I reach into the glovebox for the hip flask.

It's full.

Taking a mouthful as though it's merely a soft drink, the liquid scrapes down the back of my throat from the first gulp, as if it's laced with powdered glass; the second gulp isn't any easier. By the fifth, I have to forcibly condition myself to keep it down. By the sixth I don't even realise that tears are falling from my eyes. I'm not crying, but it is still happening. I keep the emotion inside, but the physicality of it is still present.

I think about the grid references, the girls' houses, location, their look, how we found them, the notes from the killer. I try to piece something together. I try to think of as many different things as possible to overload my drunken brain and force me to sleep.

I grip the steering wheel as hard as I can, clenching my teeth and twisting the rubber in my hands, trying to keep my frustration contained.

But I can't.

I try, but I just can't.

The twisting motion soon develops into shaking the wheel back and forth, more aggressively with every thrust. The clenched teeth soon evolve into a growl, as I tremble in my seat almost ripping the steering wheel from its bolted position. Then I explode with a thunderous, gargling scream that lasts over five seconds, my neck bulging with veins and muscle, that seems to make my head vibrate from side to side.

Releasing the tension on the steering wheel I clench my hands in two strong fists and punch at the centre where the logo is located, each blast from my hands igniting a sound from the car horn, each whack indenting my knuckles with the words 'air bag'.

I screech my lungs out until the sound fills the inside of the car; gradually the blare from the horn is reduced to faint beeps as I tire. I hug the wheel for a second, my head resting on the punished rubber until I catch my breath once more.

I take another taste of the oaky Scotch and drop back into the spongy comfort of the car seat, my hip flask in my lap, the lid still in my right hand.

With my left hand I turn the cog on the side of my seat to recline it. Staring at the ceiling of the car I notice the faint blurring of the street lamps outside that light the pathway. Each lamp creating its own burnt orange halo as the light refracts through my tears and tricks my brain.

My eyes close for several seconds and the warmth of the Scotch makes me feel lethargic. My head spins a little so I reopen my eyes, trying to take stock of my position. The halos fuse together, forming a chain of nebulous light that makes me feel cross-eyed. I close my eyes again, controlling my natural reaction to gag, to heave.

Then I sleep.

Just as I wanted.

But I cannot summon The Smiling Man. That isn't how it works. He comes to me when the timing is right. He is in command. And, tonight, he doesn't come to help me.

But I'll try anything now.

I'm ready to believe.

Girl 5

—◆—

Statistically speaking, there seemed to be a zero per cent chance of me being Girl 5. I live in London and I work here at Canary Wharf, which falls into Zone 2; I'd read in the newspapers that all the murders had occurred in this zone and that it could be a pattern, that the suburbs were more dangerous than the centre. I'm twenty-six, which does seem to fit in with most of the other girls.

Still, the odds for any girl living in the city are pretty remote. One in millions.

But, for me, less than remote.

Zero.

I'm not a girl.

Yet, I find myself waking up contorted in the complete darkness of a locked chest with little air and no room to move. I'm afraid. I'm terrified. I don't know how I got here. From the smell it is clear that I wet myself at some point. I have also been placed inside a bag or sack of some kind that is tied at the top by a piece of rope. I panic and kick around as much as I can, shouting to be let out, but there is no response. I have to calm myself down if I am going to get out of this. I need to preserve air. My only comfort is that the chest moves as I kick, so I can tell I am on a wooden floor and there is plenty of room around the outside. I should be thankful I have not been buried underground.

I should be grateful for the way that I am going to die.

Thank you, Eames. Thank you so much for allowing me to slowly bleed to death.

Thank you for turning me into Girl 5.

January

———◆———

My mouth has dried out from the booze, like I've eaten a kilo of walnuts. I wake up in my car, still outside the hospital, so dehydrated I don't need to use the toilet. I couldn't cry any more even if I wanted to. The only liquid I have is the Scotch, which I swirl around like mouthwash, burning the inside of my cheeks, thankful for the moisture.

The clock on my dashboard says 7.43 in a hazy green light that becomes clearer the longer I keep my eyes open.

I rub the sleep from my eyes and adjust the seat back to normal incline.

Some lights are on inside the hospital and I wonder what could be going through Girl 4's mind as she lies there. Is she trying to fight? Will she remember the face of her attacker?

I turn the key and the engine splutters to a start similar to my own. Instead of checking in on Girl 4, I head straight to the station. I want to be there when the mail arrives. I want to be the one that opens the next taunting grid reference. I know what these letters are now, so we can act quickly to monitor the area, but the killer is going to want to move quickly now, before Girl 4 wakes up, before she can identify him, before we are one step ahead of him for once.

He could be panicked now. Maybe he will rush his next move and leave a clue that he has so painstakingly covered up to this point. Maybe he'll get sloppy.

Maybe he is too egocentric to think anything is wrong and will continue with his plans as usual.

Maybe I am wrong.

I take three spearmint chewing gums from my inside pocket and shove them all in my mouth. I don't have time to go home and freshen up, so this will have to do. I'm unshaven and the stubble makes me look dirtier than I really am. I lift both arms and sniff under each pit once; I have some deodorant in a locker at work, so I'll splash some water on my face when I get there, but that will have to do.

I take my tie off when I get to the station so that my outfit looks different from yesterday, but Paulson and Murphy can tell from the second I walk through the door. It sends out the right message that they are here even before I arrive, though.

'In before me, eh?' I say, entering the room.

'Jesus, Jan. Did you sleep in a bush?' Paulson half-jokes, drawing attention to my appearance.

'Haven't you been home?' Murphy chips in, concerned.

'It felt wrong to be too far away,' I confess. 'Look, I'm fine. It's a new day, we have just over an hour before the post arrives. I want to freshen up a little and then we get to work on finding this fucker.' I look at them both in turn and they nod in agreement. 'Good. Now someone needs to get the coffee on, because it might be a while before we get any shut-eye.'

'I'm on it,' Murphy says enthusiastically, as if this is the most important job of the day.

I watch him race over to make the drinks and give

Paulson a knowing nod, before exiting to clean my appearance up a little.

In the changing room downstairs I spit out the gum I have been chewing for the last thirty minutes; the taste left it around twenty minutes ago. I splash cold water all over my face and wipe it with a paper towel. Then I push two more sticks of gum into my mouth to mask the alcohol and replace the act of brushing my teeth.

Taking my shirt off, I wrap it around the hand dryer, so that no air can escape, then press the button. The hot air slowly inflates the shirt circulating a warm current around the inside that I hope will have a similar effect to a tumble dryer or dry-cleaner. I wash my torso, spray it with the sports deodorant from my locker and put the warm shirt back on. I don't feel the need to change my underwear or trousers.

I lean on the sink, getting my face as close as possible to the mirror in front, and look at my face, scrutinising the lines and imperfections.

'This is it, Jan,' I say out loud. 'No more. It stops here.'

In my head I want to say, 'Come on, January, you can do this.' But, sometimes, what is said inside is not always what comes out. What is true is not always what is real.

A police constable walks into the changing rooms wearing tracksuit bottoms and a sweaty grey T-shirt with a Harvard University logo emblazoned on the front. Seeing me, he is visibly uncomfortable – obviously knowing the situation with Girl 4. It's not my wife. It's not Audrey David. It's Girl 4. It's how I cope.

'Morning,' he says, swinging the bag from his shoulder on to the bench in front of him.

'Morning,' I groan back at him.

'I just bumped into Murphy on the way in. He'd just picked up the mail.'

'Fuck.' I look down at my wrist to see the time, but I took it off to wash. It's 8.47. How long have I been down here? What have I been doing? I throw everything that isn't attached to me back into my locker and slam it shut. Without even thanking the officer I bolt through the door, down the corridor, turn left, up the stairs two at a time, left again and then right into our office.

'Where's the letter?' I ask, out of breath.

'Your coffee is cold,' Murphy jokes.

I raise my voice, 'Where's the fucking letter, Murph?'

Paulson steps forward with the envelope in his hand. It is still sealed.

'We haven't opened it, Jan. But there's something you should probably look at.'

This letter is different. On the front, in the same handwriting as all the others, it says: *FAO: Detective Inspector January David*. It is addressed to me personally. He is aiming this at me now. Provoking me. This gives me more reason to be on the case, rather than taking some time out as suggested by my superiors. It shows that I am integral to it, that I am part of it, whether I am here or not.

I start to tear at the envelope to get at the clue inside.

'He knows who you are,' Paulson says. I ignore him. 'Jan?' he persists. 'JAN!' He almost shouts to get my attention.

'*WHAT?*' I shout back at him, even louder, taking my eyes off the prize.

'This guy knows who you are.' He puts a short space between each word to accentuate his point.

'Well of course he fucking does, Paulson. Don't be so ignorant.' And I continue with the letter, eventually

229

taking out the same card we have had for the last four girls.

E3 to D8.

'So, what does it say?' Murphy pesters.

'E3 to D8,' I tell them both.

Paulson opens up a concertinaed Tube map that he already had prepared.

'Right. We've got All Saints, Poplar, Blackwall, East India, West India Quay, Canary Wharf, North Greenwich and Heron Quays in Zone 2.' Paulson has clearly ignored my slight outburst, putting it down to anxiety, and soldiers on with the investigation. 'Murph, get this down on the board.' Murphy picks up a pen and goes over to the whiteboard to write down all the locations.

'OK. What did we have?' he asks. 'All Saints, Poplar, then what?' Paulson repeats the other six locations and Murphy follows his dictations on the board under the heading of *Girl 5*.

'There's Canning Town Tube in that grid ref too, but that falls under Zone 3.'

'Forget that one. There's too many as it is and every one has been in Zone 2 so far. We have to stick with what we already know.'

We look at the list of stations. Eight in total. We just don't have the manpower to watch over all of these areas in the expectation that he will strike again soon; he waited fourteen months between the last two victims.

'Something is telling me that we should stick with the more prominent areas of the zone. Places where people tend to congregate. He chose Shepherd's Bush over Ladbroke Grove and Mile End over Bow Road, so this would suggest that Poplar, Blackwall and Canary Wharf are our three top sites.' I explain this to Paulson and

Murphy, but, of course, my reasoning is based on instinct over actual detective work.

I've got a sense for this villain now and my gut is pointing me towards Canary Wharf. But how can I say that? How can I tell them that I am basing this investigation completely on a hunch? I have to justify it with something quantifiable.

They know the struggle I have had to keep this case open and the fight I now have on my hands to keep myself involved despite my own personal attachment, but Girl 4 seems to have galvanised the focus in each of us. Whether my lead in this case is official or in a more rogue capacity I know that Paulson and Murphy have my back.

'So we're agreed?' I ask, knowing the answer.

'Poplar, Blackwall and Canary Wharf. We have to take a bit of a risk on it,' Paulson confirms.

'But it's calculated,' Murphy chips in, saying exactly what I want him to.

I feel something. Pride in my team. Optimism about this case for the first time. Like I am closer to finding out who strung my wife above a stage, fucked her and left her to die a floating corpse, a naked exhibition.

It feels, for once, like we might be ahead of the game.

But, of course, we're not.

Eames took Girl 5 last night. He is working quicker now. Always ahead. And tonight, when I fall asleep at my desk again, The Smiling Man will confirm this and I will have a huge decision to make.

Eames

It probably looks like I am panicking.
I don't panic.

Everything is planned. Everything that happens is part of the plan.

Luring a man is different from influencing a woman. I am not interested in sexual relations with someone of my gender and I won't falsely represent myself as a means to an end. Taking Richard has to be done in a slightly archaic way. No psychology, just force.

The streets all look the same. Glass wall upon glass wall, modernity replacing architectural individuality. The people fit the atmosphere. Every man is clean shaven with some kind of styling product in his hair. Expensively tailored suits and perfectly buffed shoes. Groomed is an understatement.

Women jog around the streets at lunchtime trying to stay healthy by running through the invisible smog, fooled by the sterility of this London borough.

Canary Wharf towers high over everyone, but is obscured by the presence of financial logos. Citibank, KPMG, Credit Suisse, Morgan Stanley. Bulbs light up on the side of a building scrolling the latest share prices on a constantly updated loop. Bunzl, 545, down 0.27; BP, 458, down 2.86; BT Group, 76.6, down 2.05. Balfour Beatty is up 3.13. It means nothing to me. I'm looking for my fifth girl.

They found Audrey this morning and will receive my letter tomorrow, so I have to work fast and take Girl 5 today. But this is all part of the strategy.

Audrey was not supposed to die.

I couldn't kill her yet.

I walk past a grassy area full of overly muscular men in fitted jackets perpetuating the stock-broker stereotype, sleazing over women, eating their healthy brown-bag lunch, pretending to admire the sculpture that resembles a three-dimensional Mondrian painting.

A plane goes overhead.

Two more women jog past me in lycra shorts displaying the very shape of everything they hold in place. I close my eyes for a second and think of Audrey in the air above the stage.

My greatest work.

I round the corner to Smollensky's Bar and Grill. I have lunch here. It's expensive once I add the Scotch, but every person within a square mile considers this standard. For one mile in every direction I look they are only concerned with money.

In four and a half hours I will return here to mingle with the suits and hair-gel and credit cards and fake laughter and continued work talk.

In five and a half hours I will place Richard Pendragon's arm over my shoulder, carry him to a cab, take him home, where I will keep him for a couple of days, tied up in the chest he will eventually bleed to death in.

In two days he will be delivered back to the bar that I

took him from. But first he must change. He must transform into something he is not. I can help him adapt, become something new.

Become Girl 5.

January

---◆---

We know that he stalks his prey; he has to in order to fully comprehend their idiosyncrasies, so that he can manipulate them quickly. We know that he has to research the area in advance to pick the best spot to approach the girls without them realising that they are being abducted to be killed.

The majority of the day is spent reviewing CCTV footage from the three Tube stations that we have agreed are the most likely target areas. It is a laborious, thankless task with little yield.

I don't look into Girl 4's specific case just yet. I wait. When she wakes up, we should have everything we need. Right now we are trying to compile a list from the footage we have of the areas. Faces that we could show Girl 4 when she wakes up.

She won't need a photo to remind her of his face, though. She remembers him perfectly.

I send Paulson and Murphy home to rest, still deciding that it is best not to talk to them about my dreams, about The Smiling Man. Then, I sit at my desk, only the light from my computer monitor helping me to see.

I take Cathy's file from the drawer and open it. Rubbing my face against the grain of the stubble I start to read my mother's statement. I can see why nobody believed her; it sounds insane that somebody she has never seen before would appear to her in a dream with a message about my sister. It's ludicrous.

I picture the two glasses of juice I was making in the kitchen when she was taken.

I think about Audrey's pert figure floating in natural beauty.

I remember my mother's grip on my hand.

I wonder how my father gained such pleasure, such unadulterated satisfaction from seeing the pain on my face and the pathetic stagnation and decomposition of the woman he swore to love for ever.

I close the case folder and push back on my chair. The wheels on the legs transport me out of the light and back three foot into the shadows. Staring at the screens all day has fried my brain. My eyes feel heavy. My neck is stiff. I turn it left, right, down, up, to stretch it. Yawning, my right eye becomes watery. Yawning heavier this time, I close both my eyes and rest my elbow on the arm of the chair, my cheek on my hand.

The hum of the computer hard drives soothing and sending me to sleep.

There is no blindfold this time, yet still my vision is impaired.

I am sat on the chair, with my hands and feet bound, as usual. Something weighs down on the top of my head; it isn't heavy. I look up, so that it can touch my face, so that I have a better feel for what it may be. The frayed sinews of rope push through the cloth that surrounds my entire body, scratching my face and alerting me to the fact that I am enclosed within a bag of some kind that is drawn tightly together on top with a piece of rope. But it is black.

I can't see anything and my eyes are not adjusting to make out the shapes of my limbs.

I can start to smell the fabric around me, now that my brain has registered it. I can smell urine.

Then the heat of the spotlight that switches on above me alerts me to the fact that the material is red and opaque. I try to make out shapes in the room, but it is empty.

I sigh. That is when I hear the familiar sound of the shuffling feet behind me.

And I know that someone else is going to die in the next twenty-four hours.

Girl 5.

I need to pay attention. The clues are here. They always have been. This time I have to take notice.

From side to side his feet shuffle, but something is different this time. His usual flat-footed scraping is replaced with a light click, as though he has learned to lift his feet off the ground as he moves. His heels metro-nomically keeping beat as they hit the wooden floor beneath them, hypnotically calming me.

His large hands touch my head and I flinch backwards. He releases his touch and calms me with the tap of his feet again, slowing my heart rate, gaining my trust. And he repeats his attempt. This time I remain still as he unties the knot from atop my head, allowing the air to seep in through the gap he creates.

With the knot now loose, he lets go, but doesn't pull down the sack. I sense he hasn't moved. Shaking my head vigorously, the hole on top becomes larger and larger until it drops down past my face and rests on my shoulders.

He is stood in front of me, smiling. His eyes alight with what looks like genuine pleasure to see me.

I almost smile back.

But I resist.

He turns and walks towards his spot slowly, slower than normal. As he gets further away I notice that he is taller than usual. Around four inches taller. The exact height of the high heels he seems to be wearing. I look around from side to side, as if someone might be there that can confirm I am not imagining this, scrunching my brow in disbelief.

He turns at the end like a catwalk model and places his hands on his hips. Then, he makes his way back to me, crossing his feet at the front to give a swagger; he is so comfortable and confident in stilettos.

Stopping in front of me, he bends at the waist, just as he always does, and pushes his smile into my face. His hands remain on his hips as he scrutinises me. Then he straightens his back. I haven't realised that his hands are now on my shoulders. With the cloth screwed up in either palm of his giant mitts he tilts his head to the side and distracts my concentration. Then, in one swift movement he yanks at the bag above both my shoulders.

It doesn't tear.

I don't move.

The Smiling Man holds it up in front of him, then whips it around the back of his neck and ties it into a knot like a cape. He makes his way back to his favourite spot.

I wonder when the torture will start. When he will pull a gun or knife. When he will produce a razor blade and make tiny incisions all over my body, before throwing salt over each wound or pouring my favourite Scotch over my head to painfully seal each gash.

But he doesn't want to hurt me this time.

He wants to put on a show.

I haven't even noticed the music playing.

He is my beat, my rhythm.

My guide.

Untying the knot that wedges itself underneath his immense Adam's apple, he shakes out the sheet in front of him. It appears to get longer with every flick of his wrists, rippling further, getting closer to my face and cooling me down in the process.

He stops the motion and the sheet drops to the floor at his feet in a heap, visibly longer than when it was a cape, more fabric than it had when it constricted my movement as a closed sack.

He holds his end at waist level, the top of the sheet taut from his grip. He moves it up to his chest, then back down to his waist. Back up to his chest, then returns to waist height. He does this three more times, not looking at the sheet, always transfixing his distended eyes at me, continually smiling that dirty grin in my direction. Then with one movement he throws the sheet into the air, so that it goes above his head.

Nothing could prepare me for what I would see next.

As the sheet floats downwards it shows a different Smiling Man. Almost instantaneously he has changed into something else.

He is still the same height, the same bulging eyes, the same haunting expression, the same long black coat, but my gaze is drawn away from his smile.

His hair is now down past his shoulders, peroxide blonde and in bad condition. His eyelashes are noticeably longer, his teeth whiter and his face brighter. Those dark cheeks that bookend his memorable smile are bright pink with blusher. He is wearing blue eyeshadow, mascara and a bubblegum lipstick that seems to plum his mouth up more than I thought possible.

His coat is buttoned shut. Normally I can see his trousers, his black shirt and belt buckle, but it is evident he is not wearing that now.

In a microsecond, he has become someone different.

Below his coat a pair of lightly coloured stockings display his beautifully smooth, almost attractive, legs. Where the coat parts at the chest, it is clear he has no shirt on any more. It is also frighteningly obvious that he has breasts. Ample handfuls of beautiful real breasts. Not augmented. Natural.

He is like The Smiling Transvestite.

The Smiling Transexual.

The Smiling Woman.

For the first time since he appeared I find myself wanting to look at his mouth and nothing else.

Swaying in time with the music he grabs the lapels of his manly coat, pushing his hips from left to right in an exaggerated, almost childlike, innocent way. Like he is trying to tease me.

He takes four steps forward. I count them, suddenly apprehensive.

Stopping, he repeats the hip movement, attempting allure. I try not to convey my inner cringe.

I can't avert my eyes. I am drawn in as he seductively runs his hands, now complete with white nail polish, up and down the lapels of the dirty coat, which is the only original feature left of the man that frequents my subconscious.

Two more steps towards me.

He opens the top of the jacket outwards to bare his new nubile chest, the ebony nipples pointing at me like the bullets he placed in my mouth the first time we met.

One more step.

He sways again, his breasts springing east and west, his smile remaining, his gaze fixed.

Then he stops.

And the coat drops to the floor.

There, standing before me, not four feet from where I am sat, my hands and feet bound to restrict movement, is the resemblance of a man I have learned to fear and respect. The giant Smiling Man, now naked, with make-up, wavy fake blonde hair, near-perfect breasts, lengthy muscular thighs and four-inch heels.

And that smile.

And those eyes.

And no penis.

Female genitalia. Firm and clean. His pubic hair shaved into a tidy rectangle. The transformation is beyond fascinating. I try to speak, but no words come out. So I stare at it in disbelief. And I see blood start to trickle down the inside of his legs. Her legs.

Feeling the moisture, The Smiling Man tilts his head to look down where his dick should be and sees the blood on the inside of both legs. His eyes protrude even further as his stare returns to my expression, then they glaze over. He looks like he might cry. But he doesn't.

He takes his right hand and puts it between his legs to feel what he is missing and locates what must be a wound of some kind.

Upon the detection of nothing but soft tissue and blood he brings his hand up to his mouth as if miming 'Oh no.' As he lowers his hand I count the five bloody finger marks left on the lower half of his face.

He holds his sinned hand out and takes one more step towards me.

*

I flinch and wake up, the light of day just creeping through the window of the office, the hard drives still spinning out a low-key hum.

I don't know what it means yet, but I now know that I have to share this. If this information can stop another girl from perishing, then I know that I have to tell someone about the things I see.

Girl 5

Friday afternoon in the office is always the same. I hear them talking to each other. Talking about what they are doing tonight, where they are going, who they are going with. Arranging to bump into each other or meet for a drink, but never including me.

I pretend I don't hear them.

I make out that I'm fine with it.

I'm invisible to them.

Still, at the end of every week I stay behind a little later than everyone. I tried walking out at the same time once, cool by proxy, pity invite, but all I saw were the backs of suits and blouses. Josh, from corporate, even said, 'See you next week, Rich.'

I got the message. I'm not invited.

But every Friday, I go out. Not necessarily *with* the people from work, but at least in the vicinity.

I stand outside their booth or sit at the bar on my own near where they congregate and laugh at jokes that aren't funny, drinking their livers into oblivion.

I wait. Maybe one week it will be different.

I wait for some humanity.

Every week I drink on my own and wonder what I've done wrong. But I never say anything.

I wonder if they'll even realise that I'm dead.

I wonder if I know I'm alive.

They leave the office in packs. I hear a whisper of "Ave a good one, Richard' and 'See you Monday, Rich' and I feel happy that they know I exist. But they must know that I don't stay much later than them. I don't sit here all night or travel straight home to boost my online gaming credibility.

I wait. Again. Until all the wolves have left the office. I pretend I have a few things to finish off, maybe leave a spreadsheet open on my desktop, some kind of pivot-table. I've started to use the same one each week now. They won't notice.

Standing over the far side of the office I see the crowds gravitate towards Smollensky's on the corner. The typical starting point for them and the place I usually end up staying when they all move on, the last to leave again.

Our office cleaner potters around behind me, pulling cups and crisp packets off the desks and filling her bin liner.

'Not meeting your friends for drinks tonight, Mr Pendragon?' she says in her Caribbean accent, her English less broken than when she started here.

'They're getting the drinks in for me tonight. I'm off to meet them now,' I lie to her face, grab my jacket, swing it over my shoulder and saunter out like I mean something, like I have something.

Rounding the corner of the street I see the black signage outside the bar. Through the window, hordes of people pack in, sweating on one another, sharing champagne and sampling cocktails; never the same drink twice.

I take a breath, ready for the same humiliation as last week and the week before that.

Ready to give them all another chance.

I'm not ready to be injected, tied up in a bag, locked in a casket and painted to look like a woman.

I'm not ready to bleed to death, because some psychotic maniac masquerading as an artist thinks it is acceptable to strip me naked and cut my fucking dick off.

January

❖

Icall Paulson early, when I wake up at my desk again. It's a couple of hours before he is due in. I ask him not to come into the office and to just meet me outside the Canary Wharf Tube station at 9.30. He should come with Murphy.

'What's this about, Jan? You got a lead?' he asks, audibly fatigued.

'Something like that. Definitely something that might be worth discussing.'

And I leave it at that.

Getting there for 9.30 gives me enough time to shower myself down, shave, use the toilet, change my clothes and all in record time, so I don't have to spend a second longer than is necessary in our marital home. The home we should both be living happily in.

I'm first to Canary Wharf and wait opposite the Underground exit, leaning against the concrete of the bridge, watching the share prices scroll past without really understanding what I'm looking at. I try to figure out the full company names from the abbreviations and acronyms.

Losing time somewhere in the game I have created for myself, I don't notice Paulson and Murphy have arrived together, so, when they approach and startle me, I pour black coffee down the front of the clean shirt I have forced myself into.

'Oh fuck it,' I say, looking down at my shirt, pulling it off my skin to prevent myself from being burned.

'Sorry, Jan.' Paulson fusses over me, not knowing what to do. I swat his hands away and waft my shirt in a futile attempt to dry it out a little.

I still haven't looked at them.

They're going to think I'm crazy.

'OK. It's fine. It's fine. Let's go and sit down and grab another coffee, eh?' It's clear that I'm agitated.

We walk over to Carluccio's and take a seat outside. The weather is mild, but I'm hoping the breeze off the water will help dry out my Americano-stained shirt quicker.

The coffees are brought to our tables; our usual drinks. Paulson grabs a *pasticcio di cioccolato* for himself. Not many people can handle a chocolate bread-and-butter pudding for breakfast. Murphy and I share the selection of biscotti.

I watch Paulson shovel in a portion of his breakfast dessert. Still chewing on the bits of bread he didn't swallow immediately, he asks, 'So, Jan, what have you got on this guy?'

'Well, it's difficult to say.' I pause. They wait. Total silence. Total concentration. Paulson even stops eating for a moment.

I dunk my biscotti into my coffee, then eat the soggy section of hazelnut goodness. Leaning back on my chair I tell them, 'I've had a dream.' They look perplexed, as if this is a joke. It's the same look my father gave to my mother when she tried to explain about Cathy.

I've seen it before.

I know what they are thinking.

I've thought it myself.

'A dream?' Murphy speaks slowly, elongating the word dream to convey his scepticism. Paulson says nothing.

'Hear me out.' I tell them about the dream I had last night, about The Smiling Man transmogrifying into a giant bleeding woman. I explain that the night before Girl 1 died I dreamed of having a bullet thrust into my mouth; before Girl 2 the hot pokers seared through my muscles in exactly the same positions that we found the arrows in Carla's body. I tell them that before Girl 3 I had the most vivid dream where hundreds of Smiling Men crowded around me pushing cigarettes into my mouth until I could no longer breathe.

'So . . . you think you're psychic?' Paulson asks, genuinely curious.

'I'm not psychic. I don't see exactly what is going to happen. It's like I get clues to how these women are going to die or something. I don't even really understand it myself.'

'Jan, are you sure you're OK?' Murphy asks, patronising me in the same way my mother was treated.

'Oh fuck off, Murph! I'm fine. I'm trying to explain this to you.' He sits back in his seat, shocked. 'All I know is that I have these . . . er . . . '

'Dreams?' Murphy offers.

'Visions,' I correct him. 'I have these obscure visions and the next day, twenty-four hours later, a body turns up.' I can see that Murph is not convinced at all, but that Paulson, at least, wants to believe. He's willing to give it a go.

It's all we've got.

'Look, I know it sounds crazy. I didn't want to believe it at first. I tried to fight it, but the similarities are there and you can't refute that.' I don't know why I'm even bothering to try to justify this to Murphy; he doesn't have the mental capacity to digest what I am saying.

'What about Audrey?' Murphy asks.

'What?' I say abruptly, almost cutting him off.

'Girl 4,' Paulson interjects. 'He means what about Girl 4.' He gives Murphy a look that almost turns him to ash.

'I didn't have a vision of that,' I say, trying to calm myself, knowing that Murphy is trying to catch me out, to pick holes in my theory. How dare he?

'Well, that's odd,' he continues to goad me.

I don't want to tell them about the night before the wedding, when he appeared on stage. They were there. I know they didn't see him. This would certainly trivialise the rest of my story. It would lose credibility.

'But she's alive, Murph,' Paulson says slowly, piecing things together. Murphy just looks at him as if to say *So what?* 'Maybe Jan only sees the girls that this psycho is actually going to succeed in killing. Is that right, Jan?'

'I don't know. I don't understand it yet myself.' I gulp at my coffee and look down at the stain on my shirt one more time, which seems to be drying nicely. Some men in pinstripe suits walk behind and go through the doors into one of the glass buildings that surround us. Asian tourists have already started to congregate, taking pictures in front of buildings and signs they believe might be landmarks.

I go cold. The same way I felt in the library while investigating Girl 2. The same as I did when visiting Mum. That's how I know it's Canary Wharf. At least, that's what I think the feeling is.

It's not.

This is the feeling I get whenever Eames is near, whenever I sense his presence as much as I do my own. He's watching me again. Sat in the bar next door, the same bar that he took Girl 5 from yesterday. The same bar he will have Girl 5 delivered to tomorrow morning, mutilated beyond recognition.

'That means we have less than twenty-four hours until the next girl is killed.' It appears that Paulson is willing to go along with this idea, even if Murphy is showing some resistance. He is willing to put some faith in the fantastical now that all other avenues appear to be exhausted.

I decide that Paulson and I will stake out the area this evening and Murphy can take the graveyard shift. He is there when the chest arrives in the morning containing a naked Richard Pendragon in a blood-soaked bag, his penis detached and his face painted to look like a woman.

And Murphy's thoughts instantly go back to this very conversation.

Girl 4

I've been lying here unconscious for two days now. All the nutrients and drugs that my body requires to heal and survive are administered intravenously. My five-a-day passing through a tube as a viscous liquid that absorbs quickly into my blood.

If I'm supposed to be dreaming, I don't know what about.

If I'm supposed to be in pain, I'm not. The dosage would be near euphoric if I were awake.

But I'm not.

I'm asleep with no thoughts or feelings and no control. Everything that happens now is in the hands of others. I have to trust that they get it right.

My current state is a gift. Anything that can delay me from seeing January right now is fine.

But, in two more days my consciousness will return and the first face I see will be the man who put me in this position in the first place.

This time to finish what was started.

Eames

When Detective Inspector January David thinks that he is getting close, he doesn't realise just how near he already is to me. When he looks at the scarred body of his once beautiful wife, is he torturing himself for not protecting her? Is he convincing himself that he still loves her, blocking out her adulterous behaviour? He knows what I do to each girl before I execute them. When I deliver the fifth girl to him, neatly packaged like a birthday gift, is he going to let the fact that it was once a man misdirect him like he has been doing with all the other girls?

Come on, detective, you should have figured it out by now.

I thought you were worthy.

I feel lazy for the way I have taken the fifth girl. Anybody in my line of work could have done it. A novice. An idiot. He could have been chosen at random. It could be the work of a cut-price Eames, a substandard copycat killer. That's not me. That will never be me. That is not how you create a legend.

With Detective Inspector January David avoiding his domicile of imploding marital bliss, I order a courier to collect the chest containing the very lonely, very pathetic, very dead Richard Pendragon from his address, Audrey's address.

I wait on the doorstep and hand the courier the wad of cash required to have such a large, heavy package driven through London to Canary Wharf for 9.30 in the morning on a weekday. I even help him lift the useless lump into the back of his van.

The ease of this execution is allowing me to have too much fun with it. This is where mistakes can occur. Complacency is death.

I debate whether to sign the electronic touch-screen device as J. David, not even attempting to forge his signature. A joke between us. A way to show that I am still winning. It may even buy some time while I complete the masterpiece.

But now is not the time for ad-lib.

Improvisation would be my weakness.

This is not my role.

I stick to the plan and sign it Eames.

To give him something.

Before I take everything.

Girl 5

Lying in my tomb, the blood that once gushed from my crotch is slowing to a drip; the pain I originally felt when Eames cut away the one thing that made me a man has given way to delirium as my brain swirls and my eyes roll back in my head. In and out of consciousness, I submit to death. I have no choice.

But my life doesn't flash before my eyes before I die.

Whoever said that was lying.

I have to make myself think of all the important events I have experienced in my twenty-six years.

So that I can forget that I can't breathe. So that I don't focus on the burning sensation of the glue that fastens this degrading wig to my scalp. So I can shut out that I am no longer a part of mankind.

I think about the time I wet myself at school and the way that story followed me until university; there was always someone who remembered it. I move straight on to my university years, completely skipping childhood and adolescence where, apparently, nothing happened. I think about going to the student union for the first time and being too scared to talk to anyone, even though we were all in a similar position.

I think about work and how I acted exactly the same there. Complaining inside at the behaviour of the pack without admitting any self-blame.

These are the moments in my life that I run through before my blood pressure drops to insignificance. These three incidents of nothingness are what I use for comfort as cold sweats begin to kick in, as my air hunger worsens.

No wonder there was no flash of life.

I've done worse than merely exist.

Instead of reminiscence I opt for hope.

I hope, as I edge closer in my dizziness to the next life, that there is no next life. Because I'm bound to fuck that one up too.

I don't want a bright light to head towards.

I don't want to be reunited with those that have passed before me.

In your last moments of life, just before everything ends, you find out who you really are.

I am here to feed the worms.

I am ash you should flush down the toilet.

January

I finish the shift with Paulson, but I don't want to go home. I don't want to go back to that huge house full of Audrey artefacts. Pictures of us both on the wall looking happy; the furniture we picked together; the design elements of the house that Audrey takes such pride in; the details.

So I stay at the office again with my Scotch and my sister's file. With the desk as a pillow and my self-loathing as a blanket.

If my vision was correct, it means that there are four hours until Girl 5 will be dead. I left Paulson two hours ago when Murphy took over the shift from us. We didn't really know what we were looking for in the pinstripe crowd; we were reduced to my senses. I was hoping to get a feeling for the killer's presence.

But persistence paved the way to nothing.

It was two hours ago that I lost my alibi.

And two hours is long enough for me to kill Girl 5.

Girl 6

❖

It seems unfair to me that I leave no legacy.

Girl 1, Dorothy Penn, was lucky. She was the first. She was important enough to be picked to start this entire project. Nobody will forget her.

Girl 2, Carla Moretti, proved that this was not a one-off. It was the start of a serial-killing spree, the likes of which have not been seen in London. She made it real for so many of us.

Girl 3, Amy Mullica, stayed in the capital's minds for so long. The way she died was the most brutal to date, and we were left to ponder this for over a year, wondering if this madman would return.

Girl 4, Audrey David, was obviously the most important. She managed to get away. She is intrinsically involved with the case. Her husband is investigating it. The entire mystery hinges around her regaining consciousness.

Girl 5, Richard Pendragon, was not even a girl. Of course, that will be remembered in all its crudity. Suddenly, fear for this unhinged sociopath extends further into London. He manages to double his audience overnight.

Girl 6, that's me. His latest trick.

In less than two days, I will be found. But I am just a

composite piece to the larger accomplishment. I don't have my own story. I'm here to serve the greater purpose.

I'm the misdirection.

When people look back at this in years to come, they will remember all of this information, but the details of Girl 6 will remain hazy in their memories.

Audrey David is the rabbit in the hat.

Stacey Blaine is the joke that makes you look the other way.

January

---◆---

I get a call from Paulson at 9.42.
  'Jan, Murph just called, he's got something,' he says
half-urgently, half-worried.

I stand to attention at my desk, pushing the file back
into my drawer. 'Well, we'd better get down there then.
I'll meet you there.' I start to head for the door to leave.

'No, Jan. I'm coming in. So is Murph.' I stop in my
tracks.

'What? What are you talking about?' Confused by this,
I find myself turning in small circles under the doorway.

'It's too public. Murph has called it in already and has
been told, from on high, that debriefing is to happen at
the station.' I'm angered by this and grip my phone in my
now sweaty palm, holding it away from my ear and
squeezing the life out of it as if it were Murphy's neck,
accidentally pressing buttons that beep a tune in
Paulson's ear. I take two breaths to calm myself down.

'Jan, are you there?' I hear the faint sound of Paulson's
voice checking to see whether I have thrown the phone
out of a window or dropped it in the bin.

'Yes. I'm here.'

'Look, Jan, I don't have any more information than
that. Murphy wouldn't tell me what the body looked like.
He said that he couldn't.' He leaves a pause for me to fill.

'Couldn't? What's got into him?' We had an agreement to work this case together. If any new evidence was turned up, then I should be the first point of contact.

'I don't know. I'll be there in twenty minutes, so just sit tight and wait for me. I'll see what else I can dig up in that time.' His heavy breathing is cut off abruptly as he hangs up the phone.

As soon as I press the red button on my own phone it starts to ring again. I don't even look at the name on the screen before whipping it back up to my ear.

'Murph?' I ask, anxiously, hoping that he has come to his senses.

It isn't Murph.

A doctor from the hospital is calling to update me on Girl 4's status. She is responding well to treatment and tests show that all her levels indicate repair. There are no signs of paralysis and feeling has returned to her limbs. She is stirring more now, which is a sign of brain activity and that she could wake up very soon.

If I miss her waking up for the first time because Murphy has suddenly decided to show some ambition, I will fucking kill him.

'Thanks for keeping me updated. Much appreciated. If she wakes up, please call me first. Any time of day or night. Thanks.'

Paulson is eighteen minutes away, but Murphy is only four and a half.

That means Paulson will be thirteen and a half minutes too late.

I don't know what to do with myself. What could Murphy have that is so important that it needs to be kept from me? I am the lead investigator on this case.

I sit at my desk and sort it into a neater pile where the largest item is on the bottom and pyramids up to the smallest. I walk over to the whiteboard and wipe it clean. I screw up a piece of paper into a ball and aim it at a bin around ten feet away. It misses.

I pick up a deck of cards from Paulson's desk and shuffle them a few times. I try to guess which card will end up on the top of the pack.

I grab some notes from the desk and pretend to read them. My mind can't handle this tension; nothing I look at makes sense. I'm on death row, waiting for Murphy, the officer I have mentored, to come through the door and dictate the details of my case to me.

I grab the back of Paulson's chair and swivel it around and around for a minute.

I try to ring Murphy, but he doesn't answer.

I put my mobile phone in my mouth and bite down on it with all my force.

Then he walks through the door.

'Murph. What's going on?' I plead, moving closer to him, using all my might not to grab him by the lapels and pin him to the wall.

'January,' he utters calmly. I find it disconcerting, he never uses my full name. Nobody in here is ever called by their real name.

'Yes,' I answer, trying to prompt him into discussion.

'January David, I'm arresting you on suspicion of the murder of Richard Pendragon.'

'What?' I'm stunned at this brazen display of confidence. He seems petrified yet committed to his convictions all at the same time.

He continues, unfazed, 'You do not have to say anything, but it may harm your defence if you do not mention, when questioned, something which you later rely on in court.'

'Oh fuck off, Murph. What are you talking about?' I say as if I think he is joking, but I can see in his expression that he is deadly serious. Two constables arrive behind him in case I struggle.

'Anything you say may be given in evidence.'

Oh, Murph. What do you think you are doing?

Girl 4

———◆———

There are different now. I feel more aware.

When the nurse rubs the sole of my foot with what feels like a wooden drumstick, it tickles me, so I flinch. When they prick my legs and arms with pins, it hurts. Suddenly I have feeling. I'm still asleep, but conscious of the events that are unfolding in my room.

I can hear everything that is being said.

When an enthusiastic nurse tells you to talk to a family member that is in a coma, when she tells you that the person in the persistent vegetative state can hear your voice and that your words can help them or are a comfort to them, it's not true.

Talking to somebody on that much pain medication, in that unconscious state, is as useful as discussing existentialist motifs in Russian literature with a heroin addict who has recently shot up.

I can only assume that January has been to visit me. I couldn't say whether he sat holding my hand for three days feeling guilt and shame, talking non-stop. But something is different now. I don't know how long I have been out for, but I do know that I will be awake again soon.

When I am awake, when they can talk to me properly, I could give them all the information they would need for a conviction.

I know everything.
In this state, I am useless.
Awake, I am dangerous.

January

It feels different on the other side of the interrogation desk. Automatically you feel guilty, even if you are not. I can hear Paulson and Murphy arguing on the outside of the door, while I am left to stew on my own.

'Shove your good-cop, bad-cop routine up your arse, Murph. This is Jan. What the fuck are you thinking?' I should have realised that Paulson was the trustworthy one; I should have invested my confidence in him alone. This was a huge mistake on my part in a game with no room for error.

It's all in the details.

'Oh grow up, Paulson.' I've never heard this side of Murphy before. In a strange way I'm almost proud of him. 'Dreams? Are you kidding me? Thoughts. More like thoughts. Recollections of what he's done to those girls.' Then I hear them muttering and shuffling about before the door swings open.

Murphy leads the way.

Paulson is silent for the rest of the time. His protest over this idiocy.

I'm at a disadvantage, because I don't know if this is even real. If I am awake, or at my desk, tanked up on Scotch waiting for The Smiling Man to inflict his latest dose of cryptic mental torture.

So, when I can't think where I was for two hours after leaving Paulson at Canary Wharf, I start to question myself.

Could I really do something like that?

Where was I when the other girls were killed?

This must show on my face, because I see Paulson's body language towards me change. As if doubting myself transfers uncertainty to my only ally.

I stare out at the air over Murphy's shoulder, screwing my eyes tighter, trying to recall specific moments in time over the last fifteen months. When you have nights where you don't sleep, when that turns into two days or three, it is difficult to determine a Monday from a Tuesday, a Wednesday from a Friday.

The tape recorder is not on. Murphy cannot conduct this investigation. He tries to make me think that this preamble is a courtesy to me, because of our relationship.

'Who is Eames?'

'What?' I ask, genuinely unknowing, honestly still in shock at this situation.

'Eames. Who is he? Is he your alter ego? The name you use when you kill these girls?' Murphy is really sticking it to me here. A barrage of questions to unsettle me, make me sweat.

Paulson looks at me with hope; he wants me to deny it so that he feels justified in his belief in me.

'I don't know what you're talking about, Detective Murphy.' I smirk as I say the word *detective* and he becomes visibly agitated with my petulance. Paulson thinks it's funny too.

Murphy goes on to explain how the courier that delivered a dead man in a giant chest, sealed with a padlock and sword, to the financial heart of London, collected the package from my address and that it was signed for by Eames.

'And you think I'm this Eames character,' I tell him. It is not a question.

Is it even possible that I am Eames?

Could this just be another vision and The Smiling Man is late?

What day is it?

'Why don't you get the courier in here to identify me?' I ask.

'We will, January,' he responds confidently.

They won't.

Eames may have signed for the package and it may have been electronically recorded, but it could never end there. No loose ends. No connections.

The courier had no chance.

Of course he was going to be disposed of. He'll be found later this evening. As an added insult and another declaration of his brilliance, Eames delivered the package himself, then dumped the truck with the young courier's body in the back. Nothing elaborate, a simple strangulation.

This leaves Girl 4 as the only person with concrete knowledge of Eames' identity. She is the one person that can either save me or condemn me.

'Murph, you've got nothing. Circumstantial at best and you fucking know it. And I'll say the same thing to whatever bulldog you've got coming in to try and rattle me.' He's taken aback by this outburst and, although I want to shout, I want to jump across the desk and grab him round the throat, I want to lean my entire weight on his chest with my knee so it is difficult for him to expand his lungs fully, then smash his head repeatedly into the floor, I keep my emotions down; remaining cold is only going to frustrate Murphy.

'All you are doing is hampering this investigation, Murph. If she wakes up and I'm locked in a cell because you decided to grow a set of balls all of a sudden' – I have to pause for a second to collect myself – 'God help you, Murph.'

'Is that a threat?' he asks with the comeback wit of a child.

'Oh grow up, Murph. I'm just saying, if another girl dies because we don't have enough men out there trying to catch the real fucking killer, then on your head be it.'

I'm not talking about this case, though. I'm talking about Cathy.

A moment passes where Murphy and I stare at each other, motionless, neither giving way, then the door crashes open again and two brutes steam in to replace the two officers that used to make up my team. Paulson waddles ahead of Murphy, disgusted and energised to prove my innocence. As they leave, the weight of my name evaporates; my reputation disintegrates and the level of respect I would assume at this station disappears the moment the two strangers enter to work me over.

The second session goes much the same way. This time it is recorded and my interrogators opt for a bad-cop, worse-cop approach which is laughable.

How do they expect me to answer when I don't even know whether I did it myself?

How can I remember the details of a specific date and time from over a year ago without my notebook?

I give them nothing, because I have nothing.

They leave me to sweat, my shirt still stained with

coffee, my perspiration reigniting the scent of the Italian roast as I get warmer.

They come back into the room after a short period, twelve minutes or so, and restart the recording, asking the same questions as before only in a slightly different way. The same way I was trained to do it. The same way they did when Cathy went missing. Trying to make me slip up, trying to glean an extra molecule of information or a differing response that can give something away.

It's frustrating. They keep leaving and coming back. I haven't been to the toilet; the heat in the room is stifling, overbearing. At one point they leave me for so long on my own that I wonder whether they have gone for dinner. The temperature and dehydration is draining and being awake becomes such an onerous task.

But I am still afraid to sleep.

Or wake up.

Whichever state is the opposite to what I am feeling now.

Eventually, when they realise that further persistence this evening is futile I am placed in a cell on my own to think about what I have or haven't done. To go over what I have or haven't seen. To admit to who I have or haven't killed.

But, like a guilty man, I sleep.

And The Smiling Man visits me. Perhaps for the last time.

I have no choice, Girl 6 has to die.

Girl 4

A strip of light and two patches of dark, one at either side.

Then black.

Sometime later another strip of light with the same dark towers at either side.

My eyes are open, but I cannot lift the lids to see out fully. My strength is diminished. But I am awake.

With my mouth open I suck in the dry air of the hospital. As I exhale I smile languidly, trying to lift my head from the pillow. I lick my dry lips slowly and attempt to lift the weight of my eyelids once more, but to no avail. My head falls to the side and I can make out one of the dark shapes to be a man. Adjusting slightly I see another figure only feet away from him.

Even with two guards at my door I know this isn't over. I'm not safe. Where is January?

I summon enough strength to curl my fingers and ball them into a fist, but I do not have the strength behind them to punch, to fend off an attack or kidnapping attempt. I can't protect myself. I cannot be protected.

I lick my lips again, searching for moisture, and try to speak, but nothing comes out. My body still finds a way for me to cough. My torso tightens at this reflex jolting all my organs into spasm, the tension tearing open some of the wounds that had started to heal. The rip is deafening, the sting is excruciating.

I'm just happy to feel pain again.

It's the agony that lets me know I am alive.

But now I need to rest, because as soon as I have the energy Eames won't have to figure a way to take me from the hospital. As soon as I am able to stand on my own I am walking out of here myself.

I'll be back in control.

January

The walls are white; the mattress has lost all spring and buoyancy. It used to be white too, but is yellowing with age and the sweat from many a felon's worried back. It's cold in here too, which should be a punishment but is a welcome change from the humidity of the interrogation room. All of these details go unnoticed from the other side, the side of justice.

I lean against the wall for a few minutes just to have the frigid bricks against my back. My head smashes solidly backwards against the masonry, shaking my brain for a second and making me see stars for even less than that.

But I can't fight it any longer.

I want to figure out a way to get out of this situation, but I have been awake since Wednesday, or Thursday – unless today is Wednesday or Thursday – so I slide down the wall, gradually untucking my shirt as I do so, and, before I even hit the dusty concrete floor of my cell, I'm asleep.

This is the last time I expect to be in this position. Tied up, blind, waiting for the sound of his shuffling feet. Terrified at the thought of his dark, horrifyingly cheerful, grotesque face.

I don't know if this is a dream or if he is appearing to

me in person again, like he did the night before the wedding, because the scene is different.

I am tied to the bed in my cell. Not the basic wooden chair in The Smiling Man's dark, dusty perpetual alternate reality. I'm still blindfolded like always.

It is cold this time, just as it is in the real-world cell, but it is completely silent.

And then he arrives.

The scuffing feet dragging his huge frame from side to side as he prepares to parade the Girl 6 dance to me. Telling me how she is going to die or telling me how I am going to kill her.

He whips my blindfold off, leaving me attached to the bed, my hands tied to the bar of the headboard with an oily bike chain, my feet attached at the other end by two more chains.

As soon as I open my eyes, he vanishes.

Shocked, I look around at the four walls, left right, behind my head, then he reappears in front of me. Smiling, he wags his finger at me again and shakes his head as though disappointed in me for some reason.

I want to speak to him. I want to tell him that I know not what I do. But nothing comes out. Still, he places his wagging finger gently against his beaming lips, as if to say *Sshhh*.

Then he disappears again.

Two seconds later he materialises at my bedside. He bends at his waist and places one of his shovel-like hands on my wrists, while taking one last gaze deep into my eyes. When he straightens his body, I realise that the chain binding my hands to the bed has disappeared and I can bring my arms comfortably down to my side.

He walks backwards carefully, never taking his eyes

off me. For the last four steps he points his hand directly at my chest, his fingers outstretched, and, with each step, I sit up a little more, until I am completely upright. Like an invisible force is pulling me towards him.

He turns around and faces the wall.

I wait. Mesmerised to see what will happen next. What is he going to do?

He does nothing. He just stands there with his back to me.

But I can't look away.

He raises his arms from his side and clamps his knees tightly together to form a perfect symmetrical cross.

Then he flies.

He rises up in the air by two feet, then three feet, then four.

Levitating before me, he stops at a height just above the bed frame, then his arms drop back down to his side, his head droops forward and blood begins to drip from his shoes, forming a puddle on the floor beneath where he floats.

And finally I understand.

I know what he is telling me. I've seen this before.

It makes sense now. Of course there is no link between the girls. It's the way that they are killed. The elaborate way they are all taken.

I think I know who Eames is. I know the killer.

And I wake up.

Standing at the door to my cell I make a fist ready to punch against the door. I need to get the attention of someone, so I can let them know how the next girl is going to die, so that they can save her. I need to tell them who is killing these innocents.

But I have to stop myself.

This will just incriminate me further in their eyes. It will make me look even more insane.

I wrestle with the decision for hours, pacing the room, punching the walls until my knuckles bleed. I have to scream inside, because I don't want to draw attention to myself. I perch on the edge of the bed, shaking uncontrollably.

I've made my decision.

I put my own self-interest first and the interest of my wife, who I have already let down so much. I can't let anything happen to her again and I know he will want her.

The only way I can stop this villain, the only way that I can save myself and Girl 4, Audrey, is to let Girl 6 be taken.

The only way I can prove to them – perhaps even to myself – I am not Eames, I am not the serial killer terrorising our great capital, is to still be locked in this room when they find Stacey Blaine levitating in her Hackney garage.

Who am I to say one life is more important than another?

What gives me the right to condemn to death someone I have never met?

This is not a decision a person can ever get over. So, even though I will catch him – I won't stop until I catch him – Eames has won. He's beaten me.

Eames

Stacey Blaine is the final stepping stone that takes me back to Audrey.

My prize.

The one that got away.

Girl 6 is so important to me, to the overall piece. She is the last difficulty. Suspended in the air via a scaffolding pole that is placed lovingly through her stomach, she will appear to be defying gravity when Detective Inspector January David first opens that garage door.

Another floating corpse.

The long coat I placed on her will cover the pole protruding through her back. The long wooden broom handle threaded through the arm holes of her rain mac helps to keep her arms out straight, perpendicular from her milky white torso.

Just for some religious flavour.

Just for the imagery.

He will recognise what it is straight away. But that is the idea. This is the point at which he is supposed to solve the case. Finally, he will understand the reason that each girl was chosen. Finally, he will work out why each girl I killed had to be done in such a specific way. Eventually, he will understand why I did not kill Girl 4. Why I still need her.

But that moment will come too late.

Detective Inspector January David has not learned the importance of family; he is still occupied with the case. He wants to be the hero.

In real life, the hero doesn't always win.

Good does not always triumph over evil.

One thing is certain: he will let his wife down again.

When someone has to kill, when they have a hunger for it, when that thirst for death becomes so insatiable that it doesn't matter whose life you take, when it becomes more about the killer than the work, that's not me.

The way Girl 3 died was more important than me.

The way Girl 6 is being used to send the police to the wrong place is more important than me.

Audrey David is more important than me.

If the Detective Inspector felt the same way about his wife, he might stand a chance of winning.

Girl 6

———◆———

I say goodbye to my boys for the weekend; this is always the hardest part. Ben is seven and Max is five. I cry inside every time I see them walk away from me, Ben holding Max's hand, comforting him, because he doesn't yet understand why his mummy and daddy don't live together any more; Ben doesn't even fully comprehend it yet himself.

I have full custody.

Because I am the mother.

Because I'm not the adulterous one.

Because I would never use my own children as leverage to get something I wanted.

Because it was the right thing to do.

But losing my job has put me under some strain. I have applied for jobs online, registered with recruiters, posted my CV to countless companies that aren't even advertising vacancies. I've walked the high street and spoken to every manager that will see me.

Because I don't want to claim benefits.

Because I want to provide for my children myself.

Unfortunately, this means that I have to work several jobs so that I can give them what they want, what they need. But this means relying on my ex-husband to look after them more, to do me favours. It means lumbering

278

them on my parents more than I want to. It means that I can provide for them independently, but the time I spend with them has diminished considerably.

And time is something I no longer have.

In two hours' time I will be Girl 6. Dangling in a garage from a large tube of metal that rips through my stomach.

I'm a human detour sign.

In two hours' time I'll be dead; I won't be able to help my boys. The last thing I heard from them was Max asking Ben why he couldn't just stay at home tonight.

Even if they had, I'd still be dead.

Either way, I'm about to take their already tarnished young lives and plough through them with a wrecking ball.

I don't know why he chose me, why I am significant. Why I was the best fit for the diversion. What I do know is that he isn't just killing one person tonight. Just to fulfil some twisted desire and turn an empty garage in Hackney into the scenic route on the way to justice, he is taking the life of two innocent boys.

Is that part of the art?

Is that another inconsequential section of the master plan?

An hour after the kids leave me for the last time, after I try to smoke myself to death, I leave the house unenthused about my night-job filling vending machines in a large office block for a Chinese company that appears to work around the clock.

As I crouch down at the end of my drive to unlock the chain from my bike, I feel a prick in the back of my neck and the knife through my stomach.

In the morning, a room full of men from China will

press number sixty hoping for hot chocolate with extra foam and sugar and will be disappointed with a cup of warm water.

January

---◆---

The envelope-sized rectangular hatch on the scuffed white door of my cell drops open, letting in a stream of light from the hallway outside. With no windows and no watch, the most I can determine is that I have been awake a long time, probably through the night.

I'm still perched on the edge of the creaking bed frame, my elbows resting on my thighs, cutting off some of the circulation, my head resting in my hands, which cover my face. The ring finger on each hand is wedged into the corner of each eye, acting as a tear damn, preventing emotion from showing on my face.

'Jan,' the voice whispers through the porthole.

I remain in position, my state of suspended animation, my posture of torture, retaining the pain of guilt for as long as possible; this is where I will draw my strength.

The voice tries again. 'Psst. Jan. Wake up.' This time a little gruffer, not realising that I am awake, that I'm always awake.

Paulson's podgy face blocks the opening; he tries to manoeuvre himself sideways to get a better look at me. 'It's Audrey,' he says next, expectantly.

This gets my attention.

Dropping my arms down urgently I jump up from the sweat-stained mattress. Not realising the numbness that has set into my legs, I buckle and crash to the floor. The blood oozing back to my thighs tingles with a mixed sense of pain and tickling and I have to lie on my back for a minute.

Paulson raises himself to his toes, trying to look down at me.

'You all right, Jan?' he asks, concerned.

'I'm fine. I'm fine. What's going on with Audrey? Is she OK?' I try to straighten my legs, thinking that it will make the blood flow easier, but any movement sends a string of needles through my muscles.

'She's fine. Don't worry. It's nothing major. The doctor called to say that she is moving now and stirring.'

'Is she awake?' I panic, rubbing my thighs to speed up the process.

'No. Not yet, but the doctor is confident that it won't be long now. He says all the signs are positive and tests show no permanent damage apart from some minor scarring. I thought you'd want to know.'

I stop struggling to get to my feet and release the tension in my neck, forcing the back of my head to hit the floor with a crack, momentarily distracting my brain from the sensation in my legs. I lie there for a second in contemplation, knowing I want to be with Audrey instead of helpless in this tomb. Trying to understand and justify my reason for condemning a stranger to death.

'Thanks, man,' I say, relieved.

'No worries. You won't be in here much longer, you know?' He seems so genuine.

I consider telling him about the dream. The latest vision where Girl 6 will be found, supposedly, levitating. Eames' latest sadistic adaptation.

But I can't tell him.

Paulson has shown me that he can be trusted, but I can't take the risk that actually he can't. I can't do anything that will jeopardise me getting out of here. Getting to Eames. To Girl 6.

Getting to Audrey.

I know that they can't keep me here much longer. They have nothing on me apart from conspiracy and circumstance. It's not like I'm on suspicion of blowing up Parliament. The death of Girl 6 just means that I can get out an hour earlier.

'If she wakes up while I'm in here, you keep Murphy away from me when I get out,' I say half-menacingly, half-joking.

'I'll keep him away from you anyway, I think.' And he laughs. 'Hang in there, Jan.'

He closes the hatch to the real world and leaves me stranded on the floor, legs still flailing, pins still pricking; but the sensation is wearing off and allows me to sit up.

By the time I've regained full control of my body, clambered back to the edge of the bed and resumed my position of despair, the door opens and the dimwit duo arrive to take me back upstairs for further questioning.

The two barbarians drag me back into the interrogation room to continue their predictable pantomime. I wonder if the police investigating Cathy's disappearance were like this. If they were this useless. I haven't slept again, knowing that Girl 6 will be dead shortly.

As the questioning recommences they restart the recording, again stating my name and dictating the time. When I hear this I know that she will be gone soon.

And I have let her die. That isn't any different from

pulling the trigger myself or firing the arrows or feeding the cigarettes.

'It took you two hours to get back from Canary Wharf?' the taller, balder idiot asks.

'Haven't I answered that already?' I sigh, rolling my eyes.

'Just answer the question,' his sidekick adds, getting more involved today.

'Do you want the same answer as before or something different?' I joke sarcastically, knowing that the two dummies across the table from me don't have the composure to handle my insolence.

'Don't get smart,' bald cretin bleats.

'Just answer the question,' groans Detective Halfwit in support.

I laugh.

Looking unhinged. Looking guilty.

'I stopped for coffee. No, no, wait, there were Tube delays. Actually, I walked it . . . on my hands. I've told you I can't remember.' They look at me in dismay, disgusted, for wasting police time. They are the ones wasting police time, I think angrily; Murphy is the one wasting police time. Having me cooped up inside this room talking the same conversation with Inspector Imbecile and his moronic man-friend – that is a waste of fucking time. They have me sequestered like a common criminal, forgetting everything I have done for this department, ignoring my commitment to the force, to the law and justice. They are disregarding me on a personal level, neglecting my record, stripping me of any influence I once had. Meanwhile the real killer is still out there on the streets plotting his next victim.

Conspiring to make Girl 4 his Girl 7.

'Shall we call it a day, lads? I've got nothing new I can tell you,' I ask after this cat-and-mouse game has continued for a while. I am not expecting their response.

'You like to drink?'

'What? What do you mean?' This is a cheap blow aimed at agitating me, shaking me up. And I know it's come from Murphy.

'Is that why you can't remember where you were?'

'I found my wife hanging by fishing line from the ceiling of a theatre. Her face was bleeding into a plastic coffin and she hasn't woken up since.' I speak through gritted teeth, alternating my gaze between the Neanderthals. They know they have got to me. I know I'm lying. I was drinking before that happened. I use Audrey as an excuse to vindicate my actions.

'Maybe you put her there,' the schmuck assistant proudly says, directly to my face.

I react instantly, innately, backhanding the plastic cup full of water in front of me. The liquid sprays out across the desk, temporarily compromising the vision of Detectives Simpleton and Nitwit. Almost in the same movement I launch myself forward, diving across the table, my arms outstretched, fingers stiff like talons, and grab the insensitive chump who insults my wife; one hand on the chest of his shirt, the other on his throat.

His chair falls backwards as I land on top of him, forcing his neck into the ground. His jughead partner still battling with the shock, rubbing his eyes to clear them. I only have a brief second to perform one swift punch to the face before my other arm is yanked up behind my back, my thumb locked into place and my own face forced to scrape along the carpet.

The lummox I attacked stops the tape, clarifying the time and reason for terminating the interview. Then he kicks me in the ribs as my right cheek begins to form a red burn mark from grazing the floor.

They both utter some masculine obscenities in my direction until someone knocks on the door loudly. I stop struggling at this point.

It's Paulson, and Murphy is stood behind him, partially obscured by my angle down low.

'What's going on here?' Paulson barks, exerting some authority, even though he has none in this matter.

'He attacked me,' the dipstick whimpers.

'Get him up off the floor. Now!' Paulson orders, coming into his own. 'He's not the guy we're looking for.'

'What?' The detective glances at me with his best impression of a withering look, trying to warn me not to get any ideas. 'How do you know that?'

Murphy finally steps out from behind Paulson's large frame. 'We've just found another girl. Get off him. He's coming with us.' It looks as though he has retained some of the confidence that inflated him after his backstabbing false accusation, but it will take a lot more than releasing me to redeem him in my eyes.

The bald ignoramus on my back releases his grip and eases the weight on my lumbar region. Still, I wriggle as if the struggle is two-way and, when I get to my feet, I straighten my rancid coffee-covered shirt as if to say, 'Told you so.'

'Jan, we should get going. You really need to see this,' Paulson urges.

I look almost pityingly at the two arseholes who have done their best to rattle me for information over the last two days. 'Thanks, fellas,' I say triumphantly, 'that was a memorable couple of days. Really,' I joke, and hold my hand out to the sap I attacked, a bruise already forming around his right eye. They were just doing their jobs. I guess I know that.

He doesn't shake my hand.

I smile, the better man, and head to the door.

'You.' I point my finger a few millimetres from Murphy's nose and see him go cross-eyed as he tries to look at the tip. 'You fucked up.' His eyes tilt upwards to look at mine.

'I know, Jan, look –'

I cut him off before he starts some kind of shame-faced, heartfelt apology. 'You've wasted enough time. Come on.' I motion for them both to follow me. Walking out the door I push my shoulder into Murphy, nudging him back slightly. He accepts this and they both follow me downstairs – Murphy, I sincerely hope, with his tail firmly between his legs.

The car journey to the garage in which Girl 6 has been discovered is silent, apart from the screams and obscenities that I shout with my eyes in the rear-view mirror at Murphy, who sits, sheepishly remorseful, on the back seat.

We pull up outside the garage, which is closed. It hasn't been tampered with or taped off yet. No crowds have formed; no newspapers are aware yet. They have done what they should have done with Girl 5 and come straight to me.

Nervously, I lift the door on its rails, with painful knowledge of what I will find inside. The light from the street lamps is enough to confirm what I already know.

The outline of her body depicts her in the same

position as The Smiling Man in my vision. The same way I remember it looking as a child. I swallow hard on revulsion at the grim scene.

'So, who have we got here, then?' I camouflage my real thoughts, voicing the expected response out loud.

'It's, er, Girl 6, Jan,' Murphy warbles in my direction.

'I know that much, Murph. I can count. I mean, what is her name?'

'Blaine. Her name is Stacey Blaine,' Paulson confirms, taking out his notepad.

Blaine. I say the name in my head a few times, while deconstructing the image before me.

I rub my rough, dry hands across my stubble, as if washing my face. I was hoping that I'd got it wrong, that the dreams meant nothing in the end, but this is the last clue I need.

I know the killer.

It is so clear to me now.

The way that each girl died. The reason I got involved.

It all points towards my father.

Girl 4

✦

When the alarm sounds I know it's the end.

Eames is here for me.

I have been conserving my energy for this moment, not showing the nurses that I have regained consciousness, because I don't want the hassle that would inevitably follow.

What do you remember?

Can you see his face?

Would you be able to recognise him from a photo?

I don't need all that right now.

I just need to get out of this hospital.

Despite numerous practices and training sessions, an alarm of any kind invokes panic and trepidation in even the most composed people. One of the guards instantly heads into another room, a quieter room, to make the call to January informing him of the current situation.

I pull the tubing away from my nose and arms; my left hand still has a one-inch tube protruding from it as a result of the anaesthesia. It hurts when I rip the tape away that is holding it in place.

Then the power goes out.

I know he is here.

*

The lights flicker back on and a million beeps alert the staff that the back-up generator has kicked into action. But the short lag causes pandemonium for visitors and the alarm continues to exacerbate the situation. Anybody could walk in and out of the building without being noticed amid the panicking rabble.

The second guard looks back and notices me struggling. His instinct tells him to find a doctor, find someone who can help.

His instinct is wrong.

The doctor that he finds in the hallway among the crowd of bemused medical interns and flapping family members is not a doctor at all.

My arms tire and my eyelids grow heavy. I know he is near, but I can't stay awake. I can hear everything, though. I hear the guard return with someone. It is a voice I have heard before.

'She's not safe in here. I need to move her to another room,' he says, sounding concerned. Like he knows Eames is here too.

The guard lets the doctor take me away.

He lets Eames take me away.

'Stay here in case this guy comes looking for her. I'm taking her to Level Three, Nuffield Ward, room two-forty-three. You got that?' he asks.

'Level Three, Nuffield, two-forty-three,' he repeats back to him, back to the killer's face.

He wheels me down the corridor at break-neck speed, obviously ignoring the crowds hovering around the halls. To an onlooker it gives the impression of an emergency, but when we get in the lift I feel the sensation that we are going down to the ground level rather than up to Level Three.

Still drowsy I sense each fluorescent bulb pass over my head, seeing the white through my eyelids. I count them down the corridor – four . . . five . . . nine . . . twelve – then I am hit with a blast of fresh air that blows my smock up around my waist. Almost kindly he pulls it down to preserve my dignity.

I notice the surface below my trolley-bed change, becoming rougher as we bobble over the tarmac to the car park. The air outside reinvigorates me, but still the oxygen will not pump to my muscles.

He picks me up over his shoulder and places me inside the car, buckling my seatbelt with almost parental concern.

The door slams as he gets in the other side.

'Don't worry, Mrs David. This will all be over soon.'

Eames has me again.

January

We drive back to the station and I'm apprehensive. The last time I opened up, when I went against my better judgement and discussed The Smiling Man, it backfired. His appearances support my idea, but I'm starting to realise these visions are for me alone.

Taking a breath and keeping my eyes on the road, I suggest that I may know who the killer is – that it may, in fact, be my own father. They are silent to begin with. I look over at Paulson, flabbergasted in the passenger seat. He puffs his cheeks out and curses in disbelief. In the mirror Murphy deliberately avoids my gaze, but after my false arrest they owe me the chance to follow my hunch. We still have some work to do. We need to conduct a little more research to determine the truth.

We head for the incident room, each settling into our usual chairs, falling into our accustomed poses, surrounding ourselves with the standard police paraphernalia; computers, notepads, whiteboard and, most importantly, coffee, plenty of coffee.

While Paulson and Murphy clear their desks, check for any messages and generally hunker into position ready for the task at hand, I channel into my own thoughts, focusing with precision on what I know, what I don't know, and what cannot be known.

What I do know is that my father – the man that I saw smiling through the window of my mother's eventual room of enforced rest – was not the same man that I knew as a child. He was a bitter, twisted man who took pleasure in the torture and suffering of his wife and only son.

For over a year he has been trying to regain contact with me; in the process he has tormented my wife with sinister phone calls, possibly designed to terrify her.

What I remember of my father as a child was the fun, the entertainment; that was his job. He would tour the south and east coasts performing his brand of humour, impressions and magic. Often left in our mother's care, Cathy and I were always ecstatic when he returned home from a trip. But the day Cathy went missing was the day his love died.

It died for me, because he blamed me; she was in my care.

It died for Mum, because she was insistent that she knew Cathy was all right, that she had been visited by an apparition who could confirm this.

It died for his work, because you can't make jokes when all you feel is pain and despair. You can't impersonate others when you no longer know who you are. And you cannot perform illusions when your own sense of reality has been distorted out of all proportion.

Finding Girl 6 in that position, I was immediately reminded of my father.

I remember a trick he would always perform to baffle Cathy and me. He would move over to the corner of the room, turn his back on us, but on a slight angle, put his legs close together, his arms out so that he looked like a giant Jesus, and he would levitate. He would fly.

At least that's what we thought as kids.

Obviously, he was disguising his left foot with his right foot. Simply by pushing himself up on to the toe of his left foot and keeping his right foot flat, parallel with the ground, he could give the illusion that he was six inches off the floor.

When The Smiling Man last appeared to me, and as I finally saw Girl 6, I was reminded of this fantastic moment in my childhood when I still had parents. When I still had a sister.

This trick has developed over the years and technology has improved it, whether this is through camera trickery or magnetised shoes with secret trouser openings, people recognise this trick. Many would associate it with the modern street magician David Blaine.

Summoning the performer's name ignites a dormant section of my mind.

I focus, delving into the recess, hoping to trigger the response I need. Searching for the grain that will initiate a trail of thought that leads to solution.

And it registers.

Something clicks.

Stacey Blaine.

She wasn't chosen to die at the hands of this deranged man because she had a link to any of the other girls; she was simply born with the wrong name.

They all were.

I move towards the whiteboard and in bold letters inscribe the surnames of all the girls. Under Girl 6 I write Stacey BLAINE. Under that I write *David Blaine*. Under that I write, and underline, <u>*Levitation*</u>.

Across the rest of the board I frenetically write each girl's number and her name, with each surname in capital letters.

PENN, MORETTI, MULLICA, DAVID, PENDRAGON.

'I need you to look these names up in relation to magic and magicians,' I instruct without turning around. 'I want to find out if each one is known for a specific trick and, if they are, I want to know what it is called and whether it relates to the way in which these girls died.' I am focused, purposeful. I tell Paulson and Murphy to hit the Internet and start researching. We split the research into three. Murphy looks for Girls 1 and 2; Paulson has 3 and 5, while I take . . . Girl 4.

For a few minutes, the room is quiet with concentration; only the hum of computers is audible as we weave our way through cyberspace. I see Paulson's and Murphy's shoulders hunched over their keyboards, their heads leaning close to the screens as if this will get the information to them quicker. Eager, intent, determined; on my side. I briefly savour the feeling of being back where I belong.

As we unpick the individual riddles of the case, our collective revelation is exhilarating, but, for me, also terrifyingly chilling.

Firstly, The PENDRAGONS were a duo most famous for their Metamorphosis act. A routine which sees a man lock a woman inside a chest, which is sealed with a padlock and sword. For added difficulty she is placed inside a large red sack, which is tied tightly with rope before the lid is closed on her.

The man then takes a large sheet and stands on top of the locked chest. He throws the curtain up in the air in front of him, but is only out of sight behind the fabric for a split second. As it drops, the woman that was originally secured into the case, tied up in the bag, is now stood in place on the chest, looking more glamorous than when we saw her last. Opening the case reveals the man now fastened in the red sack. This happens before an audience in a matter of seconds.

They metamorphose.

The man takes the place of the woman inside the confines of the chest. Figuratively speaking, he turns into a woman.

What we know is that Richard Pendragon, Girl 5, was treated in the same way, only this time it was a more sadistic take on a classic magic trick. The fundamental elements were all in place – the style of chest, the sword, the fabric – but the trick itself was taken too literally. By cutting off his penis and glamorising him with make-up and a wig, my father was literally taking away his manhood. Turning him into a woman.

What I know is that it goes so much further than this.

Because I know what The Smiling Man has shown me.

The magical element has been present in all of his messages, but, like all good magicians succeed in doing, I was misdirected towards something else, so that the illusion could take place behind the scenes. He made himself disappear and reappear in the last vision; the bullets emerged from his sleeve when he warned me about Girl 1 – a classic part of magic mythology; a magician always keeps something up their sleeve – and the arrows were produced from the inside of the jacket when he tried to alert me to Girl 2's impending demise.

Paulson fingers his screen as he shows me the information, invisibly underlining information that supports this theory. He can't disguise his excitement; his coffee still untouched, cooling through neglect. I try to hide my fear, suppressing my extra information from The Smiling Man.

I approach the whiteboard again, deep in my thoughts,

determined now to piece things together. Under Girl 5, Richard PENDRAGON, I write: *The Pendragons*, *Metamorphosis*.

Murphy raises a hand to signal that he's found some information regarding MORETTI.

'Performed by Hans Moretti in 1995.' We gather round his desk and Murphy plays us a video clip of the trick he has found online.

It is exactly the way Carla died.

I watch the tape, my imagination superimposing tragic images of Girl 2.

Hans Moretti is a bald magician with a laughable handlebar moustache. His wife, Helga, is his partner. He sticks two plasters over his eyes, then covers them with a black blindfold. Then he spins in a circle like a dizzy child with a crossbow in his hands pointing towards the ceiling. He stops, facing away from his wife, who has now placed herself directly behind him with an apple on her head.

She rings a bell in front of the apple.

He shoots the arrow over his shoulder to make it more difficult and misses the apple by a matter of centimetres.

Helga is not pleased. He asks her a question and she shouts 'No!' in his direction. Each of us stifle a laugh at her reaction.

They start the process again.

'According to this information, in all the times they have performed the trick, Helga has only been injured twice,' Murphy spurts, desperate to share his research; to prove himself valuable again.

Carla was injured three times before the final arrow killed her.

We continue to watch, enthralled.

This time they go through the same process. Spinning in a circle, blindfold on, crossbow over shoulder, ringing the bell, hoping he hits it. This time he is successful. The arrow cuts straight through the centre of the fruit, attaching it to a bullseye above his wife's head.

Eames didn't manage this once.

Dad didn't manage it once.

Under Girl 2, Carla MORETTI I write, *Hans and Helga Moretti*, *Crossbow*.

My shoulders stiffen with tension as I become increasingly convinced by my theory, but I am still searching for a magician with the surname David to prove it conclusively. David Blaine, David Copperfield, David Roth, but none with the surname. Damn. I have to be on the right track here. It all fits too well.

Then a random thought drifts across my mind: David. My father has the same surname. What if that was *his* trick?

'Penn & Teller.' Murphy suddenly leaps out of his seat, his whole body for once projecting excitement. 'Of course, The Bullet Catch,' he announces. 'They are famous for it.' He looks giddy, like a child would look at a birthday party if someone were performing magic in front of them.

What I know is that Penn & Teller performed an illusion on stage in 1996 that they said was the most dangerous trick in the world. A feat where both men fire a gun at the same time, both guns aimed at the opposite person, both men catching the bullet between their teeth. The bullets are fired through a pane of glass to show that they leave the guns. They are signed by members of the audience before being loaded.

What I know is that The Smiling Man placed a bullet between my teeth in a similar manner.

What I don't know is why he swallowed his.

What I don't know is why he rushed at the chair that appeared next to me.

I lean back in my seat, closing my eyes for a second and trying to clear my brain; to keep thinking clearly. Spurred on by my theory, we have made a huge amount of progress on the case in one swoop, but the things I still don't know are the things that will help put it to rest for ever.

The room buzzes with activity. Never are all three of us sitting down. Either we are crowded around one screen or writing on the board or coaxing the paper out of the printer to see the text quicker. It's the urgency we needed from the start.

I grab my pen again and stride to the whiteboard once more.

Under Girl 1, Dorothy PENN, I write: *Penn & Teller, Bullet Catch*.

'Jan, I've found the Mullica trick,' Paulson announces proudly.

I don't respond. I have just realised why I found Girl 4, Audrey David, my wife, in the position she was in.

I force myself to put those thoughts on hold; to work methodically. I turn to Paulson and listen to his findings.

Tom Mullica performs his trick on stage with a handful of cigarettes. Starting with four, he lights them individually, then proceeds to hide them in his mouth while he lights four more. These also go into his mouth, as if he has swallowed them. After a short time they reappear as a bunch of cigarettes that fill his mouth, stretching his lips around them and puffing heavily. The final part of the act sees him fill any available space within his mouth with tissue paper. Once full it appears that he completely swallows the entire contents in one swift gulp.

Obviously Eames, which I assume for now is my father's magician name, took the premise of the prestidigitation and perverted it into a colourful execution, where Girl 3 was forced to inhale the toxic smoke and asphyxiate on the sheer volume of cigarettes overtaxing her jaw.

What we know is that one hundred and fifty-six cigarettes were found, some ingested.

What I know is that there were the same amount of Smiling Men in my dream.

What we don't know is the reason for Girl 3's appearance; the jump cables and wires that bound her, the contortion of her body.

Under Girl 3, Amy MULLICA, I make Paulson write *Tom Mullica, Cigarette Eating*.

I turn back to my own computer and stare unseeingly at the screen, instead looking inwardly to my own thoughts. My research session has uncovered something that rocks my core. A definitive list of the greatest magic tricks of all time. Looking down the final fifteen, a shiver runs through me as I start to wonder whether there have been more girls that we have missed.

What I don't know yet is that Audrey is still needed.

Out of the top eleven tricks, we have found girls that correspond with six of them. It still leaves Richard Ross' *Linking Rings*, Paul Daniels' *Chop Cup*, Robert Harbin's *Zig-Zag Girl*, which I can already see as a murder scene in my mind, and Lance Burton's *Doves*.

Number five is David Copperfield's *Flying*.

She wasn't supposed to be a floating corpse; she was supposed to be a *flying* corpse.

In this awe-inspiring act of conjuring, David Copperfield flies around the stage. The background appears to be like the sky, the floor is a sea of dry ice. Just the way we found Girl 4.

The audience believes that he must be attached to strong wires that are undetectable with the human eye. To discard that theory, he flies through hoops – a concept seen in other floating tricks. However, to take the magic further, he drops himself into a large perspex box – like the transparent coffin directly below the floating corpse – and the lid is closed on him to inhibit the use of wires.

For seconds he lies on the bottom of the box until he lifts up again, flying and floating in the contained area, amazing all that watch him.

To me, this is the most impressive of all.

I wonder whether my father would have known that before he took Audrey.

Under Girl 4, Audrey DAVID, I write *David Copperfield, Flying*.

I scan the list on the whiteboard and see that every girl chosen has the same surname as the great magician who performed the associated trick – apart from Girl 4. Her surname is the first name of the magician. Possibly the most revered illusionist of our time.

What I know is that Audrey did not die.

What I don't know is that she wasn't supposed to.

I see that the only trick left untouched is known as The Death Saw. It sounds overly dramatic, but this is commonly regarded as the best trick of all time.

Another by David Copperfield.

Another for Audrey David.

What I don't know is that he still needs her. To complete his masterpiece. A series of the greatest magic tricks in history, all carried out, performed, by the same man. Only the conclusion, the reveal moment, is far more callous and brutal than ever seen.

My father, who ceased to perform in any capacity the moment that Cathy was taken, has returned for one last rendition.

He wants to conduct the most remembered piece of visual art for our generation.

The greatest trick of all time.

And cause me to suffer the way he feels only he has for the last two decades.

But The Smiling Man has not revealed himself to me. So, learning to accept his appearances as trustworthy, I know that no girl is in any immediate danger. I think the reason he didn't appear for Girl 4 was because she didn't die; there was nothing to warn me about. She will be fine, I tell myself.

I think about The Smiling Man. I recall my father's face as he voyeuristically enjoyed my reunion with my mother. As he saw the wound of Cathy's disappearance open up again when I realised my mother was right all along.

I think The Smiling Man is supposed to represent my father.

I look at the evidence on the whiteboard and compare it with the visions I have endured and I know it is him. I know it's my father.

But what we know is only what we think we know.

Eames

◆

When I look at Audrey's face as she lies in the passenger seat unconscious, her hospital smock hitched up to display some of the cuts across her thighs, I know it's nearly over.

I know he's coming to get me.

My work is almost done.

I take my left hand off the gearstick and place it delicately on her leg, running my fingertips lightly over the tender ridges of her lacerations, admiring my work; it's close to being sexual. As I stroke upwards on her thigh, my hands move against the grain of the tiny hairs that have started to grow on her legs while inactive at the hospital. I push the crumpled material up towards her waist, so that I can see between her legs.

I glance at the traffic snailing along in front of me, then flit my eyes up to the mirror to gauge whether I am being followed.

I'm not.

He still doesn't know that she is gone.

I place my hand between her legs, resting it on top, so that I can feel the warmth of her soft flesh. I don't go any further than this; I don't massage the area or insert my fingers. That's not right. That's not me.

A car makes a sharp stop in front of me and I press

down hard on the brake, moving my left hand back to the steering wheel. I'm expecting a possible impact with the car ahead and brace myself, stiffening my arms, but Audrey is still not awake and her supple frame is thrown forwards and blocked aggressively when the seatbelt locks into place.

She doesn't wake up.

The driver in front makes a gesture in his mirror to show his irritation. I imagine ramming his rear bumper on purpose, then getting out of my seat, walking over to his open window and wrapping the seatbelt around his neck tightly, his engine revving as he pushes down on the accelerator, trying to wriggle out of the situation.

Then she stirs.

I hear her voice grumble, her throat crackle.

And I want my face to be the first thing she sees.

I wonder how far away from the truth Detective Inspector January David is.

This is the final trick.

The one I will be remembered for.

Has he learned his lesson?

Timing is crucial. Detective Inspector January David must return to the last place that he found his wife. The same stage she graced with her flying naked body. This time, as with the last, she will still be alive; I can give him this much. But the entire process would have been in vain if he is not there to watch the saw drop suddenly, cutting through the waist of his exquisite wife, dividing her into two pieces, neither of which make me feel any more inclined to share her with someone else.

The image in my mind is arousing.

I turn my head to look at her again; my beguiling charm.

She opens her eyes and I smile at her.

'Hello, Girl 7, are you ready to be remembered?'

January

All three of us stare at the whiteboard like it's a floating corpse. Paulson to my left, Murphy to my right. He leaves a little space; our relationship is still tender.

'Looks pretty conclusive, Jan,' Paulson says, not turning his head away from the board.

'I don't know how you did it, but it has to be, right?' Murphy chucks his opinion into the mix.

I resist the urge to comment, to take a swipe at him for his momentary lapse of judgement when he suspected that I was behind it.

But I am involved. This is all being done for my benefit. These girls are being killed to hurt me. To make me feel the pain of the killer himself.

The evidence seems irrefutable. These are the reasons that each girl was slain in such a specific way, down to the most microscopic of details. The motives seem clear, but not decisive.

'Let's bring him in,' I tell them, still staring at the portion of the board that says *Girl 4, Audrey David.* 'Let's fucking end this.'

During the time of our estrangement I have in fact had the resources to find my father; to try to apologise or make it up to him, to try to explain my side; but I would never abuse my power as a police officer. Before The Smiling Man entered my life I would never step a foot outside the rule book. But I have a reason now.

I need to bring my own father in.

It's my job to talk to him now.

He moved back to Islington, near where we lived as a family, eight years ago. A small flat in a cul-de-sac of housing that horse-shoes around the top of a hill.

The front door is not at street level; you have to go up a flight of stairs under a badly lit arch. He is too old now to run and there is no way out for him.

I knock on the door firmly. 'Mr David,' I say in a low tone, as if disguising my voice. It feels wrong somehow to refer to him in this manner, even though he hasn't been my father for years.

I knock again. 'Mr David, this is the police. Can you please open the door? We need to ask you a few questions.'

Perhaps an understatement.

Why are you murdering innocent women in the name of magic?

Why did you take my wife and hang her from the ceiling of a theatre?

Why did you turn Mum's machine off?

What did I do to deserve this?

'Maybe he's out,' Murphy says nervously.

'Whether he's in or out, we are going through this door tonight.' I bang on the door one more time, more aggressively than before. 'Mr David!' I shout, not really waiting for a response.

I take a step back, flailing my arms to the side, so that Paulson and Murphy create some room for me. I lift my right leg off the floor, bending it so that my knee is at the height of my chest, and land my foot full force on to the door. Something cracks, but it doesn't open. I repeat the move again to the same effect. The lock is not in the middle of the door; it's slightly higher, so I barge it with my shoulder and it swings open, letting a stench release itself into the open air.

I've come across this a few times in my career. I know what it is.

And everything I thought I knew has come undone.

My father is in the living room, sat in his chair opposite the television, his dinner unfinished, placed on a tray, resting on a small table in front of where he is perched.

Where he died.

Over a week ago.

My phone rings, not giving me any time to digest the image before me. Not allowing me to confront my recent orphaned state.

It is one of the guards from the hospital.

'What's happening?' I ask, hearing a recurring siren noise in the background.

'It's a fire alarm. Everything is under control, we'll take care of Mrs David. I just didn't want you to worry if you heard anything through another source,' he tells me succinctly.

I tell him that one of them has to be with her at all times and he needs to update me once the situation is back to normal. He begins to affirm my order, but loses reception and is cut off.

A bottle of Scotch sits on the floor next to Dad's leather single-seater, the lid hidden somewhere across the room, probably thrown over there as he realised it wouldn't need to be kept fresh.

The dinner on the plate has dried and shrunk. It looks as though it may have been a steak and kidney pie with mashed potato and beans at one point; a hearty final meal. Two empty plastic containers that were once full of painkillers sit next to the plate. Under the plate is a handwritten note.

It is not the same handwriting as the Eames grid-references that arrive the day after a killing. I see that straight away.

Taking a pen from my breast pocket I lift the bottom of the plate upwards off the note, so that I don't tamper with the scene. I don't want my prints on this. Not after the recent suspicion surrounding this case.

It is not a suicide letter.

It's a letter to my sister.

Cathy, you were the best thing in my life; you were the worst thing in my life. If there is somewhere that we go after death, I hope you are not there to meet me.

I drop the plate back down over his message.

It's not the fact that he freely admits my sister was far more important to him than me or my mother. And after the way he wasted his life, after the way he waited for the instance to reap a moment of dual vengeance by legally euthanising my mother in front of me, I can't bring myself to care that he topped himself later that same day.

What really hurts is that it wasn't him. He can't be Eames. He has a concrete alibi for the last two deaths.

What we know is that these murders were most certainly all based on the works of some of the world's greatest magic tricks.

What we don't know is who planned and executed this

series of slayings. We still don't know who Eames is.

'Murph, call this in,' I croak, turning my gaze away from my rotting father and his rancorous note. 'Get someone to pick this sorry sack of shit up.' And I walk out of the flat.

My phone rings again. In my daze I don't look who is calling.

'David,' I bleat abruptly, announcing myself to the caller with a tone of dismissiveness.

'Inspector?' It is the guard from the hospital. 'We've had a power failure at the hospital, but the backup generators have kicked in until we work out what happened.'

I think I hear him gulp.

'Okaaaaay.'

'Mrs David woke up.' I panic at this news. 'She was scared and disoriented and one of the doctors suggested moving her to a safer, more secure room.'

I feel as though he has more to say, that this chaos is leading to something.

'Nobody talks to her until I get there!' I bark my orders at the young officer, still raw from finding my last living relative festering in his secreted bodily fluids.

'It is still bustling here and we are having difficulty finding which room she has been moved to.'

It's at this point I see The Smiling Man looking up at me from the bottom of the stairwell. He is wagging his finger at me in the same way he did at the speakeasy the night before my wedding.

I take my phone, the guard at the other end talking still, calling my name, and I launch it down at my tormenter, screaming, *What do you want from me?* He disappears before it strikes him and smashes to pieces behind where he stood.

And I know that she is gone.

I have let her down again.

I realise that Girl 6 was a part of the magic, but, like all tricks, it is leading to the final reveal. Every illusion requires some degree of misdirection in order to successfully accomplish the desired outcome. Girl 6 was the misdirection.

While we were busy dealing with another dead girl, while we were pinning the murder on my dead father, Eames, the illusive, deceptive orchestrator behind these atrocities, was setting up his final act: to make my wife disappear for ever.

In my mind I visualise the whiteboard.

I write *Girl 7*, *Audrey DAVID*, *David Copperfield*, <u>*Death Saw*</u>.

I know where he will take her; I feel it.

I know that I can stop him.

What I don't know is that it is too late to save my wife.

Girl 4

I open my eyes gradually, allowing the light in glimmer by glimmer.

I knew he would be waiting for me at the hospital. I can feel his presence. I sensed him a moment ago, touching me, navigating the contours of my body with his fingertips, telling me that I am special, without even saying a word. Silently declaring his love.

At first all I see is a smile, then through the beeping horns and revving engines his baritone voice greets me.

It's Eames. I knew it would be.

I don't say anything at first, I'm still a little weak. I notice his head flick to the right to keep an eye on what is in front of us, then snap back to the left, to where I am slumped, waiting for me to react.

'You . . .' I pant, taking a breath before I try again. I see his eyes widen in anticipation. He fidgets in his chair.

I close my eyes again for a few seconds, to recharge. When I reopen them the car has stopped at a red traffic light and all his attention is fixed on me.

I try to speak again. 'You . . . you've done it,' I gasp, trying to focus on his eyes, but all I see is his smile.

'I've done it,' he responds, his smile broadening.

'All of them?' I ask, puffing out air on the question mark.

'They're all dead. He should have found the sixth girl by now.' And he laughs subtly when mentioning January.

'Well done.' And I force a smile of my own.

I have just enough energy to pick my right arm up and place my hand on his thigh. Looking forward at the traffic leading back to the theatre, I drop my head back on to the head rest.

Everything is going according to plan.

Girl 1

I think falling asleep after making love is a wonderful experience to share. It's the waking up that is often a disappointment. I've been out and met men, a lot of the time as a result of a speed-dating night, and everything goes well. I take them home, we drink wine and have sex. But when I wake up, they have gone. Escaped before we even give it a chance together.

Eames is different.

I fall asleep because he drugged my wine and, when I finally wake up, I am still handcuffed to my bed, which has been tipped vertically so that I am standing up, naked, with a tall blurred figure in front of me and a smaller blur sat on my Börge chair – in black – in the corner of the room delivering her instructions.

I don't know who she is.

I don't know why he is listening to her.

When he hands me the gun I see her as the threat, not Eames; she is controlling him, but my vision is impaired and my motor skills have diminished, so when I shoot at her it misses. It goes high. I hear it slug the wall behind her.

I don't have the strength to squeeze the trigger again. Even if I could, it wouldn't matter. That was the only bullet.

Then he tells me to look at him. As things start to come into focus I see Eames standing directly in front of me with a gun pointing at my face. The red light from the laser guide blinds me temporarily as he moves it down from my head to my mouth, his hand shaking.

'If you can catch it, you live,' he says in a monotone, completely removing himself from the emotion of the situation.

'What? What are you talking about, you sick freak?' I scream. The woman in the corner laughs at me.

'Open wide,' he says, unflinchingly cold.

Before I even have time to figure out what he means, I'm dead.

I've set her plan in motion.

Girl 2

❦

'Don't move,' he says, skulking around in front of me. 'Stay perfectly still.'

Then my stomach starts to burn.

As I look down towards the pain, there is a sensation that someone has released acid inside my body, and an apple falls off my head in front of me.

I cry and whine like an injured dog.

I call out to a God that I don't believe in.

Eames strolls over to me, visibly disappointed that I am still alive, and I realise that today, the day I thought everything changes for me, things are looking up, is the day it all ends.

He brings another apple over and tries to balance it on top of my head again. But I shake it off.

'Stop moving!' he says abruptly.

But I don't.

He slaps me round the side of the face and grabs my chin like a vice. Bringing his face close to mine, I can still smell the sex on him. He tells me, 'If you stay still, you just might get out of this alive. OK?'

I nod lightly and he places it back on top of me, takes his spot on the other side of the room, turns his back, loads the arrow and places it over his shoulder, pointing directly at my head.

316

To the right I see someone else. She is outside the window looking in. I want to get her attention so that she can help me, but I'm afraid of what might happen to me if I move.

She is staring at Eames. Like she knows him. Her face moves closer to the window. She is beautiful. Smooth white skin. I wonder whether she is an angel.

Then I feel my shoulder tear open and I scream, the apple falling to the ground once more.

My natural reaction is to grab the painful area, but as I try to bring my right hand up I am quickly reminded that I am fastened to the pole in the kitchen as the handcuffs cut further into my wrists.

The angel at the window sees me now, the blood pouring out of my shoulder and trickling down my naked breast, the hole in my stomach, the tears in my eyes. I look straight at her, pleading with her to take me away from here, to a better place where I can feel no pain.

She smiles at me. And the pain goes away.

Then her smile transforms. What was once something of comfort has now become something of pleasure and enjoyment. She wants this to happen to me.

And the agony returns.

Eames continues his routine once more, this time striking me through the thigh.

I just want it to end.

And, with his next arrow, it does.

The angel gets what she wants.

January

───────✦───────

I send Paulson and Murphy back inside to wait with my father's rotten corpse after they rush out to confront my brief outburst. Plodding wearily down the stairs, dejected at the discovery of my dead suspect, I head towards the remnants of my phone.

As I bend down to pick up the pieces, I drop to one knee and black out. I don't fall over. I don't collapse. I'm just somewhere else. Somewhere dark, but familiar. And I see flashes of myself, in the chair, The Smiling Man in front of me. But something is different.

What I don't know is that The Smiling Man is trying to tell me something pertinent to the case that I missed in the first two visions.

That Eames was not alone.

That someone was there with him when he committed these obscenities.

That I need to look at it from a different angle.

While I was tied to the chair with the bullet between my teeth, another chair appeared by my side, another chair that The Smiling Man charged at. This part of the prophecy was important. This was the part of the scene that we overlooked.

This was the chair that Audrey sat in while Eames carried out her instructions to shoot Dorothy Penn in the mouth. The bullet in the wall that disappeared, that The Smiling Man swallowed, was aimed at Audrey.

The Sleep-Easy Eye Cover that he ripped from my face was the same as the one that Audrey tore off her own eyes when I woke her up, sweating over the nightmare.

All of these details that I missed the first time appear more vivid on second inspection. But I'm still learning. Still discovering which information to siphon.

What I don't know is that he was telling me it was Audrey all along.

In my second vision, as The Smiling Man backs across the room and I hear the glass smash, what I don't know is that he was telling me to look outside the window. He was alerting me to the fact that somebody saw what happened, somebody watched it.

He was trying to show me Audrey again.

When he appears to me before Amy Mullica chokes on hundreds of cigarettes, he is trying to point me to Audrey. He pulls a chunk of my hair out as he unblindfolds me, just as Audrey did when she ravaged me on the sofa.

Am I channelling The Smiling Man this time or is he still directing me?

When The Smiling Woman visited, I saw the blood between her legs as a link to Richard Pendragon being emasculated. What I don't know is that Audrey has been secretly trying for a baby and that her next period will be missed.

What I do know is that The Smiling Man appears to me only when a girl is going to die. He shows me his beaming face to let me know I have twenty-four hours to save her. If I am awake and he appears to me it is always with the wagging of a finger and it always coincides with Audrey being taken.

What I don't know is that she is not taken at all. She is giving herself as part of the larger project.

What I don't know is that The Smiling Man is my guide to solving the case. Where he comes from, I do not yet know. I don't know whether I have created him or whether he is sent from another world or time. But he is a guide, not the answer. We must work together. He is specific to this case only; he has never appeared to me in relation to any other crime. My mistake is that I associate his appearances as a link with Eames, but he is only connected to Audrey.

I snap out of my trance with more information than before, but no more answers. Still in my kneeling position, it is as if no time has passed.

What I do know is that Audrey loves me more than anything in the world and I keep letting her down.

What I don't know is that she thinks she is doing this all for me.

Eames

When Audrey wakes up it makes it feel even more worthwhile. We have done this together. I know that she feels something for Detective Inspector January David, but right now, he isn't here; that doesn't matter.

Just think how stupid he'll never feel that his wife completely betrayed him for their entire relationship. Think how lucky he'll feel not knowing that we were together until they were married. What a great man he will feel like not knowing that he could only pacify her for fourteen months before she came back to me for something extra. Something exciting. Something that gave her life meaning.

This is as much mine as it is hers.

She never had to kill anybody; I took care of that part. She just had to tell me who and how. But we both win something and lose something in this deal.

Nobody will ever know that she conceived the idea; nobody will ever know her orchestral superiority; but she will gain the worship of Detective Inspector January David. As his guilt grows, so will his need to protect.

I will have my place in history; my name will be known, even revered by those who wish to be like me. But I lose her. I have to let Audrey go. Tonight will be the last time I ever see her dark curls and succulent lips. Her rounded hips and solid calves.

She does it for him.

I do it for her.

When someone goes through their entire life without any help from another person, when they live on instinct alone, when there is nobody out there who puts them first, before themselves, that's me. That's who I am.

When someone is born into this world alone, when they do not understand the emotion of love or the concept of family, do not let that be an excuse.

I know who I am.

This is not for fame or philanthropy. It is not creative or artistic.

It's just what I know.

It's all that I know.

Girl 4

— * —

He has done incredibly well. Of course, I had to sit with him through the first stage, to keep a tight leash on the venture. Making sure everything ran smoothly. So, for the first girl, the dreadfully tacky Dorothy Penn, I was in the room with him when he pulled the trigger.

What is important is that I have not physically murdered anyone. It all had to be committed by Eames to work. That is how I planned it and that is how it has been.

In control.

Always.

Someone else does the legwork.

With the second girl I loosened my grip, knowing that I could not be there for the third girl as it was the night before my wedding, giving me an alibi. Obviously for the rest of the killings I was either the pretend victim or incapacitated, but for Carla Moretti I needed to watch, to make sure that I had the right man to finish the job. A man with a passion for what he does and an increasing lasciviousness for me.

The drugs lasted long enough for him to leave her and fetch the crossbow. I could have brought it, but allowing myself to become an accomplice would be sloppy.

Every detail covered.

His finest work was Amy Mullica and made up for his

mistakes with Girl 2. This is why I met him at the hotel afterwards, to give him his reward, to make him believe we had a relationship. By the time I realised I wanted to restart what I thought was over, he had done all the groundwork.

So he deserves the recognition he will receive when the final act is complete.

January's father was the key. Jan told me that his father had always blamed him for his sister Cathy going missing and I wanted to give him closure on this.

So that we could get on with our lives.

Without the constant guilt his father unjustly placed on his shoulders weighing down our relationship.

So I set him up.

It was easy. Easier than building a multi-million pound company from nothing; easier than convincing a man of strict moral and law-abiding code to have something else in his life other than his commitment to work; easier than making a baby.

I knew him. Despite never meeting him I knew about him; Jan would often talk about his father. Only once did he talk of his mother.

The magic angle seemed obvious. How poetic for a once-revered entertainer to come out of retirement only to complete the greatest trick of all time. To take a handful of the world's most famous illusions and distort them into a series of conjuring feats all leading to a harrowing denouement where his act of revenge would be complete.

He would take away his son's life, just as he believed his son had done to him by allowing his daughter to be taken.

In this process I give January, the man I love, some

closure, some freedom from his father's egocentric torment. I also punish his father for something that is not his fault, so that he can understand what it has been like for January all these years.

If January can let go of this, if he can realise that this is not his fault and he can put this issue to rest, then I become the most important thing in his life.

If he experiences nearly losing me, he will understand exactly what I mean to him.

He will never want to let me go again.

I occupy the spaces in his heart, not a sister he can barely remember, or a mother who detached herself from reality or a father who patiently waited for his moment of heartless, perverted vengeance.

Me.

He loves me completely.

I achieve everything I set my mind to.

I have an uncontrollable hunger. Not for killing. I am not Eames. I am not a murderer. I hunger for success. I hunger for control.

I control a successful recruitment company in the capital. I have conquered the business world. This also allowed me access to thousands upon thousands of people's details in and around London. Their names, their addresses; we even placed some of them into their jobs. This is how I found the people I wanted. The girls that had to die.

We got Dorothy the job in the bank years ago. Our temporary team handled Ms Moretti's call-centre position. Amy had registered with us, because she was looking to travel and wanted something in place for when she returned. Richard was one of our high-achievers in the financial sector in which we feature heavily, and Stacey was unemployed, calling us every other day for opportunities.

But I had not triumphed in my personal life.

January was not concerned with the wedding until it finally happened. He tried, I recognised that, but something was missing; he always seemed preoccupied.

That is why I have done this. That is why I have orchestrated such an elaborate set of incidents. I want to help the man I love, but mainly, I want to be noticed. I want to be priority number one.

I want my personal life to be as successful as my professional. I want that for January too.

I want January to desire me in the same way Eames does. Enough to kill for me.

Enough to take the blame.

We had that for a while, but the toll of not getting pregnant forced me to reignite things with Eames, to finish the trick. To let January lose me one last time.

To make him feel like he has failed before he succeeds.

Because losing Cathy made him love her more than anything in the world.

I do this for him.

At least that's what I try to tell myself.

We arrive at the theatre and I rest, while Eames sets up the mechanism for my finale.

In one hour January will watch me being sawn in half.

That is when he will realise what he's lost.

That is when he'll know how much he loves me.

January

———✦———

I can see a blue light through the window and I know I am right. Audrey is inside.

My mind flashes back to the last time I was called out to this location. Paulson and Murphy were already here, making notes, smoking, interviewing the cleaner who had found the *floating corpse*.

I think about the video I found online of the Death Saw trick and I fear what may lie inside this time. I'm scared there is no way to save her. I'm afraid that she is the last woman in my life that I have left and I am going to let her down again. Just like I did when I allowed Cathy to be taken, like I did recently when I let my bastard father take away Mum's life support, and like I did the last time I allowed this maniac to string my wife up to the ceiling of the theatre.

It ends now.

'She's in there,' I say quietly to Paulson and Murphy as the car comes to a smooth stop outside the theatre doors, one of which has been left ajar.

It feels like a trap. But Eames doesn't want me, he wants the girls. He wants to complete his magic.

'How do you know for sure?' Murphy asks, intrigued yet still not believing in my new-found abilities.

'I just know, OK?' I don't even look back at him. Both Paulson and I lean forward in our seats to get a better angle through the windscreen on the building.

'OK,' he answers begrudgingly.

We sit in silence for a few seconds, each of us collecting our thoughts. Murphy trying to make himself trust that I am not still involved, Paulson worrying at what ghostly image awaits us this time. I reflect on my emotion for my wife, now Girl 7, and envisage the moment I can get my hands around Eames' neck.

'Right, boys, you ready?' It's not really a question, so much as a polite order.

'Ready,' Murphy drills back.

'Ready when you are, Jan.' Paulson nervously looks at me, wide-eyed and worried.

We get out of the car and head for the gap in the door. We should call for backup. We should surround the building ensuring that Eames can't escape, but I don't care about protocol or the case or getting reprimanded for my actions: I care about saving my wife, who is still in a fragile state.

What I don't know is that her condition is slightly more delicate than I could have imagined. What I don't know is that her deceit runs further than this case and that she has succeeded in another area that she has been longing for over the months.

'It's like déjà-fucking-vu,' Paulson says to himself as we edge through the open door, creeping towards the main auditorium in the darkness. I understand what he means; this situation is all too familiar.

I don't feel the cold, though. The sensation I get when Eames is nearby. I can't determine whether my adrenalin is stronger and knocks it out or the sense of foreboding outweighs my hunch ability. Either way, he isn't here.

That is how she planned it.

I have to experience my wife dying before I catch the man who didn't even mastermind the operation.

The room is empty. A vast expanse of floorboards with some chairs stacked against the far wall. There is nowhere to hide except up on the stage.

My eyes adjust to the lighting conditions in here and I can make out a shape on stage. Again, it looks like a large coffin, this time from the side. This time perched on something, so it is three or four feet off the ground. Above it the light from outside catches on the shiny metal of the circular saw. It is exactly as I remember in the video. Every detail.

A light flickers outside and reflects off the surface of the saw bouncing down to one end of the coffin, momentarily lighting Audrey's tired face. Her eyes closed, not moving.

I don't know if she is already dead.

As I move forward across the empty floor, leaving myself completely open to attack, Murphy takes a step back, trying to convince himself that what he sees cannot be true; this cannot be happening again.

Paulson comes with me, but Murphy edges away, back towards the wall behind us.

As I see her, I speed up. I've seen the trick performed, I know the saw drops and cuts her in half. I know she is put back together again, but that is not how Eames works; he is altering these tricks to use them as weapons of murder.

Murphy leans back against the wall, just as the paramedic did when we found Audrey the first time, when she was Girl 4. It's different now she is Girl 7.

His right shoulder blade nudges the light switch and illuminates the room temporarily.

The brightness is blinding, but I can see the mechanics behind the saw, the pulley system, the hydraulics, then the room goes dark again as the bulb goes out.

I hear Murphy curse at the back of the room.

Then the sparks fly.

And the saw starts to rotate.

The noise is deafening.

I look back at Murphy shouting, 'TURN IT OFF!'

'What?' he shouts back at me, as if there is anything else in the world I am going to tell him to do at this moment.

I run over to where he is stood. 'Turn the fucking switch off!' I growl angrily, grabbing the switch myself and moving it down.

But the saw doesn't stop.

I wiggle the switch up and down, but nothing happens. It's dead. It was the trigger to start the saw and somehow, after sparking off the circular motion, it cut off its own circuit, rendering it useless.

There is no way to stop it.

'Fuck!' I shout, beating the wall with both my hands, slapping it until my hands hurt.

I look back at the stage and the saw is rotating at a high enough speed to blur the teeth that will cut through my wife in a matter of moments unless I can somehow pull her out.

The sparks from the top of the construction are only for aesthetics, but they drop down around Audrey's head, illuminating her face.

I pray she doesn't wake up.

330

I make a dash for it, towards the stage, to pull Audrey out somehow. To save her. To save the woman I love.

I pass Paulson at the halfway point. He is stood there in amazement, just as Eames would have wanted. His *coup de théâtre*. With around twenty feet to go I look up to see the saw wobble before dropping suddenly through the centre of the box that Audrey is contained within. I drop to my knees, sliding forward the last few feet until I hit the front of the stage, screaming '*Nooooo!*' and crumpling to a heap beneath the scene.

The saw slows to a stop.

Paulson and Murphy are statues.

I reach an arm up to the front of the stage and drag myself to my feet.

I see half a box to the left which contains my wife's delicate, perfect torso, her head poking out of the end, motionless. The box to the right contains her toned, succulent legs, her feet dangling, her ankles protruding.

Then there is a pop.

Like the noise before when the dry-ice was released.

This time it is a pyrotechnic within the hydraulics that ejects the left hand side of her body away from the now still saw to accentuate the effect of her being left in two halves.

A collective gasp from my colleagues fills the large space.

The casket wheels left for a couple of feet then stops, half my wife's body inside.

This is the reason why she didn't die as Girl 4: Eames needed her again. He needed the same girl and she had to die on the second attempt.

What I don't know is that this is not the case at all; it was Audrey that needed Eames.

Paulson comes to my side. Murphy remains at the back of the room, knowing that he flipped the switch that started the rotor.

I'm in shock. I should feel distraught or guilty or useless or a failure or alone or suicidal or something. I just feel paralysed. Physically and emotionally paralysed.

I've lost her.

I have nothing.

'Where is the blood?' Paulson says, half thinking out loud, half putting the question to me.

We both stare in silence for another ten seconds.

'Jan, there's no blood.' He elbows my arm to nudge me out of my state of suspended animation, my situation of disbelief.

He's right.

I see it.

There is no blood, just her hospital gown dropping over what should be the soggy end of her torso.

I spring into action, leaping on to the stage. Murphy takes this as his cue to run to the front of the hall and join Paulson. On the left-hand wall is a red, foam fire extinguisher hooked next to a smaller, black, carbon-dioxide extinguisher. I grab the red one, the heaviest, and hold it above my head. I bring it crashing down on to the first padlock which rips out of the wooden half-coffin. The second one takes me two strikes to remove, the last of which includes a grunt that increases in pitch as I smash down on the metal.

Once open I toss the battering ram behind me and it rolls off the stage landing next to Paulson's feet with a denting thud.

I lift the door up, folding it back on its hinges.

No blood.

I touch her back lightly; she is still warm and still breathing.

Running my hands down her back I reach the bottom where the saw cut through, but it is dry. I lift her gown. She is naked underneath and her legs drop through a hole, folding her body in two, the bottom half, still intact, hidden underneath.

'Get an ambulance here now!' I shout, not caring who performs this task. Murphy is first to his phone. Paulson waddles up the steps to help me lift her out.

We pull her from the confines of the trick box and lay her on the stage. Paulson rests his jacket over her to keep her warm; her head lies on my lap as I stroke her hair, never taking my eyes off her.

Her eyes open for a second and she puffs out a couple of words.

'Jan,' she splutters. 'You came.' And she musters enough to smile.

'Ssssh. Ssssh. Rest. I've got you.' I continue to stroke her hair. 'I've got you.'

The relief that she is still alive does not outweigh the sensation of failure and loss I felt as that saw came down and ripped my life apart.

But I should have known she would be all right. The Smiling Man did not appear to me in my dream. Just like before. He came to me to tell me everything would be all right. That Audrey wouldn't die.

What I don't know is that he was telling me not to trust my wife.

I don't understand why he has saved her. Why Eames

has let Audrey survive again. Is it to traumatise me? To show me he is better than I am? Is this how he wins?

I don't care that he has won, as long as she is alive.

I stroke Audrey's hair continually to let her know that I am not leaving her side, but I can't let him kill again. I can't let him go into hiding for another year.

'Audrey. Can you hear me?'

She opens her eyes and I see relief.

'Do you know where I can find him?' I ask gently. I know she must know; she has slept with him as all the other victims did, she clearly knows him, but right now I don't care about that, I don't want to deal with that. It isn't important.

She turns her head to the side and a tear forms that rolls down her cheek on to my leg.

Moving my hand to her face I coax her gaze back to me. In her eyes I see shame.

'Do you know?' I repeat.

For a second or two she just peers into my eyes. I see her well up, her eyes coated in two large tears, then she nods and her mouth screws up; her chest shakes, but she doesn't have the energy.

'Right, you two.' I glance at Paulson first, then focus intently on Murphy. 'You do not let her out of your sight. You ride with her in the ambulance to the hospital. You sit with her while she is examined. You stay awake next to her bed until you see my face again. You got that?'

They both nod and mutter obedience.

'Have you got that?' I ask with more vigour.

'Yes. Got it,' they respond in stereo.

I slide my leg out from underneath Audrey's head and replace it with my rolled up jacket. She is unconscious again, but breathing perfectly fine.

'What are you going to do, Jan?' Paulson asks.

'Don't do anything rash,' Murphy butts in, worried I might completely disregard the law.

'Just leave it to me. I'm bringing this psycho in.' And I walk back across the empty auditorium, leaving my wife for the third time, not knowing that this is still part of the plan, her plan. I'm still doing exactly what she wants me to do. I'm feeling what she wants me to feel.

What she doesn't know is that, with this plan, this ingenious scheme, nobody wins.

Girl 4

It was perfect. I couldn't see January's reaction, but I heard it; I heard the cry as the saw came crashing down. I heard the thud as he flopped to the floor. It does not give me pleasure to know that he is hurt; it is merely gratifying that the plan worked.

Now he just needs to live up to his end of the bargain; our tacit agreement that he knows nothing about.

I wanted it to end differently. I wanted Eames to be here, hidden in the other side of the box, acting as my legs. He changed these plans, claiming claustrophobia, saying that he would rather be taken from his home, that it would mock January one last time to find that he lived in the same area as we did; that he lived in the next street along from our house.

Not in a position to negotiate with a known serial killer, I had to let this go, but the result is the same.

He takes the fall.

He gets the glory.

I get to keep January.

Paulson and Murphy do not leave my side. They obey January's instructions. But there is nothing to worry about; I am not planning on being taken again. I want to recover; I want to get back to work, back to my husband

and his new-found longing for me.

I want him to know that we are trying for a baby.

I don't want to have to deceive any longer.

But not everything goes according to plan.

Not every detail is covered.

While I may have escaped blame, for now, I have no idea about The Smiling Man. I have no comprehension of January's ability and how it will develop.

I have no idea of my condition, because it is too early to tell, but, in two more weeks, when my final dream becomes a reality, that is the moment that will test just how much January and I love each other.

That is the moment I will discover the thing I want most.

That is the moment when I find out if this was all worth it.

Eames

—◆—

When a criminal meets his eventual captor and knows his time is up, when he uses this opportunity to divulge his inner workings, his motives, his reasons for the terrible things he has done, when he puts up a struggle and tries to get away, that's not me.

That's not what we agreed.

Just think what an anti-climax it will be for Detective Inspector January David that I don't fight back. Think how irritated he will be that I am the one who chooses when I get caught.

He won't have to kick the door down, because I have left it open.

He won't have to draw a weapon, because I will not retaliate.

He won't need to question me, because I confess, to all of it.

I wait on a bar stool in the hallway, so that he doesn't have to waste time looking around my house. I'll go easily. I will make it as simple as possible for him, so that he doesn't ask any questions. So I don't have to tell a lie. So I don't give myself the chance to have a second thought that sees me burying Audrey in culpability.

His muscular, tired frame fills the doorway with

shadow and he pushes the door open gently to meet with me face to face for the first time. I know what he looks like, but this is the first time he has seen me.

He bends at the knees slightly, widening his stance, prepared in case I attack. He holds his right arm out stiff in front of him to prop the door open and act as a barrier, should I charge in his direction.

'Eames?' he says, still unsure, still one step behind.

I nod at him to inform him he has something right.

'Don't you fucking move!' he spits as he curses, unable to contain his wrath towards me.

I shake my head at him, as if to say '*I won't.*' Then I lift my hands slowly out in front of me and turn my palms so they face upwards. As if I am fake-pleading, but inviting him to place the handcuffs on me.

'You're just going to sit there?' he asks knowingly.

I leave my hands where they are and nod slowly, smiling broadly.

Still, he is cautious, wondering whether this is another trick, some kind of Houdini escape act. But it isn't. I'm giving myself up. For her.

My work is done.

I've reached the top.

When the squad cars arrive as backup and screech into the street with their lights rotating, it's me they are afraid of. When the hero emerges from the doorway with the perpetrator's hands cuffed behind his back and neighbours stare through the gaps in their curtains, those are my neighbours, that is my doorway.

Detective Inspector January David manhandles me down the pathway to his car. I know he wants to hurt me. I know he wants to kill me. He was hoping for a struggle, something to give him an excuse, but I don't allow him the pleasure.

He presses heavily on my shoulder to lower me into the back seat, then walks around to the driver's side, opens his door, gets in and starts the engine.

We wait in silence for a minute while the car warms up.

He has so many questions in his head to which he still needs answers. I can see him deliberating. And I feel happy that he hasn't come out of this ordeal unscathed.

'You want to know why I didn't kill her,' I tell him, like I know exactly which one of the hundreds of questions he really wants to ask.

He adjusts his mirror so that he can see my eyes.

'This isn't just about your whore wife, detective,' I lie. He doesn't even blink. 'Isn't it obvious? It was love.' I lean forward in my seat, so that I can speak closer to his ear. 'I did this *all* for love.' Then I rest back in my seat, looking out the window as people emerge on their doorsteps, camera crews already arriving, police tape starting to cordon off my house.

And he thinks he has won.

The idiot thinks he has actually won.

January

---✦---

I haven't had time to think about my father yet. I haven't had the time to digest the fact that maybe he did still love Mum; that he probably blamed himself for Cathy all this time; that turning off the life support was the last thing he could take. I don't have time for conjecture, though. I just want to kill Eames.

But I can't.

I have gone against everything I ever believed in on this case. From going against the advice of my superiors to take a step back from this case, to submitting to a supernatural belief that I have had premonitions about the deaths of five innocent girls.

But it worked.

Sat before me is the man responsible for a spate of murders that has had the entire population of London looking over their shoulders. The same man who has taken my wife and tortured her to the brink of death only to spare her, twice.

We are alone.

What I don't know is that this is the final part of Audrey's plan. That somehow she has convinced a sociopathic death addict to incriminate himself for her fiendish scheme. She is guilty by association, an accessory to the fact. She is the criminal brain behind this diabolical magical massacre. But he plays his part to perfection.

He doesn't waver. He doesn't falter.

He admits to each crime.

It doesn't matter that we haven't looked into it further, that the answer is there for us to see. We don't need to find out how he could possibly know the specifics of each girl around such a vast expanse like London without a database of information, because we have the collar. Our percentages are up, and that is what is important.

I just have to accept it.

I tell myself that maybe he just wants to be caught.

Maybe that is the reason he sent me the notes; he was asking me to put him away so that he could stop this.

I am portrayed as a hero, Audrey as an innocent victim caught up in my case, and Eames receives his infamy, his place in London's bloody history.

We all get what we want, and she gets away with it.

I visit Audrey in the hospital to tell her she is safe now, that we got him, that I won't let anything happen to her again. I don't know whether she can hear me, but that doesn't matter. I need to say it out loud, to hear the words myself.

The doctor tells me that she will be fine with some rest. That she is exhausted.

He suggests I do the same. I've been awake for days. The boundaries of reality are becoming more blurred. What I feel to be fact is not the truth.

Paulson and Murphy are outside her room when I leave.

'Hey, Jan. You all right?' Paulson asks. I nod, drained. 'We got him.' He smiles proudly and slaps my arm in congratulations.

Murphy steps up to me, 'Look, Jan, I'm –'

'Forget about it, Murph. We've all got a job to do, right?' I don't need an apology from him. I know why he did it and maybe I would have done the same in his position. I just want to make sure that Eames is put away for the rest of his life; that I can give the families of these girls some closure.

Something I still don't have.

I can't talk things over with my father.

I can't apologise to my mother and tell her I believe her story.

What I have left is a relationship with my wife that is built on lies; fabrications that I am never supposed to find out about.

What I know is that this is only half of my life.

What Audrey doesn't know is that something has changed in both of us as a result of this experience.

What she doesn't know is that The Smiling Man cannot rest. He is specific to her and, while it may seem like the end, that she is smarter than everyone else, that she triumphed, the change within her that she is yet to acknowledge means that, at some point in the future, The Smiling Man will once again haunt me and this time his message will be clear.

When I finally get home the house doesn't seem so empty; it doesn't feel as scary. The phone in the hallway that was the tormenting messenger for so many months is now just a phone. The step where Eames stood to give delivery of the Girl 5 package is now just a step. The chair that Audrey seduced me on to forget about her guilt for a short while is now just the Chunky Cuddler sofa we like to watch films in.

The doorbell rings. I have no idea what the time is. It is light outside, that's all I can determine. I throw my keys down next to the phone and turn back to answer the door.

A stocky man, early thirties, Caucasian, just under six feet, is stood there with a clipboard and pen.

'Morning, sir. I have a delivery for a Mr David.' I look at him blankly, trying to work out in my mind whether I am awake. Over his shoulder I see a minivan with a courier logo on the side.

'That's me,' I say cautiously.

'If you could sign here I have a few boxes for you.' He hands me the board. I print my name and sign next to the box where he has written 9.34. I hand it back to him.

'Thank you, Mr David. I'll just get your packages. There are nine of them in total.'

I start to wonder. Maybe this is Eames' last hurrah. Perhaps each box contains the head of nine more women that we are yet to discover, I think gruesomely. But when he walks back to me with two of the heavy boxes stretching his arms to their limit, I recognise them immediately.

They are my heritage. My inheritance from Mum.

Nine boxes of journals that she has written in since 1985. Journals that she feels will be of use to me.

Right now, at this instant, I don't hate Audrey; that feeling is months away from this moment. For now, I feel protective over her. I know how I felt when I thought I had lost her and it wrenched at my heart. I love her.

For now.

But somewhere within these journals is the key to help me develop my gift. Somewhere, amongst all the gibberish, the scribbles and the illegible handwriting, are the answers I have spent my life looking for regarding my sister. Mum always knew. And it doesn't matter what convoluted formula Audrey cooks up to try to make me love her more, she is wasting her time. Nothing is more important to me than finding the truth about Cathy.

Everything I do is for her.

So, while Audrey lies in hospital, content with another success, an achievement in her personal life, the ordeal has changed her. Audrey is dead, and the person that remains is something different, something less. Someone so disillusioned that she can't see herself for what she really is.

Defeated.

A complete failure.

But she's safe. And for now, I guess that's enough.

Acknowledgements

A huge debt of gratitude to everyone at Random House who read and got behind this book, particularly my editor and champion, Ben Dunn, who just gets it.

To my friend and agent, Samantha Bulos, who is, at once, my biggest fan and most brutally honest critic. You are, I have come to find, always right. Always. You make me so much better. And to Paul Bulos for doing the jobs that nobody ever sees but I never forget and will always be grateful for.

For the few teachers who made a difference, whether you realised or not: Mrs Ireland, Jane Everton and Nic Saunders. I thank you for being more than just educators.

Jason and Belinda, thank you for allowing me to clog up your café every day with my laptop and notes; there was nothing you could do about the crying babies.

To my mother, without whom I would not be here, there are too many things to thank you for. Your endless support means more than you know. You are the best that there is.

And to my wife, Francesca, for the encouragement to go for it and write. For never letting on how worried you really were because you thought it was more important that I should do this. You are my inspiration, always.

Published by Arrow on 10th November 2011

WILL CARVER

Read on for an exclusive extract

Celeste

I don't move, at first.

It takes a few seconds to realise that, actually, I can't. I'm bound, and not just physically.

As my eyes adjust to the darkness in my windowless room I can make out a tiny rectangle of light on the wall in front of me.

And I know that I've been caught.

I know that she didn't die.

Stupidly, I think it's over.

The room is as cold as you would expect a jail cell to be; the skin on my breasts goose-pimples as a numbing chill bolts down my neck causing my shoulders to judder.

Somebody stepping on my grave.

My hands are restricted, tied to the frame of the bed which I now register as double-size. Even in the blackness, I'm also spatially aware that I have been placed in the centre of the room rather than up against a wall.

Both arms are stretched out perpendicular to my body. But I'm not handcuffed. My wrists are tethered to the bars of the bed frame with what feels like satin or some other equally sleek fabric. The loops holding me in place are not tight and yet, still, I cannot seem to move my arms. The same smooth material rubs against my ankles, binding them together then attaching them to the bottom bedstead.

What is this?

I focus on the strip of light, cocking my head to the right slightly to listen for voices, something, anything that confirms the police have finally captured me. The saliva in my mouth is thick from thirst, the acridity of smoke enveloping every taste bud.

I pull at the cloth that fetters me to the frame, trying to release myself.

Nothing.

Spiritually, my shackles tighten, paralysing my limbs, leaving my body crucified to the mattress beneath.

The back of my neck itches, then my lumbar, then the inside of my right thigh. I can't scratch. I can't move.

They can't treat me like this.

I wriggle my core violently, hoping to dislodge something, my limbs still heavy and motionless. The bed moves an inch closer to the door but my situation does not improve. So I scream. With every fibre of my intercostal muscles twitching simultaneously and the tendons in my neck trembling, I let out a cry that warbles with barbarity.

I hold the roar for five seconds, maybe ten, then wait.

Nothing.

Nobody comes.

Again I cry out, this time interspersing my howls with 'You fucks' and 'Let me outs' and 'Who *are* yous?'

I wait again, catching my breath.

Silence.

I stare intently at the illuminated rectangle ahead of me, my eyes fixed on the same spot, willing the flap to open and reveal the face of my arresting officer, the man to be hailed as a hero, the one who stopped the procession of mutilations and burnings and exsanguinations.

I want to see January David's eyes, full of pride and sense of achievement; his idiotic feeling of triumph despite the death of the five people he could have prevented if he really knew just what was going on.

But, despite my powers, I cannot open the small door to the outside of this prison.

So I wait.

Momentarily, I give up.

That's exactly what they want.

Relaxing into my restraints I take six long breaths, in through the nose, hold for five seconds then expel through the mouth, opening my eyes again on the third exhalation. On the ceiling above me I can just make out a pattern. A circle, slightly bigger than the bed that I am laying on, but it is too dark to see what is painted inside. With my vision compromised, it is only a short while before my other senses begin to compensate. I can smell the paint now; I couldn't at first. Whatever the symbol above me is, it is fresh. Like the cell has been recently decorated.

Then I smell a burning. Not like something is on fire, not like the smell a few hours ago as I knelt in front of another victim, the fire burning beneath her. Just candles. Newly lit candles, the matches still hot, the miniscule stream of smoke dancing into the air as its flame is blown out.

Then I feel something altogether alien. It's as if, somehow, the silence I have found myself in has become even more quiet. I sense something drawing closer.

The tin flap drops open, sounding like a car crash against the noiselessness of my sequestering.

I hold my breath now, my body rigid in anticipation.

353

More light streams into my cell, forming a pathway along the dust particles floating around inside.

Initially, the opening frames a bearded chin, but that slowly descends out of sight making way for vibrant pink lips against the palest of skin tones, then a pointed nose that resembles a flat owl's beak, perfectly symmetrical, eventually stopping on the eyes. Dark and bloodshot. So dark there is little colour difference from the pupil.

He doesn't blink.

I open my mouth, the viscous saliva forming a string that connects both my lips. I want to speak but can't force myself to say anything. As if attempting to call out in a dream.

The man's eyes are unflinchingly reticent. I feel my own widen further, trying to take in more than is possible through the tiny aperture I have been allowed.

Eventually, he blinks, and I jump. Every movement is exaggerated, every sound is amplified: his blink is like a whip cracking.

These are not the eyes of my arresting officer.

They are not the eyes of January David.